1812:

The Niagara Frontier

Written by:

William Mowat

CROWN & ANCHOR PUBLISHING

crownandanchorpublishing@gmail.com

Cast of Characters

Upper-Canadians
James and Laura Secord
John and Catharine Decew
Nathan Davis and Victoria Berwick
Bob and Fan Armstrong
Hector Armstrong
Richard Pierpoint
Reverend David George
John Hall
Robert Jupiter
John Vanpatten
George Martin
Billy Green
Joseph Willcocks
William Hamilton Merritt

Indigenous
John Norton (Teyoninhokarawen) - Chief of the Six Nation Confederacy
Karighwaycagh - John Norton's wife
John Brant - Chief of the Six Nation Confederacy
Tekarihoga - Chief of the Six Nation Confederacy
Tecumseh - Chief of the Shawnee Nation
Little Billy - Seneca Chief of Buffalo Creek
Red Jacket - Seneca Chief of Buffalo Creek

British Officers
Governor General of the Canadas - Sir George Prevost
Major Generals - Isaac Brock, Roger Sheaffe, John Vincent, and Gordon Drummond
Deputy Superintendent of Indian Affairs - William Claus
Lieutenants - James FitzGibbon, Thomas Evans, Dominique Ducharme, William Kerr

American Officers
Major Generals - Stephen Van Rensselaer and Henry Dearborn
Commodore - Isaac Chauncey
Brigadier Generals - John Boyd, George McClure, Jacob Brown
Lieutenant Colonels - Winfield Scott and Soloman Van Rensselaer, Charles Boerster
Major - John Lovett
Captains - John E. Wool and Cyrenius Chapin

War of 1812
Niagara Frontier Map

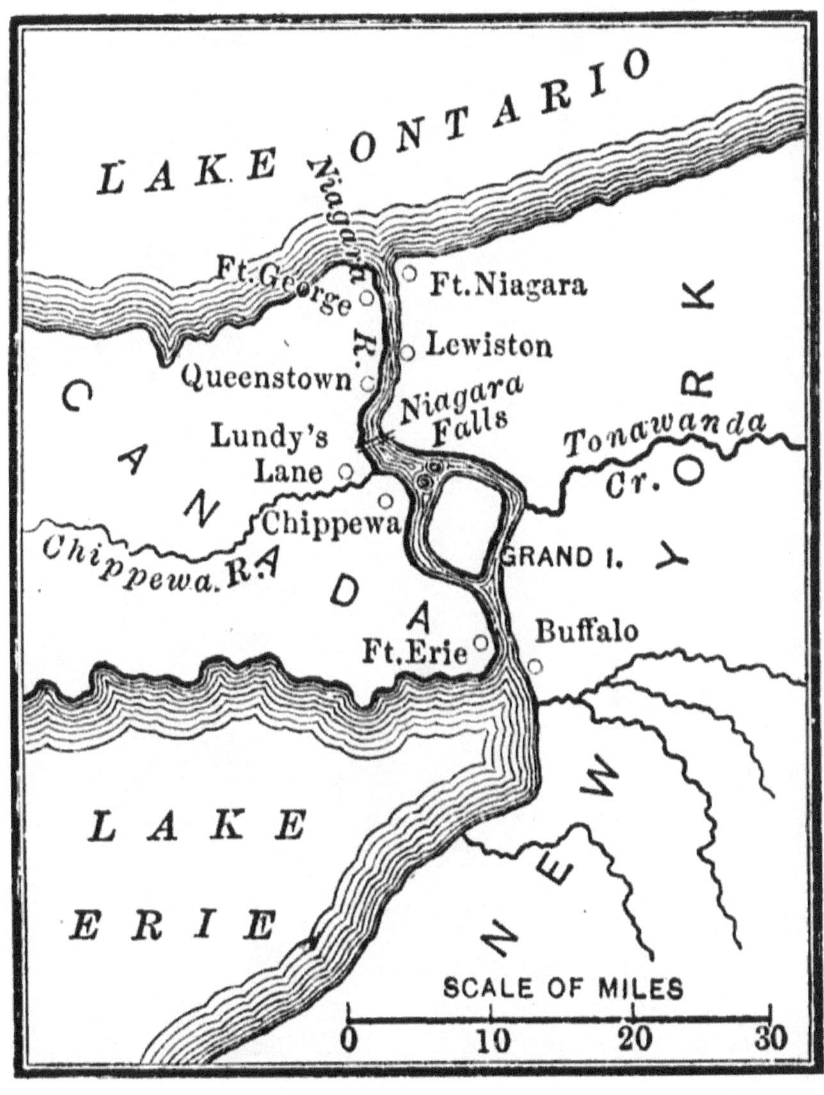

Preface:

The Niagara area is filled with rich 1812 history, from musket balls to rusty cannons, from Fort George across to Fort Niagara; students and historians alike have always been intrigued by its mystery, romance, politics, and heroics. The desire to create this true story stems from having a certain sense of pride in the residents on both sides of the border, who persisted through the struggle and an overall fascination with the time period.

The knowledge I have gained, together with my proximity to the War of 1812 and the Niagara frontier, resulted in me wanting to convey a story of perseverance, dedication, sacrifice, and community at the grassroots level on the frontier of war. This book began as a script I started in 2010, hoping for it to be produced for the bicentennial anniversary of the war. However, plans changed, and I reworked the script into a novel form that would ensure a better fit with the nature and journeys of the characters.

The people are central to this story, not just the ongoing struggle around them. I want the reader to feel and understand the internal conflict within the main characters and how they were affected by the surrounding turmoil. The decisions made by politicians and military leaders left families without homes, thousands were poverty-stricken, and everyone was in a desperate fight to survive. I have done my absolute best to be as sensitive as possible to the families and ancestors of those people from the War of 1812.

While every effort was made to maintain historical accuracy, I have taken creative liberties to weave a compelling narrative. As such, dialogue, inner thoughts, and interactions between characters, though inspired by historical records, are conjectural.

However, readers must recognize the distinction between the portrayal of these characters within the context of this narrative and the historical reality they inhabit. While their actions and personalities may reflect extensive research and interpretation, they remain products of literary creation.

As a teacher and student, I have explored the period in-depth by reading journals, biographies, articles, and novels and visiting museums, battlefields, and monuments. Yet, I still find myself fascinated by its mystery and allure. It is a period that is hard to comprehend; it consistently challenges my modern sensibilities, providing me with gratitude towards everything in my life and our society.

It must have been complicated to live in the 1800s: maintaining your livelihood, including animals and crops, educating children, providing medical treatments, heating and maintaining the home, and building your own forms of transportation. Days would have been long and exhausting enough without the threat of a major war looming overhead.

Canada in 1812 was unknown, often belittled, and misrepresented because of its population and vastness. The Indigenous tribes, including the Iroquois Confederacy, were a significant portion of the population and had been fighting the Americans for decades to have a country of their own. The British supported a grand Indian nation, from Ohio to Wisconsin, that would stop the westward expansion of the United States and provide Tecumseh and his allies with a land of their own, governed exclusively by the tribes.

At various points throughout this book, the Indigenous groups will be referred to as "Indians," "Natives," or "First

Nations," not because of insensitivity but rather because it relates to the context of the time, character, and situation. This period was also a time of borderlands, migrations, and cross-cultural diversity. In light of this complexity, all terms associated with groups of people are capitalized as "White, Black, Indian, Native," et cetera. Seeing as there were European and African people living in Indigenous communities and intermarriages everywhere, it seems careless and nonsensical to show any superiority of one group over another.

The English language continues to evolve; new titles, forms of diction, inclusions, and exclusions are constantly changing. My best intention is to highlight the strength of the people during this time rather than emphasize progressivism or show moral supremacy of one group over another. The people and the choices they make are what matter in such a hostile, turbulent time.

Tecumseh's unified tribes, along with a few Loyalists, trappers, soldiers, and sailors, made up the population of Upper and Lower Canada. Together, they had risen from the ashes of the Revolutionary War, which had happened 30 years prior.

The diverse Niagara area was a significant frontier during the American Revolution, a central hub of immigration, a major battlefield, and the borderland between two burgeoning nations, the United States and Canada. About 30 years later, in 1812, just as Americans and Canadians had rebuilt their homes and farmlands, they were again thrown into a conflict that was entirely out of their control.

President James Madison, along with his War-hawks, were outraged and fed up with the impressment of American sailors, the seizure of American ships, and the continuous and often brutal British naval blockades happening throughout the beginning of the

12

19th century. The Americans discerned it was an excellent time to take control of the entire North American continent, mainly because Britain was occupied and committed to fighting Napoleon Bonaparte on the fields of Europe. The United States signed the declaration, and the War of 1812 began.

Indigenous tribes, freed enslaved African-Americans, French trappers, British Loyalists, Irish and Scottish farmers, and, like John Norton, people of mixed blood made up the population of Canada. Without people like Tecumseh, Laura Secord, Isaac Brock, and John Norton, North America may have looked very different than it does today. The origins of Canada are full of rich, heroic, complicated stories. It is also full of bloodshed, slavery, betrayal, and corruption.

Writing from a historical perspective has been challenging and gratifying, especially trying to balance the tragic true stories and heroic independent journeys with sensitivity, realism, and precision. Contemporary audiences, including myself, may find an era laced with blood hard to fathom. War was normalized. It was almost tradition; it was constantly at your doorstep, and few people were left untouched by the cloud of war. Homes were burned, impressment happened on the seas, disease was prevalent, and life often teetered between life and death. How anybody was able to survive is a great mystery.

Very little remains from 1812: a few letters, some weapons, little to no eyewitness accounts, and a lot of conjured myth. Obviously, there were no computers, phones, cars, or trains in 1812, and electricity was still about a hundred years away. Houses were lit with lanterns and candles, horses plowed fields, and people travelled the treacherous oceans in rickety wooden boats.

I continually tried to balance real-world accounts of battles, letters, conversations, and circumstances with sensitively fictionalized dialogue and imagined situations that may have occurred.

John Norton's poetic and well-articulated journal from the War of 1812 was this story's central focal point and source. The artifact is one of the few first-person accounts preserved from this time. His real-world accounts and entries help solidify the story and provide a factual throughline for the plot.

Most of the characters within this book are real people; however, a few were fictionalized for the sake of the story and narrative. These characters, most authentic, some not, did not speak the majority of this dialogue within this book. Still, I sincerely tried to be conscious and empathetic to their thoughts and feelings throughout the conflict.

Within this fictionalized historical drama, set against the backdrop of 1812, this book delves into the hearts and minds of individual lives impacted by the frontier of war, their struggle for freedom, and the relentless march of time. The book will explore love and loss, ambition and sacrifice, and the enduring human spirit that shines even in the darkest times.

This story is designed to transport you to this fascinating period using meticulous research, imagination, and a tapestry of history and human drama. It is a time of heroes and villains, dreams shattered, and dreams realized, and a period that continues to captivate our collective imagination.

The characters you are about to meet are the architects of their destinies in a world that teeters on the brink of transformation. Together, you will witness their triumphs, tragedies, and the timeless echoes of a war that changed the course of history.

Table of Contents

Introduction

On the frontiers of the northeast wilderness in the British colonies of Canada, new boundaries were forming due to the aftermath of the first Revolutionary War of the United States. Massive migrations of British Loyalists fled to Canada seeking asylum from the newly formed republic. Tensions mounted in 1812, and all ships were on high alert on the seas.

The Six Nations of the Iroquois Confederacy, or the Haudenosaunee ("People of the Longhouse"), had been forced from their lands in the new United States (New York State) across the Niagara River into Upper Canada (Ontario). Years of bitter conflict with the American colonists led the mighty Indigenous nation to ally with the British to save the people's liberty and create their own nation.

Throughout the early 19th century, King George III and the British Empire focused on military conflicts against Napoleon Bonaparte in Europe. Thousands of soldiers were dying daily, and the Canadian Colonies were a mere afterthought of the British Empire and its leadership. The British leadership was already insecure about a significant portion of the population of Canada, given they at one time had been American. Also, the tribes of the Haudenosaunee Confederacy could choose between siding with the Americans or the British. People were generally exhausted from war. Most had seen bloody conflict during the American Revolution, the French Indian War, or the French Revolution that saw Bonaparte seize control of France and most of Europe.

The Niagara River, an extension of the St. Lawrence Seaway, connected Lake Erie and Lake Ontario and was a central piece of the North American puzzle. On one side of the river, President James Madison was being pressured to take another stance against King George; on the other side, Governor Prevost was preparing to defend against the expansion of the United States. War-hawks wanted to push the war into Canada, eliminate the British authoritarian rule in North America, and prevent them from supporting Tecumseh. The shipping lanes were the key to holding the Great Lakes, and both nations frantically began building ships to help stabilize their rightful claim on the Great Lakes.

We can only imagine people's dismay as the war-cloud intensified, casting a growing shadow on their lives. Nearly thirty years of peace had transformed the wilderness into fertile fields and thriving orchards. The log cabin had given way to ample stone and brick houses, many of which remain today as a testimony to the industry and prosperity of the people.

Though North America was modernizing, life was still harsh in 1812, but no less hostile than the previous 10,000 years. Dirt paths, horses, wagons, longhouses, stone fireplaces, lanterns, and forts of wilderness dotted the North American landscape.

Napoleon Bonaparte's success in conquering most of Europe, and with Russia as his next target, was occupying the British military forces. At the same time, James Madison, America's fourth president, was about to put pen to paper and march the burgeoning United States against the British Canadian colonies of Upper and Lower Canada.

It would be neighbours versus neighbours, friends killing friends, and, once again, families being torn apart by the civics and politics of the time. The people of the United States, especially New England, did not want another war. The Beaver Wars, The French Indian Wars, and The War of Independence were all still fresh in the people's minds; they knew it would not be long until they were touched by the cloud of war. The struggles always left families fatherless, populations poverty-stricken, and everything in general disarray. To say that the people did not want war is an understatement.

American War-hawks on the frontiers of American society pressured President Madison to take up the hatchet once more as the United States sought to expand westward into new territories and bring the war against Britain. This time, the British had Indigenous allies from the Six Nations and beyond.

Tecumseh, the Shawnee Chief, created a unified Indian nation, something that had never been done before. Seneca, Wyandot, Sac, Fox, Winnebago, Potawatomi, Kickapoo, Chippewa, Ottawa, Delaware, Miami, and Shawnee, all opposed the American westward expansion.

Tecumseh and his people had been driven from their homelands along the eastern seaboard by the United States to their current lands on the Grand River in Upper Canada. He was determined not to uproot them again.

The citizens of the United States and Canada were being dragged into another war by their governors and political leaders. The decision to march to war was something the citizens did not want, nor could they do anything to stop it.

Chapter 1 – A Shadow Looms

Laura Secord slowly and peacefully awakened before dawn and rose to her feet as her husband, James, lay sleeping beside her. The hardwood floors were cool on her feet as she put her slippers on. It was still dark outside as she began her day. Springtime was a busy time for the people of Upper Canada in 1812; seeds needed to be sown, animals fed, meals prepared, and a plethora of other chores in and around the homestead.

Laura got dressed, reflected on her dreams, and mentally prepared herself for the day ahead. Laura and James ran a busy general store at the end of their property in Queenston. Their days were usually long, rigorous, fast-paced, but ultimately, fulfilling.

Laura walked downstairs, being careful not to wake the children on the creaky stairs. She stoked the kitchen fireplace with a few pieces of knotty pine, boiled some water, and prepared a kettle of tea in the kitchen. Laura stepped outside with her steaming cup of pekoe tea, took a deep breath of the fresh morning air, and watched the sun begin to rise across the Niagara River on the New York state horizon. The sun shone through the budding forest and illuminated the dewy blades of grass as she sipped her warm, soothing tea. She was so happy to see progress in the busy village of Queenston throughout the past few years. It had become a busy port and international border crossing on the banks of the Niagara River. All the arduous work of establishing a business was beginning to pay off.

Laura and James arrived in Niagara under challenging circumstances during The American Revolutionary War. The frontier of war had left the entire area in ashes, and she had watched, over the past 30 years, orchards thrive, houses rise, pastures turn green, and smiles return to her community. She was so proud of the headway she had seen, including the growth of her five children, whom she cherished above all else.

James emerged from the front door, wiping the sleep from his eyes, and put his arm around Laura's shoulder. He leaned in and kissed her on the cheek as they enjoyed the sunrise together.

Tensions were mounting around Kingston in the early spring of 1812. With the rising temperatures and thawing snow, roads were now passable by horse and buggy. British generals and military leaders met in the small town to discuss upcoming operations and strategize a response to the imminent U.S declaration of war to take control of the North American continent.

British leadership had anticipated an attack on Point Henry in Kingston due to its relative proximity to the Royal Naval Dockyards. The docks were strategically vital to Upper and Lower Canada, as they sat at the mouth of the St. Lawrence River, a vital trade route leading to the Atlantic Ocean. If Point Henry were sacked or destroyed, the Americans could easily cut off communication between Kingston and everything east towards Québec and the ocean.

In anticipation of a potential American attack, the British had begun constructing Fort Henry, a post that would station some 2000 regulars. Hundreds of workers shuttled in limestone rocks from north of the city. Others chiselled them and hoisted them into place to create the initial walls. It was to be a massive structure that would help protect the future of the Canadas.

Major General Isaac Brock had arrived in Kingston from Fort George, his station in Newark on the Niagara River, one of the most significant, busiest towns in Upper Canada.

Brock was a tall man, six-foot-four inches tall, towering over most men and women of the time, giving him immediate stature and a distinctive leadership quality. He was a proven soldier and military tactician. Although the wildness of North America was a challenge, Brock's preference would have been fighting Napoleon Bonaparte on the European continent. The glory would be in Europe, he thought, not here in the wilderness. At 42 years old, Brock was still looking for glory in his station. He had seen little combat and was one of the few who welcomed the war.

Brock and his close friend and military ally, Major General Roger Sheaffe, took a horsedrawn carriage from the dockyards to the office of the Governor General. Sheaffe was a no-nonsense man of about 50, grizzled and fit for his age. As the carriage strolled through the muddy street, the two shared little conversation as their minds were clearly on the seriousness of the upcoming conflict.

Wearing the crimson colours, the gold guild buttons, and the feather-plum hats of the British military, they exited the small carriage, and made their way into the library of Sir George Prevost, the Governor General of Canada.

Atop nearby desks were the various maps showing the upcoming theatre of war. The Great Lakes were the centre of the conflict, as anything west of Lake Superior was considered wild and untamed country.

The maps showed the positions of Fort George, Fort Niagara, Fort Erie, and other strategic military installations and ongoing operations. Another larger map showed the Great Lakes, the towns of York, Montréal, Québec, Sackets Harbor, and various other settlements in the North American theatre.

Brock and Sheaffe sat and looked intently at the maps as Sir George Prevost entered the library carrying a steaming cup of tea. George was a smart-looking, medium-sized man about forty years old, with brown hair and about five feet, ten inches tall. As he entered the room and noticed Brock and Sheaffe, he couldn't help but smile.

"Gentlemen!" Prevost said. "I wish I could say it is a pleasure, but it seems we are about to march to war every time I see you."

"Greetings, Governor," Sheaffe said. "I wish our acquaintance was under better circumstances."

"Indeed. I see you have discovered the maps to indicate where we are engaged," Prevost said.

"Yes, we have. The thought of this war is unsettling, Governor," Sheaffe said, clearly troubled.

"We can not win this war with our forces committed to the European conflict," Brock said, getting directly to the point of the visit. "We must consider ourselves on the eve of war, and certain measures must be set, especially putting our passivity behind us. Our Upper Canadian population is not fully committed. It is constantly tempted and aroused by the writing and scribes from people like Joseph Willcocks and his rag of a paper. He persuades them that our parliament is wretched and corrupt."

"Willcocks is a scoundrel and will side with whoever is winning," Prevost said.

"He certainly can put forth an opposing argument," Sheaffe said.

"We cannot win this war with a split partisanship. I believe putting this country on a war-footing would help our efforts in creating a unified alliance among the people," Brock added.

Prevost looked at Brock with concern.

"We also can not win this war without the Indian contingency," Sheaffe added.

"Do you know where their loyalties currently lie?" Prevost asked.

Brock looked up to Prevost. "You, sir, are fully aware of where their loyalties should, and will eventually lie, with the colonies of British North America. They have been pushed too far and will not tolerate another forced migration. Tecumseh has created a grand nation of Indian alliances and will fight to the last man."

Prevost interrupted Brock: "There is no end to what the Red man wants, but critical their alliance is indeed."

"That sounds like the Department of Indian Affairs speaking," Sheaffe said.

"Like any man, there needs to be incentive," Brock said.

"Enhancing the distribution rights for Mohawk-Chief John Norton might be a proposition worth exploring," Sheaffe wisely mentioned. "He has excellent rapport and has built Native alliances all along the Grand River. He speaks many languages and promotes the lessons of the Bible."

"Exclusive distribution rights," Brock added. "He is highly motivated and stands behind the crown, regardless."

Prevost paused as he stared down at the map. "We are not one hundred percent sure of Norton's loyalties, nor are we sure that English-American bloodshed will even occur. The Canadian population is mostly migrants from the United States, which complicates the equation. It is quite possible Canadians feel more confidence in joining the U.S. after what happened during The Revolutionary War."

"There are many variables, Governor," Brock said. "That is why men like Norton are so important."

Chief John Norton sat on a rocky outcropping on the banks of the Grand River. Norton was a handsome man, carrying a calm, stoic, trusting face. Norton was born in Crail, Scotland, in 1770. His mother was Scottish, and his father was Cherokee. Norton had become a teacher for the Mohawks, a fur trader, and a British-Indian Department interpreter before rising to prominence among the Six Nations of the Grand River.

His adopted uncle Joseph Brant chose his Mohawk name as Teyoninhokarawen, meaning 'open door'. Norton quickly rose to become a leader and Chief of the Six Nations of the Grand River. He was calm, wise, and open to thoughts and opinions of all people.

Norton sat alone, gazing at the vast and swift-moving Grand River, carefully considering his next steps for the upcoming weeks. He was utterly lost in contemplation as the Grand flowed downstream. From his buckskin satchel, he removed a leather-bound journal and pen and began to write:

I have always been aware of the danger on the road ahead. I know of many secret crimson tunic meetings the white-haired fathers have held. I have heard much talk through the winds about my people and my untrustworthy stance on many empirical affairs. At this stage in my journey, I have come to grips with my nature and its stance for the common people. King George's concerns are not here, nor do the Americans revel in these lands. But I do believe when people are forced into the grips of annihilation, a bearing is always determined. Rivers flow relentlessly here. Our forefathers' pain from wars gone by, paddle up the river of my mind. Let my heart guide me to victory and avoid another dangerous walk down the road.

John Norton was meticulous in his writings, especially on the eve of war. He knew the Department of Indian Affairs and the Counsel of Chiefs would need to know particular details and information if mutual decisions were to be agreed upon.

Norton finished writing and put everything back in his satchel as his wife and lover, Karighwaycagh, arrived. Smiling, she sat down beside him.

Karighwaycagh, beautiful, young, and full of bright energy, helped balance and contrast the deep emotional feelings enveloping Norton's world. He worked tirelessly to maintain civil relations between the British and Indians, keeping communications open and truthful. He was also constantly recruiting warriors amongst the Grand River tribes, including men from the Mohawk, Oneida, Onondaga, Cayuga, Tuscarora, and Seneca tribes.

Karighwaycagh grounded him; she was the central figure who kept his thoughts and actions pure and righteous amid an escalating war.

John (Sawatis) Norton had travelled the world. He sailed the oceans, paddled down the Mississippi River, visited settlements along the eastern seaboard, and fought in many battles. Norton was now an expert translator between the British and First Nations, speaking several languages and translating various documents and messages.

Heavily influenced by the great Chief Joseph Brant, Norton promised he would do anything and everything he could for the people of the Grand River.

"Sawatis, are you writing again?" asked Karighwaycagh.

"Trying to keep my thoughts organized in these challenging times." John Norton knew war was coming, and his ability to recruit warriors and lead them into battle was going to be needed. He finished putting away his pen and journal and tied his satchel shut.

"Come for a walk with me." Karighwaycagh could sense his brooding intensity.

Norton looked at his young wife, admiring the details of her face, her brown eyes, her soft skin, and her long black hair. He smiled, put his arm around her, pulled her close, and they shared a kiss by the rolling waters of the Grand River.

"A walk would do me well," Norton said.

"I know it will," she said.

Karighwaycagh and Norton held hands as they strolled the path along the bank of the Grand River.

Sheaffe, Brock, and Prevost sat down at a large oak desk where the map of North America lay. They spoke of strategy and troop commitments as they sipped their afternoon black tea.

"Harrison, Clay, and the rest of the War-hawks are restless in Ohio and Indiana," Brock said, "They are pleading with the politicians in Washington to march to war. Tecumseh and his tribes continue to fight for the territories, and the whole thing seems unavoidable at this stage. It might be in our best interest to allow Chief Norton to begin recruiting and grant him distribution rights amongst the Grand River people. Be sure, Governor, he highly regards His Majesty and the Book of John, its distribution, and its longevity."

"Norton has great influence now, but with the U.S. so close to having President Madison sign the declaration, it proves worthy and mandatory that he influences the Grand River tribes and brings them to the battlefield," Sheaffe beseeched.

"He is a well-spoken man and speaks many languages. Did he not translate the gospel into at least a dozen?" Prevost asked.

"That he did, sir," Brock affirmed. "He also understands the people's suffering throughout the past century. They have been burdened at every turn imaginable."

"I would have the King knight him if I could persuade him to," Prevost joked.

"Agreed," Sheaffe added. "If we can secure our spot here in the Canadas, we might be able to establish a grand Indian nation in the Indiana and Ohio territory."

"The Americans are expanding quickly and unmercifully. They have no regard for anything or anyone in their path," Prevost said, leaning back in his chair.

Brock sipped from his teacup as Deputy Superintendent of Indian Affairs William Claus entered the library. A short man, about five foot five, dressed in British crimson, smiled at the three sitting gentlemen.

"Welcome, William," Prevost said. "Isaac, Roger, you remember Deputy Superintendent of our Indian Affairs, William Claus."

Brock and Sheaffe shook Claus's hand with subtle resentment and passive disinterest as they both knew Claus's agendas and genuine disdain for the Indians of Upper and Lower Canada.

"Good of you to come, Deputy," Brock said.

"We have just been reviewing John Norton's exclusive distribution rights to the Grand River tribes," Prevost told Claus.

"Be wary of that man. Though a Scot, he considers himself a true Indian. Can the Crown trust such a man in a sea of cannibals and impurities? If the U.S. wages war with the Crown, it is all but guaranteed the tribes will side with neutrality alongside the fellow savages on the American side. Be cagey of this man; the Crown should not trust him with its best intentions and its wealth," Claus said coldly.

Brock fired back. "The tribes will side with the party in control of the theatre. I insist that the President and his party of War-hawks proceed with a three-pronged attack at Detroit, Niagara, and Montréal." Brock turned to address Prevost. "Governor, as for Norton, I must insist on the man's character," he said, looking at Claus. "Like Tecumseh and Brant, Norton is a gallant warrior, wise in his youth, with a big chest full of honour. We must commend his loyalty to the King and the Canadas. Upper Canada must be defended, not abandoned, but rescued by leadership and valour by such men as Norton."

Claus would not back down from the argument. "Consider the Indian's state of affairs throughout this past decade. They are inclined not to partake in the 'White-man' wars. They insist on staying together in the area southeast of Amherstburg, smoking tobacco in the comfort of their homes. The Council Fires I have attended with the Seneca from the American reserves have indicated a strict neutrality."

Sheaffe turned to Prevost. "This isn't true at all."

"I have received many letters from Norton, full of assurances, promises, and strategic plans. Also, as bold as the man is, he does write about the Indian Affairs Department and their cowardice and incompetence. He is a great window into the mindset of our Indian brothers. We must trust our instincts," Prevost said.

"Well said, Governor," Sheaffe said.

"General Sheaffe, you are off to York this afternoon?" Prevost asked.

"Yes, sir. The ice has cleared, and the ships are sea-ready," he said. "We should be ready to set sail in a few hours."

"Good. Godspeed, General Sheaffe. You shall hear word soon, I should think. And General Brock, I understand you are returning to England to attend urgent family business?" Prevost inquired.

"Considering the current state here, your Excellency, I must insist upon remaining." Brock was an honourable man and would not miss the opportunity to defend the people of Upper and Lower Canada, White, Black, or Indigenous.

"Very noble of you. I am happy you've made this choice," Prevost said. "Make your way back to Fort George at Niagara. Relay the message to our half-Cherokee, half-Scot brother Norton, stating that his first distribution orders will come within the month. Understand, General, if England and the States come to war, we shall stay put on British soil and defend her with all our might. I am fully confident a ceasefire will be agreed upon."

"Understood, Governor," Brock said.

"We are on the eve of war, gentlemen. We must lead by example, maintain discipline, establish directives, communicate orders, and trust in one another. For King and country," Prevost said as all the men shook hands and parted ways.

Brock and Sheaffe felt uneasy after hearing how William Claus had described John Norton and the people of the Grand River. They both understood Upper and Lower Canada were not defensible without the warriors of the Indian nations. William Claus viewed Norton as a traitor and a White man posing as an Indian, though Brock and Sheaffe knew the truth about Norton; he was dedicated, motivated, and prepared to make the ultimate sacrifice.

Chapter 2 – Frontier Towns

In Newark, near the mouth of the Niagara River, Joseph Willcocks kicked the mud off his boots and entered his print shop on the main street in town. He looked around his business space, mulling over his options as he began to put the final touches on the typeset atop his printing press.

Willcocks was a well-known politician, editor, and publisher of the first newspaper in Canada, the Upper Canada Guardian or the Freeman's Journal. As war looms, he knows his publication will inevitably be shut down, so today, he regretfully prints his last issue of the paper. In the mildly successful paper, Willcocks deliberately attacked the British government with anti-authoritative political views and criticism of the British monarchical rule. Born in Ireland, he had always considered himself a Whig who opposed the Tories. Still, ultimately, Willcocks wanted to revolutionize Canada. People attached themselves to his disagreeable writings. He was witty, charming, elegant, and outright ferocious in his words.

Willcocks had been printing the renowned paper for several years with moderate success. He sold advertisements to local merchants, including James Secord, posted legal notices, and pressed announcements for Upper Canada's citizens. Willcocks fervently attacked land laws and the irrational, unpredictable powers of the King and his government. Many Canadians appeared to relish in his anti-authoritative words throughout the past few years. However, with a war on the horizon, his instincts told him that if Brock and Prevost deemed it necessary, they would force him to shut down his paper.

The past few weeks had been chaotic as he was frantically tying up loose ends, delivering packages, sending cancellation notices, and paying his final dues. His business space was a mess. Papers were stacked everywhere, and there was little evidence of organization. Crowded bookshelves, hundreds of pieces of typeface, and dusty tools were scattered around, leaving little workspace.

Willcocks set the final piece of typeface, inked his work, and lowered the iron hand of the Charles Mahon printing press. He then removed the last issue of The Upper Canada Guardian, blew gently on the fresh wet ink, and looked down to read the first paragraph of the paper:

> **_The Upper Canadian Guardian, or Freeman's Journal._** _This is the last issue of the Guardian for which we have avowedly calculated. Our goal has always been to disseminate the principles of political truth, check the progress of inordinate_

power, and keep alive the sacred flame of just and rational liberty.

Willcocks liked the attention and praise he received from the Guardian. He was admired and thought highly of, and he had built a successful career as a politician with his editorials. It was bittersweet that this was his last issue. Above all the fame, the politics, the money, and the praise, he promised himself he would be a loyal soldier for Canada when the United States declared war. He would put aside his brackishness, argumentativeness, and oppositional ways to fight alongside his fellow Canadians.

Willcocks nodded at his work as a knock on the office door startled him. He put his still-drying paper down, calmly walked to the locked door, and opened it to find a local businessman named Richard Hatt. Hatt was well-off; he wore clean, fashionable clothes, a new high-top hat, and a cane with an ivory band and golden horse handle.

"Good afternoon. My name is Richard Hatt, and I have come in response to the advertisement in the Guardian. I understand that you have a printing press for sale," Hatt asked.

"Indeed, my good man. My name is Joseph Willcocks, owner and operator of the Guardian," Willcocks said with a smile. "Come in, come in, Mr. Hatt."

"I am well aware of who you are, Mr. Willcocks. You are quite well-known everywhere," Hatt said, noting the room's disarray. "I am a big fan of your politics and editorials."

"That's very flattering, Mr. Hatt. There seems to be an increasing readership and subscriptions every day," Willcocks said.

"Then why are you selling your printing press, if I might ask?" Hatt inquired.

"In light of the upcoming engagement with the United States, I feel it prudent to sell most things here as I may be relocating and establishing a new paper away from the frontier of war." Being a shrewd businessman, Willcocks knew he had Hatt right where he wanted him.

"I see," said Hatt. "Quite unfortunate, this business of war."

"Brock has also dissolved parliament and called an election. He would likely shut down the paper within weeks. If you catch my meaning, Sir Brock seems determined to get a loyal assembly on the eve of war. The Guardian does not exactly fit into those regal plans."

"Quite understandable. It is good to hear you have a little foresight into the future of your enterprise," Hatt said, taking off his hat. "I am somewhat of a businessman myself. I will sincerely miss your advertisements and monthly listings. Everyone enjoys your editorials, and it seems that people are truly starting to understand the importance of the printed word and the factual truth. It is just a shame it has to come to a sudden halt."

"Thank you for your kind words." There was a short pause, and Willcocks spun around and looked at Hatt. "What do you say about $2000 for the almost brand-new Mahon printing press?" Willcocks opened the bidding with a beaming smile. "It has hardly been used and has all the newest features."

"Seems a little steep," Hatt said, stroking his chin. "What about $1500?"

"$1600, and I'll include all of the typeface and ink," Willcocks said as he extended his hand.

Hatt was hesitant but eventually shook hands with Willcocks. "Deal," he said.

"Wonderful. A deal between loyal gentlemen," Willcocks said. "It is a lovely machine, and you won't regret your purchase."

After a brief conversation about arranging to pick up the machine and exchange money, Richard Hatt moved toward the door, feeling like he had just made a terrific investment.

"It was a pleasure doing business with you, Mr. Hatt," Willcocks said.

"I look forward to next week. It was a pleasure meeting you," Hatt said.

Willcocks smiled and locked the door as Hatt left the building.

"What a poor fool." Willcocks knew he could buy a new printing press for a quarter of that price. His smile widened at the thought. "One born every minute; I suppose."

The village of Queenston, five miles south of Newark and Lake Ontario, was a quaint, little, bustling community along the shore of the raging Niagara River. It had a blacksmith, a bakery, a general store, a tavern, and several houses along the cobblestone streets.

The Secord house was a modest two-story white house with stonewalls and snake fences surrounding the acreage. Plants were in full bloom, and animals were grazing the new clover and grass covering the property.

Captain James Secord, 38 years old, and his two close friends, Nathan Davis and John Decew, walked through the street toward the Secord house, carrying muskets, satchels, and the small game they had just hunted.

The three friends had spent the day in the forest shooting rabbits, pheasant, and grouse. It had been a long winter, and the men were glad to get outdoors and breathe the fresh spring air. The sun shone against their sweat-filled faces as they approached the Secord house.

The Secord's five children, Mary, twelve; Charlotte, ten; Harriet, five; Charles, four; and Appolonia, one, were all at play in the front yard. The children read books, played on the swing, and conducted a tea party at the small table that James had built.

The Secords also had two African American servants, Bob Armstrong, and his wife, Fan. Like Laura and James, Bob and Fan had come to Upper Canada at the outset of The Revolutionary War in 1776. They were free citizens but were given few other options for work in the small village of Queenston.

Bob and Fan were happy to escape the hot plantation fields of the south and live in the cooler climates of Upper Canada. Now in their fifties, they worked hard for the Secords and were content in their small coach house at the south end of town. Bob and Fan earned money, ate well, and had plenty of friends and support from the local African American community.

Bob and Fan were endearingly dedicated to each other, although they publicly hid their feelings and affections. They had seen famine, sickness, and tragedy throughout their lives as they experienced the upheaval and revolution during the first days of the United States.

After 30 years of peace following The Revolutionary War of 1776, Bob and Fan built an entire life with family, community, commerce, and religion. The church was central to their lives and gave them inspiration, joy, and direction during the ups and downs of living in such an unforgiving, hostile, transitioning world.

Bob chopped wood as the Secord children played, and Fan tended to the newborn Appolonia. As James Secord, Nathan Davis, and John Decew approached the unsuspecting children, James startled them by yelling, "Hello, my beautiful children!"

James' middle child, Harriet, tackled her father and wrapped her tiny arms around his waist. Harriet was James' funniest child. She was witty and energetic, seemingly never running out of energy.

James kissed the top of her head. "Glad to see you too, Harriet," he said as she hung off his waist. He then turned to his oldest daughters, Mary and Charlotte. "I hope you two are well and getting along."

Mary and Charlotte could have been twins, and they were both approaching the age of fierce independence and general disobedience. The two girls looked at each other and giggled.

Mary rolled her eyes at her father and smiled. "Of course, father."

"Have you two been helping Mr. and Mrs. Armstrong and your mother while we've been away?" James asked with a raised eyebrow.

"Mary hasn't done anything since you've been gone. I have been the most helpful," Charlotte boasted. "I helped Mother with laundry, fed the chickens, and made biscuits, too."

"Father, believe your eldest, wisest daughter. I did the most," Mary said. "I am the one who fed the chickens and cleaned the stalls. Charlotte wouldn't help me at all."

"I know you both pulled your weight. You're both such lovely, hard-working girls," James said proudly. He then turned to Bob and Fan. "How has the day been? Any news?"

Any adult on the North American continent knew what 'news' meant. War was about to erupt, and people were generally uneasy about the prospects of another war between Britain and the United States. James was an artilleryman in the British military. He had brilliant math and organizational skills learned from his business, which made him an excellent artillery captain.

"A lot of 'Madison' news is swirling about, sir," Bob said with a concerned look. "At least, that's what Pierpoint, Jupiter, and Vanpatten tell me."

"It seems like it is coming, Mr. Secord," Fan added. "Not a lot of joy or laughter around these parts."

A curious Charlotte asked, "What is 'Madison news,' father?"

"I'll tell you later on, Charlotte." However, he was not going to. "Go and play."

Charlotte and Mary skipped around the side of the house without a worry in the world. 'Madison news' was concerning, as they would all get dragged into another war, especially living in Queenston alongside the Niagara River.

John Decew looked across the street towards the Niagara River with a look of distress. Decew, around James' age, was an intelligent, ambitious, dedicated man. He had developed a significant milling operation near Beaverdams, about 20 miles west of Queenston, and established the first library in Newark. He was a successful, well-educated businessman and had gained an admirable reputation throughout Niagara.

"I hope it doesn't come down to W-A-R," Decew spelled out.

Harriet and Charles couldn't read or write yet and were far more interested in getting attention from Nathan Davis, a handsome young man Decew and Secord hired to help with the daily operations at the lumber mill and general store.

Harriet jumped off her father and now tackled Nathan.

"Hello, Mr. Davis!" she said with a smile.

"Hi, Harriet," he grunted. "You, indeed, are blossoming into a lovely young lady." Nathan gave her a little tickle, and she jumped off.

"Thank you, Mr. Davis," she said as she giggled and curtsied.

"All right, enough of that." John Decew picked Harriet up and threw her over his shoulder. "You're under arrest for being too polite."

Harriet laughed as Decew ran her all over the front yard, kicking and screaming.

"You're not a lady yet!" Decew yelled, bobbing her up and down.

Charles came running around the side of the house and wrapped himself around his father's leg. "Daddy!"

James picked the small boy up and gave him a big hug and kiss. Laura Secord, James' wife, came through the front door. James' gaze shifted from his small boy to his wife.

Laura was a proud sight. Years of family organization, churning butter, darning clothes, tending animals, and lending herself entirely to any task the business required illuminated her. Laura was a fit woman of action and very few words. The community looked up to Laura and the Secords, as they could sustain a business, buy fashionable clothes, employ people, and promote commerce along the busy Niagara River.

As Laura stood in the doorway smiling, wearing her English lace cap, brushing the baking flour from her apron, she locked eyes with James, walked down the steps, and kissed him on the cheek.

James was utterly devoted to his wife. She was a committed, loving mother and wife and never seemed to run out of energy.

"Hello, my love," James said adoringly.

"Welcome back," Laura said as she removed her apron and took the baby Appolonia from Fan.

"Thank you," Fan said. "That is one heavy baby."

Laura looked at Appolonia and then at her husband. She loved James and treasured his affection and devotion. They had five charming, impulsive, creative children together. They raised animals and crops, created a thriving operation along the Niagara River, and were happily married for 15 years.

James looked at Laura, holding baby Appolonia, and smiled at the love of his life and the centre of his world.

Laura was the daughter of a hatmaker and a Revolutionary War veteran. Her father, Thomas Ingersoll, had moved across the Niagara River into Upper Canada when she was a girl. She had known nothing but the thriving St. David's acres her family owned and the benefits of being landowners in such a lush, productive agricultural zone.

James was also American-born and had married Laura Ingersoll in 1797. After Charlotte and Mary were born, James and Laura opened the general store in Queenston together. They filled the shelves with fresh corn, tobacco, coffee beans, spices, oatmeal, flour, sugar, molasses, eggs, milk, butter, and cheese. In the right season, fresh fruit, vegetables, honey, and maple syrup might be available for customers.

The family was prospering beside the Niagara River, along with the surrounding community members who benefited from all the trade in and around Queenston and the Secord's store. Iroquois boys would bring tobacco and cigars and trade for sugar and spice. Americans would travel across the river to get their hands on citrus fruits from the Caribbean. There were incredibly loyal customers around them who favoured the Secord's business because of their hard work and blossoming young family. Charlotte and Mary helped with stocking shelves, cleaning up, and smiling at any customer who came through the doors. It had taken years to establish the business, and the Secords now lived comfortably.

Publishing advertisements for their store in Willcocks's paper also helped bring in people from all over Upper Canada. James and Laura met people from York, Amherstburg, Port Dover, and as far away as Kingston. With war looming, business would inevitably and drastically change.

Despite the hardships and controversy, their five children, and the potential for another war, they still found time to love one another. It had been a challenging yet rewarding life for both James and Laura.

Laura oversaw the entire homestead. She was a master gardener and followed the Farmers Almanac to maximize the growing season. Her brother-in-law forced the Secords to sell the massive St. David's property. Ultimately, they had to embrace a more modest living in Queenston. Laura, James, and their children built a remarkable life together where they thought nothing could stop them.

"Welcome back, gentlemen. John, Nathan, great to see you," Laura said.

"Hello," James said as he removed his satchel, musket, and powder flask from his shoulder. "You are looking more striking than ever. It looks like we caught you in the middle of baking something delicious, no doubt."

"Baking some extra sourdough for the shelves in the morning," Laura said.

"It smells delicious," Nathan said, smelling the fresh bread in the air. "We could smell it down the street."

"How are you, Nathan?" Laura asked.

"Well, thank you, Madam," Nathan responded.

"Let us go inside and rest awhile. You have had a long day," Laura said, turning inside.

"Sorry to drop such news so late, my dear, but I figured we could set a few more places for the Decews and Nathan."

James knew Laura would have plenty of food and would not mind the extra company.

"Catharine is at the library, and I'm sure she would love to see everyone," Decew said, referring to his wife.

"Of course, Jonathan," Laura turned to James. "A friend from Shipman's Corners will also be stopping by later this evening. She is the tutor we hired to help the children with their arithmetic and literature. Her name is Victoria, and she is an exquisite young lady," Laura said.

"Ah, yes," James said, "Victoria, our new tutor."

Laura put the baby on the sofa inside the parlour. "I hope you don't mind stewed beef, potatoes, and corn," she said to Decew and Nathan.

"We don't mean to impose, Mrs. Secord," John Decew said.

"It's no problem at all," Laura responded. "Come, there is much to do."

Laura was happy to have all the additional help and sent Bob and Fan home for the day. The two servants happily took some beef, potatoes, and corn home to cook for themselves.

Bob and Fan were originally from South Carolina and were offered asylum in Canada. Though there were few options outside of servitude when they arrived, they never regretted the migration north. In Upper Canada, they were never starved, beaten, or looked down upon as they were in the tobacco and cotton fields. They attended church with the rest of the community. They were so thankful to live in such a tolerant, relatively accepting place.

Bob and Fan were married alongside the Niagara River by a Presbyterian minister named David George. Reverend George had baptized Bob and Fan's baby boy, Hector, who was now 21 and working hard on Richard Pierpoint's acreage in nearby Grantham.

Hector would always stop by Secord's general store on Mondays to drop off fresh eggs and apples to sell. Hector was allowed to keep a small share of the delivery money, but he saved every penny. Bob and Fan were excited to see their boy this evening, as they were getting off early enough to sit and have a nice meal together.

In their mid-fifties, Bob and Fan loved a good night together. They might stroll down to the Niagara Gorge or visit the sandy shores of Lake Ontario after dinner. They might play cards well into the evening or do some quality reading by candlelight.

"God bless you all," Fan said as she packed her things and thought about seeing a sunset later that night.

"We'll see you in the morning," Bob said as the two left holding hands.

Bob and Fan departed through the front gate for the evening as Laura, James, Nathan, and Decew said their goodbyes.

Chapter 3 – Council Fire

Despite knowing the nation was about to take up the tomahawk again, John Norton strolled, holding his young wife's hand, along the banks of the Grand River. Though he preferred meandering along the river with his loving Karighwaycagh, he would be part of a Council fire with the Seneca from New York State this evening. This meeting would be about Indian alliances and determining which side each of the differing tribes would join.

As they walked, he strategized the realities of living in an era prioritizing assimilation and eradication. Tribes were disappearing, and colonialism had pushed most of the eastern coast tribes to the west side of the Mississippi River. Although Tecumseh and Joseph Brant were the leaders and symbols of the unified Six Nations, Norton understood the importance of his role in bridging the gap between the Department of Indian Affairs and the tribes of the Grand.

For years, William Claus had been trying to tarnish Norton's character and reputation. Since Joseph Brant, a prominent Mohawk War Chief had died five years earlier, Norton had been battling the Department of Indian Affairs and Claus's evil plotting.

Chief Joseph Brant was Norton's adoptive uncle and, while on his deathbed, said his last words to Norton: "Have pity on the poor Indians. If you have any influence with the Great, my brother, try to do our people all the good you can."

Norton had never forgotten these words. Brant was his mentor and caregiver, and he provided a model to look up to. Chief Brant had fought against General George Washington in pre-revolutionary struggles, he helped maintain the Covenant Chain between the Six Nations, he had been a significant spokesman, travelled throughout Europe, and was introduced to several kings and queens throughout his life of dedication to the Iroquois Confederacy. Norton adored Chief Joseph and was devastated by his loss five years earlier, in 1807.

Whatever lies ahead, Norton thought, whether it be the dealings and backstabbings of William Claus or another war, he would always stand up for his Indian brothers and sisters. No longer would he stand by and let his family and relations be mistreated.

Karighwaycagh looked at her husband. "Why so quiet?"

"I'll soon be sitting at the Council fire trying to convince our brothers to oppose the Americans, to stand tall, and bring absolute freedom to our people," Norton said to his wife.

"Speak truthfully, husband. Together, we are strong. Apart, we are nothing," Karighwaycagh said. "Teyoninhokarawen, you are wise and strong and will lead us to victory. This will be our home forever," she said, indicating the beautiful Grand River and its forested banks.

The two finally made it back into the camp and the central fire of the Grand River Tribes. Hundreds of Native men and women were moving about the community. Various hides were drying in the sun, venison cooked on a nearby spit, and men were cleaning their muskets and sharpening their tomahawks and knives. Tension was mounting as the Seneca Chiefs arrived from New York. The local tribes looked upon them with reserve and mistrust.

The Chiefs began to gather around the Council fire. Tekarihoga, the oldest and wisest among the Grand River Chiefs, said, "We thank our American brothers for their journey and company."

Red Jacket, Chief among the Senecas, responded to Tekarihoga's welcome. "We thank the Grand River nations for their welcoming and their hospitality. For our cherished brothers, we bring this offering," the Seneca Chief said, handing Tekarihoga a ceremonial cloth pouch of tobacco.

Tekarihoga smelled the bag of tobacco and smiled. "Welcome," he said to the Seneca party. "Come, let us speak truthfully and sincerely about the reason for your trip from Buffalo Creek."

Once all of the different Chiefs established themselves around the fire, all nodded to one another and began to exchange various gifts of tobacco and cigars.

The other Seneca Chief, Little Billy, sat beside Red Jacket and started with the business they had travelled so far to conduct. "Brother, we have come from our homes to warn you so you may preserve yourselves and your families from distress. We discovered that the British and the Americans are on the eve of war. They are in dispute respecting some rights on the sea, with which we are unacquainted. Should it end in a contest, let us keep aloof. Why should we again fight and call upon ourselves the resentment of the conquerors?"

As the sun disappeared behind the horizon and the stars revealed themselves, John Norton couldn't help but ponder his wife's and community's safety. He understood the size and power of the Americans and the British and knew being a passive spectator would only result in demise.

Little Billy continued to express the notions of the people of Buffalo Creek; "We know that neither of these powers have regard for us. In the former war, we espoused the cause of the King. We thought it most honourable. After seven years of conflict, during which we never considered overtures from the enemy, we discovered the English and the Americans had negotiated a peace agreement. As a result of the newly agreed-upon boundary line, our enemy - the Americans - claimed our territory. We found none to assist us in obtaining justice. We learned to rely on ourselves and make the best of it." Little Billy was a wise man and had seen much bloodshed through the decades and was reminding the Six Nation Chiefs of the hapless policies and treachery of the two warring nations. "Our experience has taught us we will be neglected until they want something from us. Why should we endanger the comfort, even the existence of our families? To enjoy their smiles only for the day they need us?"

John Norton understood Little Billy's rationale for not getting involved in another European conflict. Norton also admired his dedication to Buffalo Creek's people and preserving the peace. However, the Seneca people were at the complete mercy of the United States. They were allocated a plot of land and given no choice.

Prevost, Brock, and the rest of the British leadership offered the people of the Grand River an entire country of their own as well as help with establishing the Indian Nation in the Ohio and Indiana territories. The British had promised not only to put the nation into place but also to allow it to govern itself.

"You all understand this upcoming war. Side with the British King and fight the well-prepared Americans or come, with open arms, to our American country in the west, said Little Billy." He did not want war and was opting to side with the Americans. The Seneca had seen many wars and battles with the Americans in New York State and were now taking a position to avoid further conflict.

Tekarihoga, the wise Grand River Chief, began to speak, "This is Canada. Here is where the bones and ashes of our ancestors are buried. We must not forsake them. Should the kind invitation of our American brethren entice us to forget these silent objects of our regard, we shall never forgive ourselves."

All the Chiefs around the fire nodded their heads in affirmation as Tekarihoga continued. "We speak only with affection, yet the old and the feeble, the young and the helpless, our parents, our wives, and our children, will call loudly upon us to be cautious and consider well if we attempt to conduct them to a strange unknown country. To undertake a long journey where we may leave their bones on the road and make no provision for them is inexcusable."

John Norton nodded again in agreement at the Chief's wise words. No more long journeys away from home, he thought. No more deaths on the migration road. His people have suffered and been displaced long enough.

Red Jacket responded to the wise words of the Mohawk Chief, "The American agent who lives in our neighbourhood has told us that the U.S. does not require our assistance. Their number is endless and adequate to every emergency of war. This entirely meets our sentiments; we are in their power but do not wish to join them in war."

Norton broke his silence. "Brothers, you know that we removed ourselves from the country of our ancestors when overhung by the power of the Americans to place ourselves under the protection of the King. He does not desire to invade the Americans, but if they follow us here to attack our father King, we cannot be passive spectators."

Little Billy spoke in opposition to Norton's words: "In standing between the English, the Americans, and the French, many valiant warriors have fallen. Although we have thus been weakened and deprived of our independence, it has not been by the victories of a conqueror; it has been the neglect or unkindness of our friends. Seeing that no good can be derived from war, we are of the opinion that we should follow the example of the Quaker people, who never bear arms in war and denounce the principle of hostility."

Norton quickly responded to the newly formed pacifist nature of the Seneca Chief. "What you have said certainly applies to those of you who remain on the other side. The Americans have gained possession of your country except for the small part you have reserved. They have enveloped you; it is out of your power to assist us. You would not hazard your families, nor do you have a motive to assist them. King George does not want to take your lands nor injure you, and the Americans will not give you more for assisting them. Even should your actions or courage merit a glorious report, they will hardly allow you that which they bargain for themselves. It is, therefore, both in your interest and your duty to remain peaceable at home."

This was the message Norton wanted to send to his brothers in New York. The Seneca tribe of Buffalo Creek would die if they met the Six Nations in battle, and it would be all for nothing.

Red Jacket could sense the escalating frustrations around the fire. "Brother, we implore that you all sit in your habitations, regardless of the tempest of battle. You may thus escape unhurt and unobserved by the enraged combatants. Let us now pledge ourselves to each other to observe a strict neutrality. When the storm of war has blown over and left the sky clear, we may then meet again with our hearts unclouded by disagreeable circumstances. We hope our words may penetrate your hearts. Take this wampum, in token of our sincerity."

Red Jacket gave Tekarihoga the wampum belt, and the entire Council began to smoke their pipes as the big sky passed overhead.

Norton was happy his message was heard by the reserved, trapped, and seemingly helpless Seneca. They were reserved at Buffalo Creek, in New York State, and had no reason to engage in battle with the Americans. Every scalp the unified Grand River Nations would take would be from the blue-coated Americans and none from their Seneca brothers.

Chapter 4 – Friends, Old and New

Laura and James were preparing dinner: a beef stew with potatoes, carrots, corn, and freshly baked biscuits. The spring evening was cool, and the fire had been stoked. The Secord children were winding down upstairs after a long day. Nathan Davis and John Decew helped set the table with candle holders, silverware, serviettes, and new European porcelain plates.

There was a knock at the door. Laura put down her wooden spoon, wiped her hands on her apron, and went to the front door.

Laura opened the door to Victoria Berwick, a young, pretty tutor James and Laura had recently hired to help guide the children's education. The children were all coming of age and would need constant instruction and special attention as they prepared for adulthood. Laura and James had become increasingly busy the past few years and needed help teaching grammar, arithmetic, and the sciences.

"Victoria. So nice to see you this evening. How are you?" Laura asked with a smile.

"I am wonderful, thank you, Mrs. Secord," Victoria said. "The aroma smells terrific."

"Why, thank you. Come in before you catch a cold." Laura took the young Victoria by the arm and guided her into the warm, cozy house. "James dear, you remember Victoria, our new tutor?"

"It's wonderful to see you again, Mr. Secord," Victoria said.

"Please, call me James. The children are very excited to meet you. Come upstairs, I'll introduce you. They're just winding down for the day." James led Victoria towards the staircase. As they passed the dining room, Victoria caught Nathan's eye. Victoria looked at Nathan and smiled as he clumsily dropped a few forks on the floor while setting the table. Victoria smiled at his clumsiness as she went up the stairs.

"Mary, Charlotte, Harriet, Charles, and Appolonia are their names, born in that order. I'm quite sure they'll all adore you," James said as he guided Victoria up the stairs. "Children, I'd like to introduce someone to you," he announced. "It's really nice to have some extra help around the house."

Catharine Decew, John's wife, came through the back door carrying an armful of firewood for the evening ahead. They had been married for 15 years and had eleven children. The children were home with their aunt and uncle this evening, which gave Catharine and John a rare evening together with friends.

John Decew was an important man throughout Upper Canada. He was an assessor, collector, and warden. Decew was among a few founding members of the Niagara Library Board, the first circulating library in Upper Canada. The Decews also owned a successful lumber mill near Beaverdams, which had been thriving for years.

"John, could you help bring in a few more loads of wood for the Secords?" Catharine asked her husband.

"Of course, darling," Decew said without reservation, making his way out into the cool night air.

The children had an early supper and were winding down for bed as usual. Victoria read them a short story called 'The Green Snake and the Beautiful Lily' that she had brought to build rapport and relations with her new pupils. Laura and James were so grateful to have Victoria's help, as they knew education was crucial in a progressing world of literature, business, knowledge, and commerce.

Laura and James brought the cast-iron stew pot and basket of biscuits to the dining room. Nathan, John, and Catharine sat conversing, patiently waiting for the hot meal.

After meeting the children, introducing herself, and reading them a bedtime story, Victoria went down to the dining room and was the last to be seated amongst the five others.

"It smells delicious," Victoria said as she sat down. "Thanks for waiting for me."

"How was your first meeting with the children?" James asked Victoria. "I heard you reading them a story."

"They are delightful, Mr. Secord. I read them a relatively new German story called 'The Green Snake and the Beautiful Lily.' It is about the outer senses and human aspirations. I think they liked it."

"Oh, that's just fantastic," Laura said. "You will discover the children have wonderful and very active imaginations."

"Mr. and Mrs. Secord, I thank you for the opportunity and sincerely look forward to our future lessons and adventures together," Victoria earnestly said.

"Call me James, please," he responded. "I could tell straight away they loved you already."

"They can be a handful," Laura added. "Charlotte and Mary are also super helpful with the little ones. Don't hesitate to ask them for their help."

"Victoria, I would like to introduce you to…" James was saying until Nathan interrupted.

"Mister Nathan Davis, my lady. It is a pleasure to meet you," he said, pushing his chair back from the table and rising to his feet to shake Victoria's petite hand.

Laura looked at James and smiled. James smiled in return, acknowledging he also saw that Nathan and Victoria had just made a connection.

"It's a pleasure to meet you, Mr. Davis," Victoria said.

"Victoria, this is Mister John and Catharine Decew. They are great friends of ours," James said. "We've known each other for years."

"I'm very familiar with your dedication and commitment to the library in Newark, Mr. Decew," Victoria said. "Having a new education and innovation centre here in Canada is wonderful."

"Well, aren't you just lovely," Decew said.

"The Decews also run a milling operation near Beaverdams," James added.

"Mr. and Mrs. Decew provide me with a lot of work at the mill throughout the year," Nathan said.

"This is such an exciting part of the country. So much is progressing and developing," Victoria said.

James shifted the conversation. "Well, shall we eat?"

The six friends shared a hearty meal. They talked about education, milling, the spring seed plotting, the new baby foals, and planning for the busy season ahead. They drank wine, laughed, shared memories, and got well-acquainted. As was tradition, the ladies cleared the table, and the men smoked tobacco from their pipes, drank wine, and shifted the conversation to the looming war.

"Have you noticed the preparations at Lewiston, across the river? President Madison is close to signing that declaration, I swear it. A matter of days before word hits here and Fort George," James said.

"By God, who wants this war?" Nathan asked.

"It's the American War-hawks in the west that persist with Washington and the president," Decew added.

"The War-hawks and the general public call for war. I've read articles from Baltimore and Washington. British marine impressment on the sea, naval blockades, and trade restrictions are sharp wounds that run deep. Remember the Chesapeake? Why not attack the Canadas and use her as a bartering chip against the British," James said as he lit his pipe.

"How can Britain and the Canadas possibly fight the United States when the entire British military is at war with Napoleon?" Nathan said, obviously concerned about his future and business.

James grabbed the last issue of The Guardian from atop the dining room hutch. "This is Joseph Willcocks's last issue of the Guardian. If that is not a prelude to war, I don't know what is." James read from the paper:

It is not my intention, Gentlemen, by a recital of sufferings, to influence or irritate the minds of an injured, insulted, and loyal people. No, but it is my intention and my wish to impress upon the public mind the indispensable necessity there is of sending men to the new parliament, whose livelihood or prospects in life do not depend upon the will or caprice of any tyrannical individual and whose principles are unambitious, and beyond the reach of corruption.

"Willcocks does not love the King, does he?" Nathan said.

"No, he does not," Decew said.

"Willcocks says he is 'the enemy of the measures of the King's servants in this colony.' Dangerous rhetoric in such a fragile period," James observed.

"I think he is loyal to Canadians. Hell, most Canadians were, at one point or another, American. Friends or family all seem to be opposed to this war. Hell, I'm American and still have family in New York," James said. "His hate for a tyrant 3000 miles away has more to do with selling newspaper subscriptions, I suppose."

"Nothing ties these Canadian colonies together. We are a land of refugees, trappers, and Indians. The Americans believe this will be their second revolutionary war while we're all still trying to settle ourselves and build a civilized society after the first revolution," Decew added.

"In the New York Gazette, I read an article that said former President Jefferson stated that invading Canada would be 'a mere matter of marching'. He might be right," James said, taking another draw from his pipe.

"Easy for him to say," Decew joked.

"Willcocks sounds like he's taking a page from Jefferson," James said.

"When will there be a generation of leaders who are not so dedicated and single-mindedly focused on killing one another?" Nathan asked philosophically.

"Perhaps in a couple hundred years," Decew said.

"Or until the powders run dry," James added. "American victory will be cutting off our supply routes, you realize. They aim to cut off Upper Canada completely at Kingston or Montréal."

"What about Detroit?" Nathan said.

"And here at Newark and Queenston?" Decew added.

"Word from Fort George says that Major General Brock has asked to remain here, not wanting to return home to England. Yet another indicator that war is forthcoming." James had confidence in Brock. He was a credited soldier, leader, and tactician. If anyone could lead a counter-offensive against the Americans, it would be General Brock.

Decew nodded in agreement. "Have you heard anything from our Cherokee brother John Norton?" he asked James.

"His backbone is, no doubt, hard at work, gaining respect amongst his people somewhere, trying to assemble the reluctant pieces of a fragile puzzle. He does assure great numbers though, which may well be the deciding factor in the war," James answered.

"Scalps of slain neighbours drying in the sun, flesh sides stained with vermillion dyes; drawn from these lands. Not exactly the warm thoughts I had when I envisioned starting a family around here." Nathan was still young and dreaded the thought of having to kill his fellow man. "Those poor Indians, having to be dragged into another war, fighting for fathers they know nothing of," Nathan said as he shook his head.

"The King has given them complete freedom and equality here in the Canadas. They are treated as equals, whereas the U.S.

treats them like farm animals herded into tiny pastures," John said to Nathan. "Tecumseh and his tribes have just as much a reason to defend these lands as we do."

"Prevost, Brock, and Sheaffe all look upon us as though they do not know where our loyalties lay. Brock wants the British legislature to pass an act that forces us civilians to take an oath of allegiance," James said to his friends.

"And what of those Canadians who would gladly join the American effort?" Nathan asked.

"In all likeliness, the King would have them shot, to be made an example of," James answered.

"They truly must be worried that we will join with the Americans," Decew said.

"There will be traitors, deserters, Loyalists, and mutineers throughout this war. It will not be pretty," James added. "There are family members on both sides of the river, friends, relations, and associates. I think that is why Brock is pushing hard for legislation to guard against treasonous acts."

"I don't know if I have the stomach for war," Nathan said.

"I don't think Madison and his army care much about your stomach, Nathan. Have no fear; we will pinch our pennies and support our neighbours, no matter the cost," Decew said.

"Brock will need a victory to win the favour of Canadians right at the outset of the war," James said. "Word will need to spread quickly."

Laura, Catharine, and Victoria came from the kitchen carrying two steaming pies from the oven, a stack of small plates, and dessert forks. The men put out their pipes, sat up straight, and smiled at the thought of sweet, delicious pie.

"Fannie made some delicious apple and blueberry pie," Laura said.

"Sounds wonderful," Nathan said.

"Fan makes the best pie. We sell out of them every time we put them on the shelf," James said.

"Fannie's pies are famous," Decew said, smiling. "You're going to love them."

The six friends shared the hot pies, drank pekoe tea, and played cards by candlelight well into the evening. Though the thought of war stirred in their minds, the fresh spring evening surrounded by old and new friends trumped any dark thoughts of war and bloodshed.

Chapter 5 – Fort George

It was another beautiful spring day at Fort George, where the Niagara River spilled into Lake Ontario. One thousand soldiers had been cooped up for the harsh winter months. They were relieved to finally be outdoors without fearing frostbite, pneumonia, or other sickness. Illness had taken its toll over the winter, with some deaths and long recovery lists.

William Hamilton Merritt, a newly appointed Captain of the Provincial Dragoons, tended to the horses' stall at Fort George. He fed them apples and topped their troughs with hay from a local farmer. Merritt's love of horses and pride in his new role stemmed from his father's passion in nearby Shipman's Corners.

General Brock and General Sheaffe opened the stable doors to see the young 19-year-old working hard.

"Congratulations on your Captaincy, Mr. Merritt," Sheaffe said.

Merritt finished filling a trough with hay. "Thank you, Generals," he said, putting the pitchfork down and saluting.

"We will need your youthful energy and riding skills before long," Brock said.

"I will be ready," the young Merritt said.

"So long, Captain," Sheaffe said. "Keep up the good work."

Brock and Sheaffe left the stable and continued their daily stroll around Fort George. They next stopped at the general barracks, where Joseph Willcocks sat polishing his boots.

Joseph Willcocks had recently taken up arms with the British after leaving political life, the printing press, and propaganda behind. He was one of the soldiers who had become severely ill in the wintertime and still had a persistent cough and general fatigue.

Willcocks was a long-time member of parliament and official opposition. General Brock had attempted to push through assembly measures meant to quicken preparations for war. It was politicians like Willcocks who stiffened the resistance to Brock's plan. Now, at Fort George, Brock was his superior officer and governor of Upper Canada in wartime. However, Willcocks welcomed Brock as a highly decorated leader, mentor, and role model for the 49th regiment. Things were different now; though Willcocks was still suspicious of Brock and his motivations, he did respect him. Willcocks applauded Brock's expectations of his soldiers regarding discipline, hard work, and loyalty to the cause.

General Brock and General Sheaffe approached Joseph Willcocks, who was putting the final touches on his black military boots. He put them neatly on the bench beside him and wiped his nose with the sleave of his jacket.

"Mr. Willcocks, good to see you looking better," Brock said.

"Terrible flu this winter through the barracks, sir," Willcocks said, rising to his feet. "I was on the brink of death," he said, saluting the Generals.

"Well, it's good to see you back in good health," Brock said. "Mr. Willcocks, I have a special mission for you and your talents."

"Oh, yeah?" Willcocks replied with intrigue. "Ready for duty, sir."

"Mr. Willcocks, we need you to visit the Grand River. Your priority is to help convince the Haudenosaunee people of the Haldimand area to join in our defence of Upper Canada," Brock said.

"Indians, sir?" Willcocks asked, coughing hoarsely.

"Yes, Mr. Willcocks. We need you to help convince the tribes of the Six Nations to join our effort," Brock said. "They seem hesitant, as there are differing perspectives and opinions amongst the tribes."

"I would be honoured," Willcocks said.

"Good, Willcocks. We will discuss the details on the morrow. That is all for now." Brock saluted Willcocks and carried onward with General Sheaffe.

Willcocks was pleased, knowing being selected for such a critical mission was an honour. He watched Brock and Sheaffe stroll off as he thought of his future role in creating alliances in Upper Canada.

Brock trusted Willcocks' leadership abilities. When it was published, he had read The Guardian and agreed with many of Willcocks' sentiments. He believed his personality and fame would perfectly fit such a mission.

Activity was abundant about the fort as the military leaders inspected soldiers and their duties, monitored behaviours, and checked the general cleanliness of things. Soldiers prodded their weapons and ate freshly arrived Caribbean fruits. Some men carved and whittled wood, some were smoking and playing cards, while others were working on maintaining the fort's structure and walls.

Brock and Sheaffe kept the soldiers highly disciplined and insisted on cleanliness, health, and regular maintenance. There were some disgruntled soldiers, but they were primarily upset at the terrible Canadian weather rather than the highly regimented discipline of their superior officers.

There had been attempted mutinies at Fort George in the past, but Brock, Sheaffe, and the rest of the military leadership quickly vanquished them. Four mutineers and three deserters were captured and sent to Québec, where they were executed by firing squad. Since then, Brock took great pride in the 49th regiment, their well-being, and their immaculate record of being without crime, major incident, or desertion in a decade. The soldiers were incredibly loyal to Brock, and he reciprocated with love for the men.

The newly arrived John Norton and his party, guided by Lieutenant James FitzGibbon, a grizzled Irish veteran of the 49th regiment, joined Brock and Sheaffe.

"Captain Norton, welcome," Sheaffe said.

"Thank you, General," Norton responded as they shook hands.

"You look well, Captain Norton," Brock said as the group continued to walk about.

Brock smiled and nodded to a group of soldiers cleaning their weapons. "Can you confide in the Grand River peoples? Do you think they will be faithful to you? Tell me without reservation," Brock asked Norton. Brock was a man of few words, and Norton respected that.

"They are unfortunately divided into parties. There are some plausible men who delay in coming forward, but when we engage and confront them, I have no doubt they are so depraved as to be allies." Norton knew in his mind that all of the Grand River people would eventually join the fight, it might just take some persuasion.

"You can see, Captain Norton, from the activity here and across the river at Fort Niagara, tensions are high. The War-hawks continue to press their President, and I anticipate he will soon sign the declaration of war. Your relations and leadership are crucial to preserving the order of Upper Canada," Brock said.

"I am aware of the urgency, and so is Tecumseh and his brother, The Prophet," Norton assured.

Lieutenant Thomas Evans approached as Norton and Brock continued to stroll the grounds. Evans was a young man of about 25 and carried himself with confidence. His regiment looked highly upon him and both Brock and Sheaffe knew he had a promising future and would soon climb the military ranks.

"General Brock, sir, the American party is en route across the Niagara," Evans said as he saluted his superiors.

"Excellent, Evans," Sheaffe said. "Be sure someone is there to guide them up from the shore, even if it is yourself."

"Yes, General," Evans said as he departed the fort with two soldiers he called upon.

"American Major General Van Rensselaer, his cousin Solomon, Major John Lovett, and a few others will join us for dinner tonight; would you care to join us, Captain Norton?" Brock asked.

Norton did not want to dine with the potential enemy; a group of men he knew looked down upon him. At least in Upper Canada, he was respected and looked upon as an equal. "Thank you for the cordial invitation, sir, but I must decline."

"You are a busy man, I understand," Brock said without delay.

Norton stopped walking and turned and addressed Brock and Sheaffe directly. "Sirs, I must say, regarding my Native family and friends, that it will be necessary to oblige them to return to their usual occupations and homes to ensure support for their families. You understand their present situation is very different from what it was. They no longer possess extensive land, abundant in game and wide ranges for their cattle."

Brock understood that Tecumseh and Norton could not dedicate thousands of grown men solely to a war effort without directly affecting the well-being of their people. He knew they would need men to remain on the farmlands to raise the crops, harvest hides, and build structures in preparation for the winter seasons.

"Quite different from the time when they were protected from enemy assaults by a desert frontier," Brock said as he nodded in agreement with Norton. "Of course, Chief Norton, Family should always be the priority. Clear as the blue sky. Before you set off west, perhaps arrangements can be made for more suitable offerings for your people, courtesy of the Crown. This might answer the purpose better than money."

"You have, again, hit the mark, my friend," Norton said. "Seed, grain, flour, weapons, powder all make better than coins. I shall gather with my allies, and you shall hear word soon. My prayers are with you. General Sheaffe, General Brock, I hope we can remedy this conflict before it escalates."

"The Saint Lawrence River has just thawed, so we will be able to arrange for provisions within the month," Sheaffe said confidently.

"Walk well, John Norton. Pass the news on to Prophet-Town. Be united in whatever you undertake and communicate freely your sentiments on whatever suggestions may arise from your ongoing discoveries," Brock said as he shook hands with Norton.

"Goodbye, good Generals."

Norton exited the fort with his accompanying warriors as they returned to the Grand River settlement. Norton was happy the British knew the Six Nation warriors would be with their families until called upon. It would mean they do not stand idly by waiting for action, as is the case with the soldiers of Fort George.

"The Indians are a much-injured people," Sheaffe said to Brock.

"American-Indian policies are hapless. However, we will remain allies with the Canadian-Indians no matter the cost. I would give them the coat off my back," Brock said.

FitzGibbon added his two cents: "The Indians are an enterprising, hardy race and uncommonly expert on horseback with a rifle."

"We will need the island of Mackinac at the outset of the war if the Great Lakes are to remain in British hands," Sheaffe said to Brock.

"We must get off to a good start," Brock said with determination.

Along the lower Niagara River shore, a sixteen-foot boat landed carrying American Major General Van Rensselaer, his cousin, Lieutenant Colonel Solomon Van Rensselaer, Major John Lovett, Lieutenant Colonel Winfield Scott, and two aide-de-camps.

Lieutenant Evans and two British privates greeted them as they began to disembark.

"Nothing like nice, fresh river air to work up an appetite, eh Solomon, old boy?" Van Rensselaer said to his cousin.

Van Rensselaer was a longtime businessman, landowner, and politician in New York state. He inherited wealth and 1200 square miles of land in upstate New York because of a grant to his ancestors. He was in the midst of advocating for a canal connecting Lake Erie to the Hudson River. He was not a military man, so his cousin Solomon was appointed First Lieutenant as war appeared on the horizon.

Solomon had been in the military since 1792 and had seen many battles. "This river never ceases to amaze me," Solomon said in response to his cousin.

"A pathway of power-producing prosperity," Van Rensselaer said.

"There is great potential here," Solomon responded.

"Hello and welcome, good sirs," Evans cordially said to the newly arrived Americans.

"Hello, good sir," Van Rensselaer said. "Thank you for coming to meet us."

As passive and delightful as Major General Van Rensselaer was, John Lovett, his biographer, was not as cheerful. Lovett knew the war was coming and was there to investigate the British preparations in Newark and at Fort George.

Winfield Scott, a gigantic man, six-foot-five, weighed at least 230 pounds and was as equally as cautious as Lovett was. Winfield and the New York military were eager for Congress to declare war and he would gather as much information this evening as he could.

"That is one rough river," Van Rensselaer told Lt. Evans.

"Indeed, sir. Not your typical swimming hole," Evans said, smiling.

As the party made their way up the steep embankment towards Queenston, Van Rensselaer tripped on a tree root and fell to the ground.

"Lord, I miss my wife," he said, lying face-first on the ground.

"Come, sir, to your feet," Winfield Scott said as he picked up the Major General.

John Norton paddled down the Grand River toward the Iroquois settlement with his accompanying warriors. He was looking forward to his home, his young wife, and a meal around a nice warm fire. The rocky shores and towering forests were reminders of his time in the United States a few years earlier. He had made his way through Ohio, Kentucky, and finally to Tennessee, the land of the Cherokees - his people. He dreaded the thought of fighting those he had met along the way. Wyandots and Cayugas in Ohio, Delawares and Chickasaws in Kentucky, and friendly settlers and outposts everywhere in between.

Norton knew this continent could be peaceful amongst such a vast landscape. Still, it might take a war to truly establish the ordinance of things. Norton had seen the plantations run by enslaved people in the south, the gigantic cities on the eastern seaboard, and the hurried, unfiltered, westward expansion into the territories of the Lakota and the Cheyenne. He would need to stand tall with Tecumseh and the tribes of Canada to avoid possible slavery and eradication like so many others before him.

The officer's dining hall at Fort George contained a sizable wooden table, chairs, and a hutch for service. The hutch was painted white earlier in the spring to provide a more welcoming decor.

Brock, Sheaffe, FitzGibbon, Van Rensselaer, Solomon, Lovett, and Winfield Scott sat at the table. It was the end of the meal, and a few servants cleared the dishes from the table as the officers sat drinking wine.

Brock stood and raised his glass. "Gentlemen, if I may, I'd like to propose a toast. If the sudden eruption of war is to come upon us, let our battles be that of professional and courteous soldiers," he said.

"Hear, hear. To our neighbours and our health," Van Rensselaer said. "And to a wonderful meal and even better wine."

They all clinked their glasses together, rejoicing in being merry and a bit impaired. All except Winfield Scott, who hadn't taken a sip of wine, and was now staring down the competition, trying to determine weaknesses.

Lt. Evans entered the room with a concerned look as they settled down after the accolades. He strolled past the American end of the table and whispered into Brock's ear.

"Come now, let there be no secrets among friends, General," Winfield Scott said with a false smile.

"You brought this news on this night, June 27th?" Brock said with a shocked expression.

"Speak, General. You stalk the table," Soloman said. "What is it?"

"I stalk the table because I fear the response to my words," Brock said.

"If you deem it fitting and appropriate, General, please share," Van Rensselaer cordially suggested.

"It seems your President Madison has signed the declaration of war against our King on the 18th of June, eighteen-hundred and twelve," Brock said humbly. "Nine days ago."

A silence fell over the dining hall. The tension was palpable. No one was sure how to react to the news. They reserved their emotions and looked at one another to see who would make the first move.

Van Rensselaer's writer and biographer John Lovett interjected: "And so begins the second war of our neighbouring countries under the most peculiar circumstances. A moment ago, salutations to health and happiness, and now I seem caught in the hesitation of pulling out my pistol and making a gallant run for the American shore."

Everyone laughed at Lovett's notion of running away and trying to swim across the torrent Niagara River.

"Don't worry, he's a terrible swimmer," Van Rensselaer jokingly told his newly anointed enemies.

Everyone shared another laugh.

Brock considered the uneasiness of the situation. "Gentlemen, please let us proceed with dessert and reverie, and assume this news has yet to come. I will ensure a clear journey home to the east bank of the Niagara. So please relax and enjoy these moments of peace amongst friends."

Van Rensselaer, Soloman, Lovett, and Scott were relieved to hear such peaceable words from the British leader.

"Honoured and humbled by your generosity, good General. We salute the Crown for its grace and principle," Van Rensselaer said.

"Well, while we're all here, face to face, where do you suppose you'll strike first?" Sheaffe joked. Now that the tension had left the room, everyone laughed.

"Honestly, I hope to be on peaceable terms as soon as possible. An armistice would be the most desirable and beneficial course of action for us here at Fort Niagara. We hope this war lasts only weeks," Van Rensselaer said.

Lovett was a learned man and quite poetic compared to his military superiors. "My brothers, it pains me this evening to learn of such hostilities that we are so not closely linked to. Furthermore, I pray that we do not see each other's faces in battle, for it would bring about memories as warm as my wine-filled cheeks and as fuzzy as my head will be tomorrow morning." Everyone shared a laugh as dessert was served to the table.

Brock admired Lovett's sound and poetic words. "Well said, Major." Brock once again rose to his feet and raised his glass. "Let our combat remain on the battlefield, and our memories and friendships endure and be lifelong."

"Hear, hear!" everyone proclaimed, as they joined together in another salute.

"On behalf of the Crown, Governor General Prevost is certain an armistice will develop. Let it be known, we do not intend to be on the offensive until we receive word that a ceasefire is out of effect," Sheaffe said with sincerity.

"You are all men of great honour and I hope and pray this war is over as suddenly as it has developed," Soloman said.

Chapter 6 – Prelude to War

Karighwaycagh waded in the cool, knee-deep waters of the Grand River near her home in Haldimand. She missed her husband, as he had been gone for what seemed like weeks. Though fiercely independent, her youth drove her desire to be near her husband and lover.

Karighwaycagh occupied herself with beading, cooking, and other chores of the day, but today, she realized she was with child. Morning sickness, nausea, and continuous waves of fatigue had gripped her for several days straight.

Karighwaycagh rubbed her stomach and watched upriver as she saw two birch bark canoes approaching on the horizon. She held her reserve, though internally, she was delighted to see her diplomatic husband returning. Though she worried about her husband's reaction to her pregnancy, she knew he would ultimately be excited for their growing family.

78

Norton drove the hand-crafted canoe ashore, jumped out and embraced his wife. She was his life, his world, and everything he fought for. He adored her beauty, poise, and devotion.

As he turned to bring the canoe onto the bank, the spirited Karighwaycagh playfully ran away.

"Karighwaycagh, why do you run away?" Norton asked with a smile.

"Catch me if you can, Teyoninhokarawen," she said.

"You're too quick," Norton joked. Norton followed her behind a large maple tree and grabbed her around the waist.

"Kwe," (*Hi*) Karighwaycagh said softly.

"Shé:kon!" (Hello) Norton said, looking into her beautiful dark eyes. "Shé:kon, skennenkó:ken?" (Still, is everything peaceful?) Norton asked.

"Hen," (Yes) she said, looking back into his eyes.

"Skennen'kó:wa ken?" (How are you?) he asked.

"Yoyanerátye," (I'm well), she said with a coy, deceptive look on her face. "Iáh tewakata'karí:te," (I am not well) Karighwaycagh added.

Norton was puzzled at his young wife. "Oh niiawenhátie?" (What's happening?) John inquired.

"Wirahninòn:re," (I am pregnant) she said, holding her belly.

"Raké:ni?" (Me, a father?) John screamed and picked his wife off her feet.

"Konnorónhkhwa," (I love you) she said with a beaming smile.

"Konnorónhkhwa," John said with enthusiasm. "Ha' ki' ó:nen tsitiahtén:ti." (Let's go home now).

"Hen," Karighwaycagh said, smiling.

"Yeksá:'a táhnon raksá:'a?" (A girl or a boy?) John asked.

"To:ka," (I don't know) said Karighwaycagh.

Karighwaycagh was so happy that, on the eve of war, her husband accepted and welcomed her pregnancy.

The news of Karighwaycagh's pregnancy had cleared the negative thoughts and feelings Norton had been experiencing at the prospect of war.

She held out her hand, and Norton interlocked his fingers as they strolled down the wooded path.

The two returned to the community where the Seneca party had come to sit at the Council fire on the Grand River. Little Billy, Red Jacket, and a few other Buffalo Creek warriors had once again come to the Grand River to reconcile and plead with the Iroquois not to go to war.

In Queenston, James, Laura, Bob, and Fan began to remove all of their inventory from the shelves of the general store. They knew that outposts, general stores, and landowner homes would be the first raided in the event of war. They carted the bundles of flour and sugar, the jars of cured meats and seeds to the small village of St. David's, where they would store them in a small, discrete dug-out cellar outside of town. Though war had not immediately come across the river into their lives, it indeed was on its way.

Bob and Fan's young son Hector also helped move goods. Hector knew that if the Secords were affected, he and his parents would be too.

The brave young Hector had recently joined a group called 'The Coloured Corps' under the leadership of Richard Pierpoint. It was a small group of formerly enslaved people from the United

States that came together to fight the threat and distinct possibility of American victory and re-enslavement.

In 1793, under Governor Simcoe, Upper Canada passed an act preventing the further introduction of slaves into the province. England was amid gradual abolition, and in 1812, most men and women were free. However, in many circumstances, their skin colour inhibited them from obtaining prestigious jobs and positions in society.

Hector, along with the rest of The Coloured Corps, thought that if they fought alongside the Indigenous tribes and the British King, it might help pave the way for future generations of young Black men and women throughout Canada and the rest of North America. Though Hector had known nothing but freedom, he had heard hundreds of horror stories that convinced him to fight for his right to liberty.

Bob and Fan rode up front and steered the horse-drawn wagon while Hector sat in the back with all of the provisions from Secord's store.

"I'm proud of you, boy!" Bob yelled back to his son.

"For what?" he yelled back.

"I'm just thanking you for all your hard work in preparing for the oncoming war. Trust me, boy, war is coming," the proud father said.

Bob, Fan, and Hector arrived at the small St. David's barn, tucked away behind a thicket of evergreens. Nathan Davis and Richard Pierpoint stood waiting for the wagon.

Richard Pierpoint was Bob's oldest friend in Niagara. Pierpoint lived in Grantham, near St. David's, which Bob and Fan visited regularly.

Pierpoint was now 68 but didn't look a day over 50. Given his tumultuous life journey, he had undoubtedly earned the 200 acres he owned.

Pierpoint was born in West Africa in 1744, in an unruly, chaotic and diverse place called Bondu, which Fulani Muslims ruled. The Fula people adopted Islam, which emboldened them to feel religious superiority over the surrounding people of West Africa. The Fuluani captured Pierpoint when he was sixteen. Ultimately, he was sold and brought to North America in chains.

Pierpoint always spoke of his memories of Bondu, painting vivid pictures of a rich and thriving culture. Griot traditions, sports, hunting, music, and dance filled Pierpoint's earliest memories in West Africa. He shared them with his fellow African-American community members wherever he went.

When war erupted in 1776 on the North American continent, Pierpoint, 32 at the time, fought and was granted freedom by the British.

Being stationed at Fort Niagara during The Revolutionary War, he was ultimately given a parcel of land in Grantham, where he farmed the rich Niagara soils. Today, in 1812, Pierpoint was a leading voice, business entrepreneur, and community organizer in the Black community and the entire region.

"Hey, old boy!" Pierpoint yelled to the oncoming wagon.

"Hay is for horses, old man!" Bob yelled, smiling back at his friend.

Pierpoint had given Bob and Fan Armstrong room and board after The Revolutionary War and introduced them to the Secords in 1802. Bob and Fan had always shown gratitude for what Pierpoint had done for them and would forever be indebted to them.

The wagon came to a halt, and Bob jumped off. "My, my, you don't look a day over 40," he said to Pierpoint. "What brings you way out here?"

"I ran into Nathan in Newark, and he told me you'd be doing the rounds for the Secords," Pierpoint said.

"I'm glad you could come," Bob said. "You remember Hector?"

Hector jumped off the wagon and shook hands with Pierpoint. "Hello, Mr. Pierpoint."

"Hector, how are you, son?" Pierpoint asked.

"Doing real well, Mr. Pierpoint," Hector said proudly.

Pierpoint smiled at his newest recruit. Earlier that week, Hector had been pruning trees in Pierpoint's orchards when he approached and asked him to join his contingency. Hector had wondered why Black soldiers were not a part of the British military, and Pierpoint had explained that it was coming, just not yet. Pierpoint explained that was why he was actively creating his own military division, composed of Niagara's most capable Black men from Niagara.

"I'm glad to hear of your high spirits, Hector. Have you told your father the news?" Pierpoint asked.

"What news?" Bob asked.

"Hector is my newest recruit in Niagara's Coloured Corps," Pierpoint said.

"Coloured what?" Bob said confusedly.

"Coloured Corps, Dad," Hector said.

"That's exactly why I'm here," Pierpoint said. "Bob, I've come here to ask you to join our military outfit with your son."

"What?" said Bob, looking at Fan, who was not impressed.

"You old fogies will drop dead of a heart attack before you go on and get yourself killed in battle," Fan said.

Hector gave a little laugh.

"That's not funny!" Fan snapped at Hector.

"I'm now Private Pierpoint, reporting for duty, and you will be Private Robert Armstrong," Pierpoint said, grabbing Bob's shoulders.

"Are you sure this is a good idea?" Fan asked.

"Well, I don't know," Bob said, pondering the ramifications.

"Come on, Father, we should do it together," Hector said.

"I haven't fired a musket in 15 years," Bob said, being modest. Bob was an excellent marksman.

"Come to my place in Grantham tomorrow morning, and I'll re-introduce you," Pierpoint said. "Our boys can not stand idly by. The American army is frothing at the mouth, and we must be at our best."

"Can't the British soldiers handle this?" Fan asked.

"The Americans are endless in numbers, and the Brits only have a few here at Fort George. They're going to need all the help they can get," Pierpoint responded.

"Well, if it is alright with Fannie, okay, I'll join your Coloured Corps," Bob said, turning to see his concerned wife. "For our community, freedom, and everything we've built."

"You old fools. You're going to get yourself killed," Fan said, shaking her head. Though she knew they were fool hardy for rushing into war, Canada would need all the help it could get.

"Hector, bring your father to my house in Grantham tomorrow, and we can get him back into shape," Pierpoint said.

Pierpoint and around 30 others were determined to fight for their freedom. The signatures were slowly accumulating, and Pierpoint would soon have a list worthy of submission to British leadership.

"Honey, I don't know if this is a good idea," Fan said.

"Mamma, don't worry, I'll take care of Paps," Hector said. "Now, come on, we still got tons of work to do before the sun goes down."

Pierpoint mounted his horse. "Bob, Hector, I'll see you two in the morning. Fan, it's always a pleasure." Pierpoint tipped his hat, smiled at Bob, Fan, and Hector, and waved goodbye as he descended the forested path toward Grantham.

General Brock had recently appointed Joseph Willcocks to help secure the alliance between the tribes and the British. Brock was worried about a war happening on two fronts and asked Willcocks for cooperation in determining the intentions of the Grand River tribes.

Willcocks, famous for owning The Upper Canadian Guardian and admired for his wit and boldness, was now free of political position and commitment to his newspaper. He was loyal and determined to help Brock and his country by recruiting local militia and by helping to secure the ever-so-important Iroquois alliance.

Little Billy and Red Jacket, the Seneca Chiefs, had returned with their party to continue the talks around the Council fire. They were welcomed by the Six Nation Chiefs, Willcocks, and a couple of accompanying British soldiers.

Shawnee Chief Tecumseh had also made the journey from Amherstburg to plead with the Seneca to remain home during the upcoming calamity. The night was cool, and the full moon overhead lit the forest floor.

"Brothers, feeling that tender anxiety for your welfare, which should always influence people of the same blood and kindred, we have come to you to explain the sentiments of our hearts," Red Jacket said as he lit his pipe. "We intended to have abode with you some days on the Grand River, to gratify our eyes with a sight of our brethren, but the gathering clouds of war, covering the earth with the gloom of darkness, forbid us from passing this place. We shall, therefore, deliver immediately what moves within our breasts," he said, holding his hand over his heart. "Brothers, our hearts overflow when we look upon you. We lament that you are on the eve of being plunged into the miseries of war, and we pray you to avert them by remaining peaceably at home, unmindful of the clash of arms."

Beside Red Jacket sat Little Billy, who continued a seemingly planned and rehearsed speech by the Seneca: "We know that war is destructive, its conclusion may be ruinous, and it is well ascertained that misery is its constant attendant. Brothers, the people of the great King George III are our old friends, and the Americans are our neighbours. We grieve to see them prepare to imbrue their hands in the blood of each other. We have determined not to interfere, for how could we spill the blood of the English or our brethren? We implore you, therefore, to imitate our determination. Remember, we are in the power of Americans, and perhaps when you have spread destruction through their ranks, they will change their language and insist upon us joining them. They may compel our young men to fight against their kindred. Like devoted animals, we will be brought together to destroy one another."

Red Jacket pleaded with Tecumseh and the other Grand River Chiefs: "Friends, we view you with apprehension and suspicion: we think you are so zealous to serve the King that you are inclined to draw after all these people without considering the difficulties in which you may thereby involve them. Perhaps you also imagine we have come here entirely under the influence of the American agent, prepared and rehearsed the lesson he may have given us. To convince you that we act from the disinterested love of our people and to ensure their welfare and preservation, we shall lay before you the reasons that induce us to recommend neutrality."

Little Billy supported Red Jacket's words: "The gloomy day, foretold by our ancients, has departed from us; we find ourselves in the hands of two powerful nations, who can crush us when they please. They are the same in every respect, although they are now preparing to contend. We are ignorant of the real motives that urge them to arm themselves. Still, we are well assured we have no interest therein, and neither one nor the other has any affection towards us."

Tecumseh, Norton, and the rest of the Grand River Chiefs sat beside each other and contemplated Little Billy and Red Jacket's words. Tecumseh had gone to great lengths and effort to form a massive alliance with the tribes of North America. He had difficulty understanding the reasoning of the Seneca tribes. Tecumseh knew the importance of the unification between the tribes and the vulnerability and weakness of their disconnect. He held his reserve.

Red Jacket spoke again: "We know that our blood, shed in their battles, will not even ensure their compassion to our widows and orphans, nor respect to our tribes weakened in their contests. Has not our nation participated in every war where the English were engaged, even when joined in hand?"

Tecumseh spoke directly to Red Jacket: "If the King is attacked, we must support him. We are sure such conduct is honourable, but how profitable it might be to submit to these mighty men without resistance, we can, by no means ascertain. We know we would feel it highly disgraceful, and we remember the fate of those who have thought a passive inoffensive demeanour would be a sufficient protection."

Joseph Willcocks turned and looked at John Norton, whom he respected throughout the weeks leading up to this moment. Brock had highly praised Norton and said he was to be treated with the 'utmost respect.' Norton had given Willcocks abundant advice regarding Indigenous affairs and local traditions. Willcocks was beginning to enjoy his status on Brock's staff and was looking forward to his future Loyalist ambitions.

It was Norton's turn to support his friend and ally, Tecumseh. "We can not lay at ease when our Father-King is threatened. He has not yet given us the hatchet, but should the enemy invade us; we hope many of your young men do not become subservient to the Americans. Our Father-King has been loyal to his promise of protection and peace since the Americans raised their arms against our King in the name of brothers."

Tecumseh nodded at Norton's words and looked at Red Jacket and Little Billy. "Brothers, we will never consider you to belong to them. We will caution all our Western brethren not to hurt you by striking at the Americans who dwell around you. May the Great Spirit preserve you in peace."

Little Billy could identify Tecumseh's stubbornness and leadership. "We see our words have no effect, but we are easy; we have done what we judged our duty and perceive you have made your selection. Therefore, we shall not exhort you further, as you will join with Europeans in their wars, imitate their example, and inhumanely treat your prisoners. Let the warriors' rage only be felt in combat, by his armed opponents. Let the unofficial cultivator of the ground and his helpless family never be alarmed by your onset, nor injured by your depredation." Little Billy was saddened.

Red Jacket calmly offered his parting words: "We encourage that as the nations listen to your words, you will help them and endeavour to make them happy in favour of the great King, and should you pass through the chance of war, be to them a protector. May he who dwells above the clouds avert every evil from your heads and lead you by the hand. Goodbye, great Chiefs."

Everyone rose to their feet. The opposing tribes' feelings were ominous yet peaceful. They had no idea when they would see each other next, whether it was a peaceful gathering or war. The Seneca departed for Buffalo Creek in their canoes down the Grand River.

Tecumseh, Norton, and the other Chiefs were left around the fire, and they shared stories and premonitions about the upcoming war. Tecumseh rose and spoke: "Proud Mohawks, warriors, I depart for Amherstburg to rendezvous with General Brock. I have received word that our northern brothers have captured Fort Mackinac without injury, and our next venture will be to take Fort Detroit. I'll leave you now. Be on guard. Be brave for your people. It will not be long before we are reunited."

"Goodbye, Chief Tecumseh. We will miss your wise words and your leadership," Tekarihoga said. "Good travels to you, John Norton. May you lead our warriors into glorious victory."

Joseph Willcocks looked on with great admiration for the tradition of the tribes. They exchanged gifts, ate heartily, smoked, and smudged in front of comfortable, warm fires, and were genuine in their exchanges.

"Goodbye, John Norton," Willcocks said.

"Travel well," Norton said, shaking hands with Willcocks.

"I shall bring word of the Grand River commitment to General Brock and General Sheaffe at Fort George," Willcocks said as he shook the hands of the surrounding Chiefs.

Tecumseh and John Norton began preparation for departure along Lake Erie to Fort Amherstburg, across the river from Fort Detroit. At the same time, Willcocks and his aide-de-camps mounted their horses and started the journey back to Fort George and the town of Newark. Willcocks was proud to carry and deliver such important news to the military leadership. The intentions of the Six Nations' commitment to the war helped bolster Willcocks's confidence in Canada's ability to repel the Americans at the outset.

Chapter 7 – War-Cloud

War was slow to develop, especially in Canada, when weather and resources significantly affected where and when to attack. Seeds needed to be sown, animals needed tending, and supplies were mandatory before any army invaded anywhere. Cannons were pulled by man or horse, powders needed to be dry, and orders needed to be given.

Fort Mackinac, a crucial outpost for controlling what was happening in the northern Great Lakes, had been captured by the British at the junction between Lake Michigan and Lake Huron. The Americans had not yet heard of the declaration of war and were surprised by the 600 regulars that stormed the island structure. Fort Mackinac was a great success for the British and was precisely what they needed at the war's outset. It boosted morale amongst the civilian population and throughout the military ranks.

Brock and his men marched to Fort Amherstburg, where he met up with Tecumseh, John Norton, and about 500 warriors. They prepared to engage General Hull at Fort Detroit. One of Brock's men managed to capture dispatches from American General Hull, outlining the low morale of his army, and relayed the letter to Brock. Brock learned of Hull's fear and dread of the number of Indians across the river. Fort Detroit was also getting short on supplies and would be susceptible and vulnerable to an invading force.

Tecumseh entered the officers' mess at Fort Amherstburg, where Brock and a few lieutenants were looking at a map of the surrounding area. The air was smoky, and the chatter was loud as the great Shawnee Chief entered the room.

"Chief Tecumseh, welcome, my friend," Brock said, waving Tecumseh to enter. "Happy you have arrived."

Tecumseh shook hands with Brock.

"How are you, General?"

"Morale is high." Brock rose and looked right at Tecumseh. "I have arranged a special letter to fall into American hands outlining our exaggerated force here at Amherstburg. I have put our fictitious number at five thousand," Brock said with a smile.

"Smart man," Tecumseh responded.

"They fear you and your warriors," Brock said with a smile. "In fact, they dread the thought of you. Do I have the support of you and your warriors when we move against Fort Detroit?"

"You have our support, General, and I assure you our full cooperation," Tecumseh said seriously.

"Good, we will play on General Hull's fears. We will parade you and your warriors past the opening on the field opposite them, giving the impression your force is much stronger than it is. I need you and your warriors to be loud and full of terrifying war cries," Brock suggested. "Bestow upon them the fear of the devil himself."

"Sounds like a good plan, General," Tecumseh laughed and turned to his fellow warriors. "Here is a man!"

"How many times should the same group pass the opening in the field?" Norton asked.

"At least three separate times, in different, unassuming order," Brock added.

"A bold plan," Norton responded, "They will not be happy."

"I am indebted to you, sirs. More sagacious and gallant warriors do not exist," Brock said.

"This should be fun," Tecumseh said as he turned to the smiling Norton.

The following day, Brock sent a letter by messenger, under a flag of truce, to General Hull at Detroit that read:

> *The force at my disposal authorizes me to require of you the immediate surrender of Fort Detroit. It is far from my intention to join in a war of extermination. Still, you must be aware that the numerous bodies of Indians who have attached themselves to my troops will be beyond control the moment the contest commences.*

Tecumseh and Norton paraded their 500 troops through the opening in the woods, hollering and whooping, instilling terror into the fortified American troops. Brock had sent the letter and demanded an immediate surrender to the frightened Hull, who was petrified and isolated within his office.

A British twenty-pound cannon opened up on Fort Detroit. The first shell landed inside the officers' mess and exploded, sending three American soldiers hurtling through the air. General Hull was in the next room and was thrown to the wooden floor from his desk.

As the smoke cleared and the ringing in his ears stopped, Hull rose to his feet, grabbed the rum bottle he had been drinking all morning, and took a long swig. He was paralyzed with anxiety and fear. His army was in short supply, and the surrounding enemy outnumbered his forces. He thought of his family, the dozens of women and children, and the lives of his dedicated American soldiers, all within the fort walls.

Brock's letter requesting surrender lay across Hull's desk, and he felt nauseous at the thought of Indians scalping his entire force. He sent a letter under a white flag of truce to Brock, surrendering his 2,500 troops without a fight. Tecumseh and Brock's plan had worked. Not a single warrior or army regular lost at Detroit.

Norton thought this was the exact type of start Brock and his allies would need if they were going to be successful in the war. They would need to gain the favour and confidence of the population if they were to preserve their culture, lands, and lives.

A month later, the Americans were outraged at Hull's defeat and ashamed of his cowardice. Hull had been sentenced to death in Washington but was ultimately saved by President Madison due to the General's Revolutionary War record.

Major Lovett and General Van Rensselaer played a game of cards inside the officer's mess at Fort Niagara on the American side of the Niagara River. They discussed General Hull's mistakes at Detroit and how he allowed his emotions to distract from his sworn duty.

Grey skies and early autumn rain did not help American spirits around Fort Niagara as they prepared to invade Upper Canada at Queenston.

"How is your cousin's health?" Lovett asked Van Rensselaer.

"Solomon is in poor condition," Van Rensselaer responded. "This weather has not been good to him."

"If any man wants to see folly triumphant, let him come here, let him view friends by friends stretched for hundreds of miles on these two shores, all loving and beloved; all desirous of harmony; all wounded by being coerced, by a hand unseen, to cut throats," Lovett said with great sincerity. Lovett knew, as much as everyone else, that neighbours would be killing neighbours.

"Our nations, once again, must follow its great leaders without questioning their decisions, Mr. Lovett," Van Rensselaer said. "If we are to succeed, there must be no indecision or coercion within our ranks."

"The people must awaken; they will wake from destructive lethargy and stupor. While recording our folly, history will dress her pages in mourning, the showers of posterity's tears will fall in vain, for the sponge of time can never wipe this blot from the American name," Lovett poetically said.

Lovett was an intellectual and a master of words. In his contemplations, he was also very aware of the aftereffects of war; the poverty, desolate communities, starvation, destruction, and chaos that would ensue.

"It is folly that we are such good friends with the enemy. We dine with them, drink to new health and introduce our families to one another," Van Rensselaer said as an American messenger entered the room. "Hello, Private. Do you bring news?"

"I do, sir, of the unfortunate kind. Our American General Hull's army has been seen marching up the Niagara pathways, captured by General Brock at Detroit. The sensations being produced are inexpressible, sir. The remnants of our defeated army are being prodded onward by their British captors. They are shoeless, ragged, dispirited, sir. The wounded are groaning in open carts, heard across the river to us here," the messenger said, clearly upset.

"Thank you, Private, that'll be all," Van Rensselaer said as the messenger left the room. "That damn Brock."

"Parading our captured troops does not help our situation, General," Lovett said.

"Alarm pervades the country and distrust among the troops. Not only are Hull's defeated shoeless, but my own, as well, not to mention they are clamouring for pay and wanting to attend their families and harvests," Van Rensselaer said.

"This parade will produce rage, distrust, mortification, indignation, fearful apprehension, suspicion, and jealousy, General," Lovett said.

"Along with dismay and madness. While we are thus growing weaker daily, our enemy is growing stronger." Van Rensselaer was deep in contemplation.

"Sir, we may be deluged in water, storms of rain I've never experienced, every three days like a muskrat. No burning heat by day, nor blasts of the evening air, shall take my breath away if God be with me…I feel safe; it is my duty, and I am glad I am here. My state is first-rate, and the soldiers will be as well if there is a call to action," Lovett said, trying to reassure his General.

"I'm glad to hear about your ox-like condition. Solomon, on the other hand, has had enough salts, castor oil, and calamine to render an ordinary man immobile and numb."

They both shared a laugh.

"Let us wipe this Detroit disgrace from the American campaign," Lovett boldly said.

"Our best troops are raw, many of them discouraged by the distress their families suffer by their absence, and many do not have the necessary clothing. We are in a cold country; the season is far advanced and unusually inclement, and we are half-deluged by rain. The blow must be struck soon, or all the toil and expense of the campaign will go for nothing, and worse than nothing, for the whole will be tinged further with dishonour," Van Rensselaer said with distinct urgency in his voice.

Winfield Scott entered the mess carrying a letter with a determined look.

"For you, sir," Scott said, handing Van Rensselaer the letter.

Van Rensselaer read the letter: "By putting on the best face that your situation admits, the enemy may be induced to delay an attack until you can meet him and carry the war into Canada. At all events, we must calculate the possession of Upper Canada before the winter sets in. Signed 'Granny' Dearborn." General 'Granny' Dearborn was the Secretary of War and, as his name suggested, was an old, short, grizzled veteran of The Revolutionary War.

Musket shots could be heard in the far distance. Lovett quickly grabbed his possessions and made his way through the door toward the commotion.

"Come back. Come back!" Van Rensselaer yelled.

Scott and Van Rensselaer walked through the door after him. They saw Lovett mount his horse and dash towards the musket shots without hesitation. Both men looked at each other and smiled.

"He is quite the eager beaver, isn't he?" Winfield said to Van Rensselaer.

"More of a curious kitten, I suppose," Van Rensselaer joked.

"Do you suppose we'll ever see him again?" Winfield said, laughing.

"Perhaps. I believe this is all quite exciting in his eyes," Van Rensselaer said, turning to Winfield Scott. "Tomorrow morning, we are set to launch. I need you at your absolute best, Major. Dearborn calls for action. Washington calls for action. We must have Upper Canada before the winter sets in."

Lovett arrived on horseback at a cliff overlooking the Niagara River. Five American soldiers were firing musket volleys upon a rowboat crossing the river about one hundred yards from their position. In the rowboat, two Americans frantically rowed towards the Canadian side of the river.

The musket fire was loud to Lovett's untamed ears, but he dismounted his horse and looked at the soldiers with excitement and curiosity.

"Private, what is happening here?" Lovett asked a reloading soldier.

"Major, do not ride into that hollow, for the balls fly dreadfully there," the soldier replied.

"Why all this musket fire?" Lovett asked.

"American deserters headed for the Canadian bank, sir."

"Cowards," Lovett said as he looked through his small telescope.

As the soldier finished loading his musket, he was shot through the cheek, and blood splattered onto the front of Lovett.

The soldier fell to the ground in agony. Lovett quickly jumped behind a nearby tree and tucked his arms, laughing to himself.

Lovett peered around the tree. "Soldier, are you alive? Are you much hurt?" he yelled.

The soldier moaned in agony while Lovett continued to crouch behind the tree.

"I am going to get you to a doctor," Lovett said as he rushed to pick up the soldier and helped him onto the horse. "Musket balls certainly do fly dreadfully here."

Across the river on the Canadian side, there had been a handful of soldiers, including James Secord, John Decew, and Nathan Davis, who had been firing at the Americans across the river.

After the deserters had made it to shore and disappeared into the thick wooded forest, James, Decew, and Nathan made their way down the dirt road to the village tavern in Queenston.

Joseph Willcocks was inside the tavern, drinking with some friends. He had just returned from his successful mission to the Six Nations and was quite proud to have been part of establishing the alliance between the British and the First Nations. He was also excited and motivated in anticipation of his next orders from General Brock.

James, Nathan, and Decew entered the tavern, ordered some beer, and sat down at the table next to Willcocks and his friends.

"Willcocks, how are you?" James asked.

"Besides this string of bad luck, I am doing quite well, I suppose," Willcocks responded.

"Good to see you, Willcocks. I heard you sold your printing press?" James asked.

"Yeah, I traded it in for a musket and some powder," Willcocks joked, and everyone laughed.

Both tables of men played cards and drank as day turned into night. The smoke became thicker, and the noise became louder. The bartender lit lanterns and candles and spread the dim, warm light across the wooden room.

"James, you seem to be losing quite a lot. When you're ready, wave the white handkerchief you have there and save yourself any further embarrassment," Nathan said confidently.

"By the end of the night, dear boy, I'll have won all of it back," James said.

"Come to grips, man," Decew said.

"This just is not your night, Captain," Nathan joked.

"Both of you, prepare yourselves to witness my great redemption." James had trouble admitting defeat sometimes. Either way, he loved playing cards and getting out of the house from time to time.

The tavern continued to buzz as Brigade Major Thomas Evans entered the front door. He was clearly winded from the sprint from Fort George. Evans ordered a drink from the tavern keeper, took a long chug of the beer, turned to the crowd and spoke: "All listen here!"

The tavern slowly began to quiet.

"Quiet!" James yelled with his best captain voice.

"Orders from the General!" The bustling stopped immediately. "Brothers in arms, this afternoon I was sent by Brock to Fort Niagara for a prisoner exchange. While on the American side, I noticed boats covered in foliage hidden within fissures. I asked about the terms of the exchange, and the American major responded that nothing could be done until the day after tomorrow. When I continued to press the issue, he told me the prisoners had been moved to Albany. He then told me again that all would be settled on the morrow. At this point, I find myself on high alert. The newly swelled numbers of Americans, the boats, and the harping of the morrow have me believe an attack on our shores could not be prudently delayed for a single day. Keep yourselves on alert. I'm off to Newark to warn the town." Evans had regained his breath and took another swig of beer.

"You're certain there will be an attack in the morning?" Decew asked.

"I would bet my last shilling on it." Evans moved toward the door. "Be brave. Every able man, prepare yourself for invasion."

Evans left the tavern, and everyone began to shuffle about and depart for home.

"I must get home and get the children safely to St. David's," James said. "We'll rendezvous across the street at the Hamilton House at dusk."

Nathan, James, Decew, Willcocks, and the other tavern-goers went their separate ways to prepare for the morning's potential invasion. They would need their physical strength and mental fortitude for the inevitable battle ahead.

Laura frantically drove the horse and wagon along the dirt road to St. David's. She had woken the children in their beds, packed a bag of provisions, and hurried out the door around midnight. Queenston would be too close to the invasion, and their house would undoubtedly get caught up in the middle of the battle.

In St. David's, she would off-load her groggy children under moonlight at her brother and sister-in-law's house, where they would be protected from the direct harm of the oncoming assault.

The night was cold and wet as the harsh autumn wind blew against her face, but Laura was able to keep her horse and wagon on the straight and narrow.

"Are you alright back there?" Laura yelled back to her confused, shivering children.

"We're fine, mother!" Mary yelled as she clung to baby Appolonia.

"I'm cold," Charles said.

"We're almost there, sweetie," Laura said.

"Why are we going to Uncle Charles' house?" Charlotte asked.

Laura could not help but feel emotional. The combination of the cool wind and the panic in her children's voices made her eyes swell, and she began crying.

"Uncle Charles isn't feeling well, darling. We are all going to help take care of him."

"I want to go home," Harriet said.

"I know you do. You're cold, tired, and confused. We'll get you all warmed by the fire and have some hot apple cider when we get there," Laura said over her shoulder as she kept her eyes on the path ahead.

Chapter 8 – Invasion

Just before sunrise, the Americans, led by a sick and miserable Solomon Van Rensselaer, began loading the bateaux on the bank of the raging Niagara River. There were two long boats, each containing 80 men, and another dozen smaller boats, each with 25 soldiers. The plan was to get the first wave across the thunderous river, then row back and pick up the second wave of soldiers.

The Americans wanted to cross at the narrowest part of the river, which was also the lower Niagara River's most hazardous, rapid, and turbulent section. Solomon signaled to his army to begin paddling across. As they disembarked, the batteries from the bluffs above Queenston had anticipated the Americans and opened up on the weary invaders.

As the cannon and musket fire erupted, the crossing boats became separated, and panic set in among the American rowers.

Solomon did his best to try and maintain the composure of his soldiers. "Press on, dear boys, press on! Face your fears head-on!" Solomon yelled.

The 18-pound cannon balls and a hailstorm of musket balls bombarded the crossing boats. The American soldiers screamed, yelled, and lost the organization and rhythm of rowing the boats in unison.

James, Decew, and Nathan were among the 50 or so soldiers firing at the crossing Americans from the bluff above.

"Like fish in a barrel!" Decew said as he fired his musket.

"The 18-pounder is going to rip them apart," James said.

The militiamen were smiling at having an enemy that was not firing back and was in such a vulnerable place.

Joseph Willcocks and a few local recruits arrived at the bluff and joined the action.

Aiming with his musket, Willcocks yelled, "Leave some for me!"

Chief John Norton and 19-year-old John Brant led 200 Grand River warriors along the narrow, jagged paths of the forested Niagara Escarpment. Brock had sent word to the Indian camp the night before, and they were only a few miles outside of Queenston when they heard the cannons from afar.

Norton knew they were close by the sound of the cannon atop the bluffs. He had been waiting for this moment for months and was ready to engage the enemy.

The warriors moved stealthily among the autumn's colourful leaves. The uneven terrain was cool and easy to move on. The Grand River warriors were determined to be victorious on this day. They were fighting for their right to exist and remain free men; they would sacrifice themselves for their families, their elders, their ancestors, and for a nation of their own.

Major John Lovett commanded the artillery battery at Lewiston, directly across from the village of Queenston. Three 18-pound and two six-pound cannons were wreaking havoc on Queenston. To relieve the pressure felt by the crossing boats, Lovett controlled the commands of loading and firing each gun, aiming to destroy the homes and surrounding buildings of Queenston.

General Stephen Van Rensselaer and Winfield Scott watched from Fort Niagara as they viewed Solomon struggle to cross the river. Both men knew Solomon was deathly ill and worried he wouldn't be able to lead an army under such sickly, miserable, and hostile conditions.

Three American boats lost their course and drifted downriver away from the rest of the army. They desperately tried to regain their course, but the river's power was too much.

"Look there! They've broken their oars!" screamed Van Rensselaer.

"Damn," Scott added.

"Alright, Winfield. It's time for you to get down there and lead the second wave," Van Rensselaer said with a concerned look.

Across the river, Solomon's boat was the first to arrive on the Canadian shore among an onslaught of bullets from the 50 soldiers firing from the redan above, a pivotal cannon location looking down at the disembarking Americans. Solomon was the first out of the boat and could hear the bullets whizzing past his ears.

The American General was immediately struck in the thigh with a musket ball and blew out the back of his hamstring. He hobbled but maintained his balance. The next musket ball hit his other thigh, and he stumbled to his knee.

"Damn it!" Solomon yelled in pain.

An American soldier picked Solomon up and was trying to bring him to a nearby rock but was hit with a third bullet through his calf, and a fourth mangled his heel.

Solomon was devastated by his injuries. Though sick, he had been looking forward to this day for months. The first American ashore, only to be shot and removed from the battlefield. Though incapacitated, his soldiers still looked to him for leadership.

American Captain John E. Wool came running from a nearby landed boat and knelt beside Solomon. "Sir, we are pinned down. If something is not done quickly, all will be dead or taken prisoner."

Solomon looked at Wool, and then his gaze moved to the hail of bullets raining down on the nearby landed boats; then he looked to the river as an entire boat filled with 15 men was lost due to cannonball fire. Boats were drifting downriver, men were screaming, and all was chaos. Solomon eventually snapped out of it.

"We can not hit that redan head-on," Solomon said, trying to think of a plan.

Captain Wool pointed up the river. "I've heard word of a fisherman's path leading up to the redan's bluff," he said.

"And you know where?" Solomon asked.

"I do, sir. May I have this assignment?" Wool responded.

"Take 60 men and head up that fisherman path. If any man turns tail, shoot him," Solomon commanded.

Wool smiled. "Yes, sir." Wool turned to go and gather his sixty soldiers.

Solomon noticed a gunshot wound on Wool's buttocks. "Captain, you've been shot."

"Through the buttocks, yes, sir. Embarrassing, but surprisingly painless."

"Good luck, Captain," Solomon said.

Captain Wool led the 60 soldiers into the thick, rocky bush toward the fisherman's path with a desperate plan to surprise the unsuspecting militia atop the bluff.

At the Redan, General Brock came galloping from Fort George on his trusted horse, Alfred. The gunners continued firing cannonballs into Lewiston and down at the landing boats below. James, Decew, and Nathan were still amongst the militia guarding the valued Redan position.

Brock dismounted and had immediate orders for the redan soldiers: "You are coming up short of the target. Use longer fuses." Brock turned to James. "Captain Secord, take five men, get down to the village and reinforce the Hamilton house. We shall hold here."

"Yes, sir," James said as he took Decew, Nathan, and a few others to reinforce at Queenston.

Brock had been up early in anticipation of the invading force but was surprised at how early the Americans had begun their incursion.

"General, look!" a soldier yelled.

Brock peered through his telescope at Captain Wool leading his 60 troops up the fisherman's path and was nearing a bluff above their position at the redan. Brock snapped his telescope shut. "Damn. Protect this redan with your lives. Victory depends on it!"

Wool had made his way to the top of the bluff and was now looking down at Brock and the redan. "It's the General," Wool said. "Charge!"

Wool and his brave sixty men charged the redan with fixed bayonets, screaming their loudest war cries.

Brock did not have enough men to defend the redan. He ordered his men to spike the gun. The gunner captain took a 10-inch barbed steel spike and drove it through the touch hole of the cannon, rendering it ineffective.

"Good job. Now, let us regroup at the Hamilton House," Brock said.

Brock and his dozen or so men ran down the hillside and hid behind a stone fence at the Hamilton House in the village below.

"This is the first time I've ever seen the 49th turn their backs," Brock told the group of scared, out-of-breath men.

200 British regulars and militia were ready at Brock's side at the Hamilton house, including James, Decew, Nathan, and the newly arrived Joseph Willcocks. Brock was regaining his confidence and strategized the next few steps.

"Good of you to join us, Willcocks!" Brock yelled.

"Thank you, sir!" Willcocks yelled back.

"Take a breath, boys. You will need it in a few moments," Brock said, taking a deep breath himself.

Brock knew the importance of the redan as his adrenaline was firing. Upper Canada was under his protection. He thought of the families, the soldiers, and the progress Upper and Lower Canada had made since The Revolutionary War and was determined to defend it with his life. The Americans needed to be stopped here and now.

"Alright, brave men of the 49th. Follow me! Charge!" Brock yelled as the newly formed 200 soldiers charged up the hill behind their General to the redan above. The Americans fired a volley at the charging soldiers.

Brock, with his feather plume hat, sword in hand, and still at the head of his column, was struck in the chest and fell to his knees. Blood trickled from his mouth as he grabbed his chest. He spit blood out onto the ground as two nearby soldiers grabbed the General and laid him on his back. "Fight on, brave boys."

"Stay with us, General," one of the soldiers said, squatting down at Brock's side.

Joseph Willcocks had seen Brock fall to the ground. As he continued forward, he tripped and fell. He kept his nose down, too scared to raise his head into the oncoming musket fire.

As Brock lay dying, he reflected on his life, his country, his duty, his travels, his fellow soldiers, and the battles throughout his career. He realized he loved this country and was glad to die for it. Brock spit more blood onto the grass as he took his last valiant breath before closing his eyes forever.

James Secord also saw General Brock fall. Secord looked at Brock's motionless body below and couldn't help but feel a sense of hopelessness. James ran over and helped carry the lifeless Brock behind the stone wall at the Hamilton House.

After he dropped off the body of the General, Secord rose to his feet and carried on up the hill, following the orders of his fallen leader. As he charged up the hill, Secord was hit. The first shot went straight through his left shoulder; he grimaced but remained on his feet. The second shot exploded his left knee as he buckled, screamed, and fell to the ground, thriving in pain. He had never felt agony like this before. The burning and stinging of the throbbing wounds tormented him as he lay on the cold ground. He looked up the hill and saw Nathan, Decew, and the rest of the British regulars getting pushed back by the sharpshooting of Captain Wool's gunners.

James lay dying on the frigid, damp ground. The pain in his knee was excruciating, and he could barely move. He wanted to see his wife and his children one last time.

Major John Lovett continued to oversee gunnery operations across the river at the battery of Fort Grey. It was hazy from all the exploding gunpowder and noisy as his troops worked feverishly to load and reload. The gunners lobbed cannonballs across the narrow ravine of the Niagara River at Queenston, where the British were pinned down, and James Secord lay dying in agony.

American spirits seemed to be lifting since the initial launch early that morning. John Lovett had a painful grimace on his face as General Van Rensselaer and Winfield Scott arrived at the battery.

"Major Lovett," Van Rensselaer called.

"What news, General?" Lovett answered with a grimace still on his face.

"Winfield and I are leading the next wave across the river," Van Rensselaer said.

"Sorry, sir. You're going to have to speak louder. My hearing is lost, and my ears ring incessantly," Lovett said, pointing to his ears.

Van Rensselaer pointed across to the battlefield at Queenston. "Scott and I are going over there!"

"Right. Good luck, sir," Lovett yelled as he continued to direct the artillery operations.

Van Rensselaer and Scott reached the bank of the river and left toward the shore, where they disembarked aboard a long boat filled with 20 determined-looking American soldiers.

Scott was excited to get into the battle. He had watched on for too long as casualties began to rise.

Scott and Van Rensselaer were surprised at the river's power as the boat launched. They had crossed the river before, but this section was highly turbulent and challenging. The soldiers rowed frantically as they drifted off course almost immediately.

"Steady as she goes!" Scott yelled, staring at the opposite shore.

At the Hamilton House in the village of Queenston, the British officers and their allies began to strategize with the dead body of General Brock lying a few feet away, covered in a blanket, on the dining room floor.

"I'm not going to march up that hill and make the same mistake Brock did," Sheaffe said as his head turned toward the dining room. "I'm going to form up with our forces behind the warriors at Elijah Phelps field on the right flank of the Americans," Sheaffe said. "Brock was certain the heights were the key. We need the warmth during winter, the waterway, and a clear path to Fort Erie. If we fail, Upper Canada is all but lost," Sheaffe said.

"This is a good plan. The Americans will be preoccupied with terror and the surrounding warriors. You should be able to push them right off the edge," Lieutenant Evans responded.

FitzGibbon came storming into the room, carrying a smoking musket, as sweat dripped from his nose. "Hundreds of soldiers are out there starving, sir. Do we have your consent to dig the potatoes in the Hamilton field to feed our army?" FitzGibbon pleaded.

"Of course," Sheaffe said, as he departed to begin the second wave.

FitzGibbon signaled to a few officers, and they rushed outside to begin digging up potatoes. The Irish Lieutenant soon followed and addressed his fellow soldiers outside: "All able-bodied militia are to report to General Sheaffe as he is about to deploy the flank to the plateau above the village."

After a few minutes, in Hamilton's field, several fires were started, and water was boiling everywhere. It was an atypical sight to see amidst such a gruesome battle, but it had been hours since the outbreak of the battle and soldiers needed fuel.

Richard Pierpoint led The Coloured Corps militia along the Niagara Gorge towards the battle at Queenston. Bob and Hector Armstrong and about 30 others ran along the rocky paths beside the roaring Niagara River. The group of highly motivated soldiers had organized at first light and began their journey soon after the sound of cannons began.

"We're going to miss it," Hector said to Pierpoint.

"We're not going to miss anything," Pierpoint responded. "This battle is just getting started."

"By the sound of it, Americans have landed and taken the heights at Queenston," Bob said to Pierpoint.

"The redan cannons have stopped, which means they've been spiked and abandoned," Pierpoint said.

As Pierpoint's militia moved stealthily through the forest, the sun shone brightly through the slightly overcast skies.

"We are close. Load and prepare for battle," Pierpoint yelled. "Keep your powders dry and your barrel clean!"

Ahead in the distance, they saw John Norton, John Brant, and their 200 warriors at the American position. The warriors, dashing in and out of the wooded thicket, kept the Americans on edge.

Pierpoint and his soldiers joined the Six Nation forces in their fighting as Sheaffe arrived with his 600 British regulars. Sheaffe hailed Norton, and he ran through the bush.

"Captain Norton, glad you and your contingency are here," Sheaffe said. "We are going to flank that American position atop the hill. We'll cut through Elijah Phelps' fields and, hopefully, catch them off guard. I need you and your men to keep harassing the piss out of them until we arrive. Place the fear of God in their hearts, Captain Norton."

"We are here to support you, General," Norton told Sheaffe. "We'll give them all we've got."

"I'm going to lead the regulars; you get up there and give them hell. Captain Merritt and his Dragoons will join you. When we arrive, you and the Dragoons protect our flank," Sheaffe said as Norton nodded in affirmation. "Good luck, Norton." Sheaffe turned and left, heading toward his men.

Norton motioned to Brant to gather the warriors. Once all the men had gathered and focussed their attention, Norton took a deep breath, looked toward the battlefield, and then back at the Grand River warriors.

"Comrades and Brothers, be men. Remember the fame of ancient warriors, whose breasts were never daunted by odds of number. You have run from your encampments to this place to meet the enemy. We have found what we came for."

Norton inspired his fellow Haudenosaunee. He had helped to bring prosperity along the banks of the Grand and continued to fight for their rights, lands, and freedom, and now, he was leading them into battle.

"Let no anxieties distract your minds. There they are!" Norton said, pointing to the Americans. "Let us ascend that path, by which, unperceived, we may gain their rear. Your bullets shall soon spread havoc and dismay among those ranks. Don't let their numbers appall you. Look up." Norton pointed to the big sky above. "It is He that shall decide our fate. Our gallant friends, the redcoats, will soon support us."

Pierpoint approached Norton as he was addressing his men. "Captain Norton, shall we join your efforts?" he asked.

"Welcome, Captain Pierpoint," Norton said. You and your men can join us in pressuring the Americans at the redan. When Sheaffe arrives with his reinforcements, we will protect his flank."

"Lead the way, Captain Norton. We're ready and willing," Pierpoint responded as he motioned to his men.

Norton, Pierpoint, and their men began their gradual march to the American position.

On the battlefield, through a maze of wounded lying everywhere, James lay isolated on the hill. The Americans still controlled the redan, and the Iroquois were engaging the enemy. The sounds of musket and cannon fire and the clashing of tomahawks, swords, and bayonets filled the autumn air. Through the smoke and the haze, James' adrenaline was fading, and the pain was starting to set in. His breathing was getting deeper, and panic was overcoming his once-stable emotions.

About 50 yards away from James at the Hamilton House, John Decew and Nathan Davis sat and leaned against the stone wall with the dead General Brock only meters away inside the house. Nathan peered over the short stone wall to try and spot his friend. He could not see anything amongst all the bodies, the falling leaves, and the smoke that stifled his vision. Nathan hunched back down behind the safety of the wall and let out an enormous exhale.

"James is out there, and the General is dead," Nathan said to Decew.

"Reinforcements from Chippewa and Fort George should be arriving any time now," Nathan said, trying to reassure his friend.

"Look there!" Decew said, pointing to General Sheaffe leading a thousand redcoats alongside the edge of the farmer's field. "Reinforcements are already here."

"Damn right! Let's retake control of those damn heights!" Nathan yelled.

"We need to retake them. Brock knew this, and so does Sheaffe," Decew said as he rose to his feet. Come on, let's rejoin this fight."

James Secord had wrapped his knee with a piece of cloth torn from his shirt and tried to crawl down the massive hill toward the Hamilton House. Each movement was excruciatingly painful. The field was still too dangerous to send soldiers out to find survivors, so James, inch by inch, tried to save himself. Finally, with there being too much pain, James collapsed on his back and looked toward the cloudy blue sky.

As he lay writhing in pain, three American soldiers approached the helpless Secord, ready to stab and club him to death.

Laura Secord had made her way to the Hamilton House and scoured the premises for her husband. From a distance she noticed the three nearby American soldiers approaching James. She ran up the hill as the three soldiers raised their muskets to finish off her helpless husband. Laura rushed in between them. "Spare him!" Laura pleaded.

"Get this wench out of here," one of the Americans said as he slapped Laura across the face.

Another soldier grabbed her by the hair and pulled her close to his face. "What's the matter, little lady?" Laura could do nothing. All three Americans laughed.

"Please!" Laura pleaded again. "He means nothing to you."

Captain Wool had seen the commotion and ran down to investigate the scene. "What the hell do you think you're doing?" he said in a stern voice to the three men. "How dare you attempt such a thing? All three of you are cowards, and I shall see you court-martialed if you do not release that woman."

Wool signalled to a few of his trusted soldiers to bring the rough, vulgar, abusive Americans to Lewiston. There, they might be tried and sentenced to imprisonment for their breach of discipline and cowardly malice. Wool also ordered a party of men to take the wounded James to his own house with Laura at his side.

Both Laura and James had come close to death and were relieved to make it off the battlefield under protection.

"We will forever be grateful for your kindness and decorum, Captain," Laura said to Wool.

"It is the least I can do for a neighbour," Wool said as he returned to the top of the heights.

Laura, with James around her shoulder, arrived to see the horror of their general store burning to the ground. All of the windows in their home had been smashed, along with the front door being torn off the hinges. As if a near-dead husband was not enough, she had lost her family's primary source of income, and her home was in ruin.

James, exhausted, draped from his wife's arm, looked up to the burning building but was in too much pain and too close to death to care about his store or his house.

Laura got James inside the plundered house and, laid him on the dining room table and prepared to clean his wounds and apply fresh bandages. Laura knew he was losing a lot of blood, but no major organs had been hit, and she was fairly confident that if he survived the night, there was potential for him to be nursed back to health.

Colonel Winfield Scott and General Van Rensselaer arrived on the Canadian shore below the heights, aboard a 16-foot boat, carrying a dozen frightened-looking soldiers. The whooping and hollering of the native forces heard in the distance greatly concerned the newly arrived soldiers.

118

They witnessed soldiers swimming back across to the American side, some drifting downriver, others disappearing entirely. Wounded fighters were everywhere. Demoralized soldiers pleaded with Van Rensselaer. Some soldiers lay hiding in bushes, some were scrambling aboard boats, and some sat, immobilized by melancholy and terror.

Scott knew his duty. He was going to bring morale to his soldiers. He would lead by example; it was just too bad he wasn't there to lead the first wave.

Van Rensselaer noticed his cousin Solomon in a beached boat. "Solomon!" he yelled.

"Cousin!" Solomon weakly yelled.

"Have you been hit?" Van Rensselaer asked.

"My heel is destroyed, calf mangled, and bullets in both of my thighs," Solomon said, groaning.

"We are going to get you back on the next boat. Winfield and I are going up to the heights."

"Take the fisherman's path that Captain Wool took. Just about 50 metres upriver," Solomon said as he laid his head back down.

As Winfield Scott led his reinforcements to the fisherman's path, Captain Wool returned to the shore while being helped by a couple of other soldiers. He was losing too much blood, and the pain was starting to set in. Though his day was done early, his good deeds and heroic actions were enough. Wool had discovered the fisherman's path, been shot twice, held the heights under heavy gunfire, demonstrated honourable behaviour, and motivated his troops to the last second.

Van Rensselaer saw Wool and rose to his feet. "Captain, how goes the battle?"

"Indians have arrived, sir. The men are terrified they will lose their scalps and worse."

"Fear not the savage, Captain Wool. They breathe the same air and drink the same water," Van Rensselaer said.

"Of course, General. Spirits are not high, though," Wool added.

Van Rensselaer was worried. His only hope lay in Winfield Scott and fortifying their position.

General Sheaffe and Lt. FitzGibbon led the regulars through the farmer's field. The militia were on their flank, including the newly arrived Black Coloured Corps, with Pierpoint in front leading the way. Norton, Brant, and the Grand River warriors continued to harass the Americans, who were barely holding on at the redan.

The clouds had cleared, and the sun was now bright overhead. The smell of gunpowder and autumn decay sifted through the neighbouring forests as Winfield Scott made his way up the fisherman's path.

Scott finally reached the top of the plateau and consulted with his engineers. The spiked cannon was unusable. Clearly upset, Scott noticed Sheaffe's crimson column forming on Elijah Phelps' field and knew he needed to take immediate action. He sent a messenger to Van Rensselaer below requesting immediate support, as Sheaffe was almost in attack formation.

Scott's forces were tacked down and harassed by John Norton and the Natives. They waved their tomahawks in sporadic movements as they dashed in and out of the forest cover. Scott and his troops were being pushed to the edge of the cliff.

An American soldier, fearing the attacking Indians, jumped off the cliff to his certain death in the ravine below. Then, a second and third soldier jumped to their doom. Winfield was furious. He just needed some reinforcements. As his soldiers ran and jumped in various nooks and crannies of the escarpment, Scott looked over to the American side of the river and saw no troop movement or boats leaving the banks.

"Reinforcements are not coming, my brave fellows. I urge you to die with your muskets in your hands. Redeem the shame of Hull's surrender," Winfield shouted.

Scott's troops cheered him as Sheaffe, Norton, Pierpoint, and their forces continued pushing the Americans down the cliff. The Americans struggled to get down, clutching branches and various out-croppings. Scott was among the last few men atop the redan. He again peered down to the river and noticed the hundreds of Americans waiting at the shoreline for a boat that was not coming. Scott approached two American couriers.

"Tie your white handkerchiefs to your muskets; it might be our only way to avoid a complete massacre," Scott said.

"Excellent, sir," the courier responded.

The two couriers fixed their handkerchiefs to their bayonets and jumped out of hiding, moving toward the oncoming British. The first courier was shot in the head and fell immediately. The second courier was charged and clubbed by two rushing Mohawks.

Scott noticed the fallen couriers, pulled a scarf off a nearby officer and tied it to the blade at the end of his musket. He bravely approached the ruthless enemy. John Brant and another warrior jumped and tackled the monstrous Scott. On the ground, Scott managed to pull his bayonet free and plunge it through the neck of the attacking warrior.

John Brant allowed Winfield Scott to stand as the two began to duel in hand-to-hand combat, as John Norton approached, watching the scene unfold.

Van Rensselaer arrived back on American soil with the injured Captain E. Wool and Solomon Van Rensselaer. Solomon was barely conscious, his face ghostly white and his clothes soaked with blood. Captain Wool was no better, as the day's fierce combat and climbing had drained him of all his energy.

"How is your rear, Mr. Wool?" Van Rensselaer asked.

"Embarrassed, General, embarrassed," Wool responded.

"Hang in there, Solomon. Not much further," Van Rensselaer said, looking upon a group of demoralized, unenthusiastic Americans. "Form up, brave men, for one final push!" he yelled. "The heights can still be won. I have promised reinforcements and ammunition."

Once ashore on the New York side of the river, Van Rensselaer looked around and saw the failure of the day. He knew reinforcements would not reach Scott, and he was alone.

"Take a note for me, Captain Lovett," Van Rensselaer said, looking at the dirty, exhausted Lovett.

Lovett did not respond. He had almost completely lost his hearing while working the Fort Grey battery all morning. Cannon blast after cannon blast, a steady ringing dominated the ear drums of Captain John Lovett.

"Take a note for me!" Van Rensselaer yelled and waved his arms at Lovett.

"Of course, sir. You'll have to speak loudly," Lovett said louder than usual.

"Never mind, Captain Lovett, I'll have someone else take the note," Van Rensselaer said, waving at another soldier. "Do you know how to write?" he asked the soldier.

"Yes, sir," the soldier said.

"Please write this," Van Rensselaer said, handing him a pen and paper. "I have passed through my camp; not a regiment, not a company is willing to join you. Save yourself by a retreat if you can. Boats will be sent to receive you," Van Rensselaer said as the soldier wrote the message. "Make sure this message gets to Major Winfield Scott." The soldier nodded in agreement and left immediately towards the battle.

Van Rensselaer was dismayed as he knew that the message might not even reach Scott in his most desperate time of need.

Winfield Scott thrust his bayonet with the white flag still attached, and John Brant dodged the weapon.

John Norton came running to the engagement and intervened in the duel between Brant and Winfield Scott. "Halt! This officer carries a flag of truce!" Norton yelled.

"Two of our Chiefs are dead. We need to exterminate our enemy," Brant said to Norton.

"No more, young Chief," Norton sternly said.

Winfield Scott collapsed to the ground from exhaustion. A bugle of cease-fire was sounded in the distance, but many of the Grand River warriors paid no attention and continued the onslaught. They raged in the fight for their homes, families, and futures and would not rest until complete victory was achieved.

Norton and Brant brought the captured Scott before General Sheaffe and Lt. FitzGibbon. Scott noticed the relentless

Natives continuing to attack the Americans that were scaling the escarpment cliffs and trying to escape the massacre.

"I demand to return to my troops and share their fate. These are not the ways of war. It is said the Crown has control over their savage allies," Scott said. Enraged at what was happening, he threw his hat to the ground and looked at Sheaffe directly. "I demand you give up your command and go home if this does not cease." Another bugle sounded and Scott threw his sword to the ground. "This has to stop!"

"Brothers!" Norton screamed to his warriors.

Sheaffe looked at the enraged Scott. "I am sorry for their behaviour. They have lost much and carry a heavy vengeance in their heart."

"Brothers! The day is won! Put down your muskets and tomahawks!" Norton yelled.

Eventually, the warriors stopped fighting and spared the lives of the remaining Americans. It had been a long, bloody day for both sides.

At the chaotic Secord house, Laura tied a handkerchief around James' wounded leg as he screeched in pain. She handed him a glass of water, and he had trouble as he was shaking uncontrollably.

"Lay back, darling," Laura said as she helped hold the glass still so he could drink.

"I'm so light-headed," James said.

"Rest now, and we'll have a doctor look at it later."

"I was lying on the battlefield for what seemed like hours," James said.

"The children and I were worried about you all morning, jumping at every cannon burst and musket blast."

"Take me to them."

"They are still at your sisters in St. David's. You will see them soon enough. You need rest and some food. Be calm, darling," Laura said as she wiped her husband's dried, bloody face.

James eventually drifted off to sleep. Laura stayed by his side, cradling his wounded body. She could not imagine losing her husband. They had built so much together, and everything was now in jeopardy. Laura was relieved her husband was alive, but she was emotionally torn as everything in and around her home was destroyed.

Richard Pierpoint, Bob, and Hector sat together on a log in the nearby forest with the rest of his militia beside Elijah's Phelp's field. Pierpoint was proud that he only lost one man from his militia.

"You boys did well today," Pierpoint said to Bob and Hector.

"Not too bad yourself, old man," Bob responded.

"How are you doing, Hector? This was your first battle, wasn't it?" asked Pierpoint.

"Yessir, it was," Hector answered.

Hector's adrenaline was still surging through his body. He had shot a man and watched him fall to the ground; he had seen men get blown apart by cannon blasts, watched soldiers commit suicide and many other bloody realities of war. Though Hector was a young, strong man, he would likely carry this engagement and its memory for the rest of his life.

"Might have to get this boy a beer or two tonight, Bob," Pierpoint joked.

"He made me really proud today," Bob said, putting his arm around his son's shoulder. "I'm real proud of you, boy," he said, giving him a gentle shake.

"Thanks, Father."

Nathan Davis and John Decew were relieved the fighting was over, but now their concern was James Secord's health. They both had spent the hours following the battle helping with the wounded and clearing the dead soldiers from the field.

The two men walked into Queenston to the Secord house and noticed the devastation and destruction amidst their friend's smouldering property. They stuck their heads inside the broken front door to see James lying on the dining room table, sound asleep, and Laura sitting beside him, crying.

Chapter 9 - Sacrifice

Four days after the Battle of Queenston Heights, the weather was ominous and gloomy. Though the British and Upper Canadians successfully defeated and pushed the Americans back, they experienced a significant loss. Major General Isaac Brock was to be buried at Fort George along with General Macdonell, another leader who had fallen days earlier.

Over five thousand people had come to the funeral, an enormous crowd for such a sparsely populated area. Grand River warriors, colonial militiamen, citizens, and soldiers lined the route to Fort George, where Brock and Macdonell would be laid to rest.

A dozen pallbearers lowered the two caskets into graves, amongst them were John Norton and Thomas Merritt, father of William Hamilton Merritt. At the northeast corner of Fort George, General Sheaffe, Lt. FitzGibbon, and other officers waited in

128

formation to pay their respects to their fallen General. Brock's tombstone read:

> *Here lies the earthly remains of a brave and virtuous Hero, Major General Isaac Brock, Commanding the British Forces and President administering the Government of Upper Canada, who fell when gloriously engaging the enemies of his Country at the head of the Flank Companies of the 49th Regiment in the Town of Queenston, on the morning of the 13th October 1812.*

Lieutenant Gregg, Brock's aide-de-camp, the man in charge of the funeral arrangements, addressed the thousands in attendance: "Friends, soldiers, ladies, and gentlemen, we are gathered here on this sombre, overcast October morning to remember and honour a true hero, Major General Isaac Brock. When faced with the threat of invasion from foreign power, General Brock stood tall as a symbol of courage, leadership, and unwavering dedication to the cause of liberty."

Lt. Gregg was well aware of Brock's aversion to extravagant displays, but people from all over the province wished to pay their respects this morning. Gregg was full of sadness but also pride. He had not realized how much the General had meant to the people of Upper Canada and the Niagara area.

"General Brock was a man of exceptional character. Born in Guernsey, England, in 1769, he came to Upper Canada ten years ago, in 1802, and quickly became a key figure in defending this land. His leadership on the battlefield and his ability to inspire his troops were legendary. Brock was a brilliant military strategist and a man of principle and honour. He valued the relationships he built with the Native peoples of this land and worked tirelessly to maintain their support in the face of adversity. His commitment to justice and fairness was evident in all his actions."

John Norton stood by and considered the consequences of losing Brock. He looked at the thousands of people and pondered their future without the heroic leader. Brock's tactics, ability to act, and leadership skills would be hard shoes to fill.

"As we remember General Isaac Brock today, let us commemorate his military achievements and dedication to the ideals of freedom. His sacrifice in the defense of Upper Canada shall never be forgotten, and his legacy will continue to inspire the generations to come."

Brock had never married, although it was generally understood he put his position and responsibilities before all else. He loved the company of women, but his duty, especially in times of war, trumped his urges, desires, and jealousies.

"In conclusion, Major General Isaac Brock was not just a hero of his time; he was a hero for all time. His courage, leadership, and unwavering commitment to the cause of liberty make him a figure worthy of our deepest admiration and respect. We honour his memory and his sacrifices for the land that he, and all of us love so dearly."

A few soldiers, including Joseph Willcocks, proceeded with putting soil on the caskets. Everyone rose to their feet as the British fired a twenty-one-gun salute in three salvos as a gesture of respect to the departed General.

James, Laura, and their children did not attend the funeral but were able to watch the procession pass by from their parlour window. James was still in tremendous pain as he fought an infection and a horrible fever. Laura had been unwavering at his side since the battle and did her best to rehabilitate her husband. Laura looked out the window on the dreary, wet Queenston street as James lay on the sofa.

Victoria was with the children upstairs. She had become increasingly important around the house after the war had broken out, helping to take care of the children at St. David's during the invasion and now taking on other caregiving duties besides schooling.

Nathan Davis and John Decew had attended the funeral and had promised to stop by the Secord's house afterward. The two men came up the front pathway of the Secord home and knocked on the door.

Victoria came down the stairs and opened the door. "Hello, Mr. Davis. Hello, Mr. Decew."

"Lovely to see you again," Nathan said earnestly.

Nathan was utterly in love with Victoria; she could sense his desire and affection.

"Hello, Victoria," Decew said.

"Come in out of the rain," she said.

Nathan and Decew followed Victoria into the parlour, where James lay incapacitated. Barely conscious, James raised his head to see the newly arrived guests.

"Still alive, you old dog?" Decew joked.

James had lost his sense of humour. The past four days had been miserable as he could not put any pressure on his knee. "Just barely," he meagrely responded.

"Were you able to get the bullet out?" Nathan asked.

"It's still in there," James said while trying to sit up. It is a permanent resident."

"Do you need us to get you anything?" Decew asked Laura and James.

"Nathan, thank you for boarding up the windows. I could not have done it without you," James said.

"Yes, thank you, Nathan. Other than that, I think we are fine for the time being. Perhaps some fresh bandages would be helpful," Laura said.

Victoria stood in the doorway and yelled upstairs to the noisy children. "I'll be right up, Mary." She then turned to Nathan and smiled. "I really should be going. It was nice to see you again, Mr. Davis."

"It was my pleasure," Nathan said as he bowed. He had never bowed before. After he rose, he looked around to see everyone staring at his strange behaviour.

"Goodbye, Mr. Decew," Victoria said, smiling as she went up the stairs.

"I'll come with you," Laura said, following Victoria, leaving the three men alone.

"Any news?" James asked.

"There must have been five thousand people at Brock's funeral this morning. They came from miles around," Decew said.

"This will prove to be a huge loss for Upper Canada," James said.

"Winter is coming, and there will not be another campaign until spring. In all likeliness, the Americans will stay put in New York at Fort Niagara," Nathan said.

"Try and get better this winter, Captain. There is sure to be action," Decew said.

"I shall try my best," James said as he rubbed around his knee.

Along with hundreds of other captured soldiers from the Battle of Queenston Heights, Winfield Scott found himself, hands tied, aboard a ship about to depart for Québec. It had been days since they were captured, and no one had told them what was happening. But this morning, soldiers and sailors began stirring about and preparing the ship for departure.

As the different ships prepared for open water, a few British officers came aboard, assembled the prisoners, and calmly began to separate the Irish from the rest of the Americans.

"Those who have declared themselves Irish will be sent to England and be tried for treason. Once a Briton, always a Briton!" the British officer explained.

Many Irish men deserted the British army and joined the newly formed United States. Ireland had been poverty-stricken for generations and the people were given little opportunity within the constraints of the British Empire, so many joined the U.S. military in their search for success and prosperity.

Among separation of prisoners and the noise and confusion on the ship's deck, Winfield Scott boldly rushed to intervene. He found himself face to face with the officer who had just announced the fate of his Irish soldiers.

"I object!" Scott said boldly.

"I order you to go below deck, or I'll have you whipped for your outburst," the British officer sternly said.

"I again, object!" Scott turned to the rest of his soldiers. "Refuse to speak, and don't give them any reason to call you Irish."

Twenty-three soldiers had already been separated for being Irish, and Scott pleaded with the officer to let them go. The weary 23 were rowed to a different frigate where they would take a long voyage back to Britain and face death under a dark cloud of remorse.

"You shall ever regret this. I shall bring this outrage to the President, and we will retaliate against your actions here today. Once I am exchanged, I will immediately go to Washington and tell the Senate what occurred here today." Looking on as his Irish soldiers were being loaded onto another ship fueled his rage.

"Take him below deck!" the British officer demanded.

Two soldiers grabbed hold of Scott's arms and forcibly led him below deck against his will.

"Prepare for departure!" the British Captain yelled as the sailors prepared the sails and rigs for the long easterly journey.

Chapter 10 - Winter Repose

Word had reached North America that Napoleon was on the retreat from Russia. His Grande Armeé marched into the hostile lands with nearly half a million soldiers and returned with a meagre force of 10,000. The Russians captured over 110,000 prisoners during the campaign, and many more were lost to desertion, malnutrition, sickness, and the fighting itself. The harsh winter, violence, poor preparation, and overconfidence led to a disastrous retreat back into Europe.

American leadership in Washington knew that Napoleon's faults in Russia would relieve the pressure on Britain and their efforts in fighting the French Emperor. With room to breathe, the King could send reinforcements to the North American theatre and help relieve the already taxed British regulars.

As the snow fell on upstate New York, General Stephen Van Rensselaer sat in the dining hall at Fort Niagara reading the latest news from Europe. Months had passed since the battle of Queenston Heights, and it was still fresh in his mind. The plan was solid, but too many variables contributed to the catastrophe: the boats, the river's current, fear, lack of support, and general instability. Van Rensselaer was now thinking about his spring campaign and how he might redeem his status in the eyes of the people and President Madison.

Stephen Van Rensselaer's cousin, Solomon, entered the dining hall looking ghostly and limping with a cane. Though he had been shot four times, he was on his feet. Surgeons had patched him up nicely. The pain of having the bullets removed was more painful than being shot, he would tell people.

"Hello, cousin," Solomon said with a smile.

"Welcome back, Solomon. How goes your recovery?" Van Rensselaer asked.

"Every day, there seems to be some sort of small improvement."

"That's encouraging," Van Rensselaer said, smiling. "I've just received a letter from Major John Lovett. He is also on the upward swing of things, although the battery barrage rendered him permanently deaf."

"Poor fellow," Solomon said. "The man was such a master of conversation and dinner wit, now silenced by the very war that initially excited him."

"Now he studies with the hearing impaired." Van Rensselaer paused in reflection. "I remember him riding off towards some gun fire; I was yelling, 'come back, come back'."

"Where is he now? Where is he doing his studies?" Solomon asked.

"After the Queenston Heights battle, he returned home to Washington. There is a special school there for the deaf and hard of hearing, where they teach a language that uses hand gestures to convey words."

"Fascinating," Solomon said. "I am quite sure he is in good spirits, and the people at his new school love him and his company."

"I don't doubt that," Van Rensselaer replied.

"And what of poor Winfield Scott?" Solomon asked.

"Likely still imprisoned in Québec," Van Rensselaer responded.

"I hope he is in good spirits and pray we can arrange a prisoner exchange," Solomon said.

"Me too, Solomon, me too."

"Cousin, General Dearborn and Commodore Chauncey have put into action the strategy for the spring." Solomon pointed to a sprawled-out map of North America on the table. "They will attack York and Kingston. Following these attacks, they call to immediately land at the mouth of the Niagara and capture Fort George. An amphibious landing, backed by 16 warships and 7000 men."

"Monumental failures in 1812 have inspired our dear commanders to rebound and take revenge in the spring of 1813. From Fort George to Fort Erie, sparsely guarded by 800 or so British regulars; if Chauncey's fleet and these 7000 are with us, the British will have no chance at holding," Van Rensselaer said.

"Let 1813 be more fortunate than 1812," Solomon said.

"It will not be long until British reinforcements arrive from Europe," Van Rensselaer said.

"Doesn't Napoleon have them occupied," Solomon responded.

138

"Things have changed," Van Rensselaer said as he handed Solomon the newspaper. "The Emperor's army has been decimated in Russia. The little man could not help himself. He occupied Moscow for too long. Now, only a handful of soldiers return. It will not be long before he is captured and brought before a tribunal."

"Let this burden not cloud our objectives. The spring campaign will change everything," Solomon said. "Let their reinforcements come."

The Grand River peoples, including John Norton, carried a tiny bit of hope throughout the winter, as they had helped to repel the Americans at Queenston. Though they were still at war, they felt their livelihood was not in jeopardy for the time being. Many men were out hunting and trapping in the bountiful Grand River valleys. Others found themselves on surrounding lakes ice fishing for perch, trout, salmon, and muskie.

It was a busy time of year, as winter was at its peak and wood needed to be gathered constantly to warm the long-houses and smokehouses. Winter was a social time of year, as bonds strengthened, and interactions were intimate.

Norton helped tend to the horses and livestock that needed special attention during the frigid winter months. Karighwaycagh, now with a newborn baby boy wrapped around her back, helped feed the horses and cows underneath the various shelters.

Norton was anticipating a small group of Cree from Lower Canada making the trip to engage in trade with their neighbouring allies. It was a yearly tradition to trade clothing, weapons, gunpowder, dried meats, carvings, beadwork, and dressings. As

Norton gave special attention to the horses, Karighwaycagh approached him from behind and put her arms around him.

"Hello, lover," Karighwaycagh said.

"My, my, these horses are hungry and happy," Norton said as he stroked the cheek of his favourite black horse.

Karighwaycagh spun Norton around to face her. "You seem vacant. You stare through me as if you see ghosts on the other side. Tell me what you are thinking."

"I do not wish for you to see the things I have seen, but the visions I've had are still fresh and become increasingly more painful as these winter months pass," Norton said.

Karighwaycagh embraced Norton and smiled. "I am here, Sawatis. I am here." Karighwaycagh held on tight as Norton pinched the tiny cheek of his newborn son.

Norton could not help but think of the thousands of Americans he had seen at Queenston. He knew there were endless soldiers to call upon, and his people might one day be overwhelmed by the new nation.

"The horses, the river, and you are helping to see me through these unstable, forbidding times. I fear these dark times are just beginning, and the sinister shadow will loom for months to come," Norton said, clearly thinking about the future of his people.

"Your victory has helped the spirit of our people. The great counsel recognizes your bravery in maintaining our place here and in the universe. Your pain and sacrifice will be remembered," Karighwaycagh said.

"You are wise beyond your years, Karighwaycagh," Norton said.

"You and our people are strong. We will succeed. We will endure."

Norton and Karighwaycagh embraced as the newborn boy let out a joyous scream. The two laughed together as the snow fell upon the Grand River valley.

Victoria and Nathan strolled along the streets of Queenston, holding hands as the cold weather flushed their faces red. The two had become close from the onset of the war until now. Nathan would often help Victoria with tutoring the Secord children, and together, they would help James and Laura with various tasks around the house. Though the war had arrived, the young couple were quickly falling in love.

"Charlotte and Mary are growing up so fast," Victoria told Nathan. "It's quite remarkable how quickly they have attached themselves to their studies."

"They are both bright, charming young ladies," Nathan responded.

"I hope to have such bright, caring, thoughtful children one day," Victoria said, clearly playing on Nathan's heartstrings.

Nathan could only blush at the thought as the two made their way up the front steps of the Secord house. John Decew sat on the porch, bundled in winter attire, arms crossed, smoking from his pipe.

"Hello there, strangers," Decew said, smiling.

"How goes it, friend?" Nathan said.

Decew tapped the ashes from his pipe and opened the door to go inside with Nathan and Victoria. "Things are well," he said.

Decew, Victoria, and Nathan went inside the boarded-up house. James sat in front of the fire with a cane, and Laura sat with the children at the dining room table. Mary and Charlotte crocheted yarn while Charles and Harriet practiced reading and writing together.

Laura and James had done their best to hide their feelings and attitudes from the children. War had taken its toll on the citizens of Upper Canada and the United States. Everyone, including James and Laura, remembered what The Revolutionary War had done to communities. Though they were children at the time, they still remembered the burning homes, the dead bodies, and the starving families across the lines. Laura and James loved their children and did their best to keep the children's eyes blind to the war on their doorstep.

"Hello, James," Nathan said as he approached his friend.

"Hello, Mr. Davis," James said.

"How is the recovery going?" Nathan asked.

"It will be months before I can take more than a few steps," James said, stoking the fire before him.

Victoria entered the dining room and joined Laura and the children at the table.

James was full of doubt and melancholy. His knee had made him near useless, and he had to depend more on Laura, Victoria, Bob, and Fan. His stagnation had been heavily influencing his reasoning and thought process. He could not plow and sow fields, ride a horse, or pick up his children. Though depression weighed heavily on him, he still managed to believe in his road to recovery and would do everything in his power to persevere.

Decew and Nathan knew his pain and did their best to reassure him that he would mend, and things would return to normal.

"Spring is just around the corner. Do you plan on staying here when the war resumes?" Decew asked James.

"I do not have much of a choice. I cannot travel. I hope if there is any occupation, I am treated as a citizen rather than a soldier," James said.

"Hopefully, the warm spring weather will help remedy your wound. Did the bullet get removed?" Nathan asked.

"A permanent American souvenir," James said as everyone shared a laugh.

In Grantham County, just west of Queenston, Bob and Fan Armstrong entered the local African-Canadian church on a cold, snowy Sunday in January 1813. It was a quaint structure, with a few pews on each side of a central aisle. A single wood fireplace warmed the space and gave a pleasant aroma to the sacred room. Richard Pierpoint and his three friends, John Hall, Roger Jupiter, and John Vanpatten entered the church and sat waiting for the sermon to begin. Hall, Jupiter, and Vanpatten were in their early fifties and fought alongside Pierpoint, Bob, and Hector at the Battle of Queenston Heights.

Hector and his friend George Martin arrived at the church together. George Martin, the son of Peter Martin, had gained notoriety when he witnessed an enslaved girl, Chloe Cooley, being beaten, bound, and transported across the river to the United States. Concerned that Chloe might be freed, her owner hastily went across the river from Queenston to make a sale on American soil. Peter Martin presented his firsthand testimony of Chloe's abuse to the Executive Council of Upper Canada. Following this incident, the Act Against Slavery was introduced into legislation.

Hector asked George to join Pierpoint's men, and being the proud son he was, joined The Coloured Corps to take up arms with the Upper Canadian militia.

Reverend David George came to the podium to address the mass. "Ladies and gentlemen, brothers, and sisters, as we gather here on this day, amidst these challenging times, we find ourselves seeking solace in the Lord's house and reflecting upon the uncertainties of our hereafter. Our beloved Canada stands at a major crossroads of history where snow falls hard, the wind blows fierce, and the nation hangs in the balance. Before we delve into our sermon today, let us first bow our heads in prayer, seeking guidance and strength from the Almighty."

The mass bowed their heads in silence, considering what they might do to help protect their homes, lands, and communities.

"Amen," Rev. George said. "My dear congregation, it is no secret that we, the children of this great nation, have been tested by the fires of conflict. We again find ourselves caught in the turmoil of this insensible war. Our brothers and sisters are called to the frontlines to defend our homes, our families, and our way of life. We must remember them and pray fervently for peace to descend upon this land. In times like these, it is easy to be consumed by fear and doubt. Our community has known adversity and triumph, sorrow, and joy. Our friends, family, and ancestors, the Black Loyalists, sought refuge on this land, and in their trials, they found the strength to build communities, to till the soil, to raise families, and to worship the Lord."

Everyone in the church replied enthusiastically, 'Amen.'

"Today, we gather in this church not only as a congregation but as a testament to the faith that sustains us. Just as our forefathers and foremothers leaned upon their faith to endure hardships, so must we."

The mass responded with another 'Amen.'

"The Bible reminds us that in times of tribulation, we are not alone: Yea, though I walk through the valley of the shadow of death, I will fear no evil: for thou art with me; thy rod and thy staff they comfort me. We must find solace in these words, for they remind us that even in the darkest of times, God's presence is our strength. Blessed are the peacemakers, for they shall be called the children of God. In our prayers, let us ask for the safety of our loved ones and the wisdom and compassion of leaders who seek a just and lasting peace. Through prayer, we find hope, courage, and the grace to face whatever trials come our way. Together, as a united congregation, let us commit ourselves to pray for our nation, our families, and the healing of our land."

As the congregation continued, the Reverend's words of courage, strength, and unity seemed to uplift spirits. Bob squeezed Fan's hand a little tighter. He interlocked his fingers with hers, turned his head, and gave his wife a subtle wink and smile.

Pierpoint, Jupiter, Vanpatten, Hall, Martin, and the rest of the small congregation rose and sang hymns led by the Reverend George. The songs filled the space with energy and optimistic feelings. Though it had been a bloody first year of war and the snow descended heavily, they knew they would endure; they would fight for their belonging.

"In closing," George continued, "Remember the words from the book of Isaiah: Thou wilt keep him in perfect peace, whose mind is stayed on thee: because he trusts in thee. May the Lord bless you; may the Lord keep you, and may the Lord grant us all the strength to endure these times of trial and tribulation. Amen, amen, amen."

Chapter 11 - Spring Campaign

A small group of Queenston citizens gathered by the shore of the Niagara River beneath the canopy of newly budded trees. Nathan and Victoria stood at the altar, preparing to exchange their marriage vows.

Despite the past year's turbulent times and desperate measures, the couple had fallen in love. Their bond's power and faith had triumphed over the dark cloud of war and was about to be consecrated before their friends and family.

Catharine and John Decew, James and Laura Secord, and other local friends and family joined them. The Secord children, Mary, Charlotte, Harriot, Charles, and baby Appolonia were also in attendance as the Priest continued his poetic benediction.

"May the Lord bless and keep you, Nathan and Victoria, as you embark on this sacred journey of marriage on this 23rd day of April, in the year of our Lord, 1813. May your love for each other grow stronger with each passing day, just as the roots of the ancient oak tree deepen with time. May you find a source of comfort, joy, and strength in each other as you face the challenges that life may bring."

Nathan looked at his bride with adoration and absolute certainty. From the moment he first saw Victoria, he knew he had fallen in love and would forever go above and beyond for her. Though the uncertainty of the war loomed, nothing could break the bond of their young love.

The thrushes and finches chirped, the Niagara River roared, and the cicadas buzzing harmonized to create a perfect symphony for a springtime wedding.

"May your home be filled with laughter, understanding, and the warmth of love's embrace as you build a life together in God's grace. May your union be a shining example of love and commitment to all fortunate enough to witness it. And now, by the power vested in me as a servant of God, I pronounce you Nathan and Victoria Davis, husband, and wife, in the name of the Father, the Son, and the Holy Spirit. Amen."

Everyone smiled as Nathan and Victoria embraced in a newly wedded kiss.

The American fleet returned from York, the young, developing, new Upper Canadian capital on the north shore of Lake Ontario. The fleet and the army had burned the entire city to the ground. It was a great American victory, sending General Major Roger Sheaffe, the Canadian militia, and British regulars fleeing into the surrounding districts.

The York public buildings, the library, the post office, law and clerk buildings, and people's homes were all looted, burned, and left in ashes, something the British were not accustomed to in all their years at war. The American's only significant loss in the battle was General Pike, who was bombarded with debris and shrapnel from the exploding magazine at the battery near the shore of Lake Ontario.

President Madison and the rest of the Washington leadership vowed not to make the same mistakes they had made the previous year. So, after Hull's surrender at Detroit and the failure to take Queenston Heights, the Americans had assigned new leadership and assembled a massive fleet to combat the British and take over the Canadas once and for all.

With York in smouldering ruins, the Americans redirected their attention again to Fort George, near the small town of Newark, on the Niagara Frontier.

Along the foggy shores of Lake Ontario, where warm spring air mixed with cool lake waters to create a misty haze, General Dearborn, a Revolutionary War veteran, and Admiral Isaac Chauncey rode aboard the flagship USS Madison.

Chauncey, a wise, weathered man of about sixty, approached Major General Henry 'Granny' Dearborn, a short, heavy-set man, sitting in his wooden wheelchair pondering the great victory that could be coming his way.

Almost every citizen in the United States was familiar with 'Granny' Dearborn; his reputation frequently preceded him. The explorers Lewis and Clark, appointed by Thomas Jefferson, named the raging Dearborn River in Montana after the General in 1803. The recently established Fort Dearborn in Chicago was also named for him. Dearborn often talked about his time with General George Washington and the Continental Army at Valley Forge in the winter of 1778. He was the Secretary of War, had the common touch, and was newly appointed United States Army Commanding General.

Dearborn was recently and specially assigned by President Madison to reverse the American fortunes in the War of 1812. His goal this spring was to invade Montréal, Kingston, and Newark in a newly conceived plan designed to overwhelm the British strongholds.

"The loss of General Pike at York was a great one, but in retrospect, our victory was completely one-sided," Chauncey told Dearborn.

"I don't think the British took too kindly to us burning their public buildings," Dearborn said. "It may come back to haunt us."

"We need to achieve absolute victory this spring," Chauncey said.

"We are in a good position as we approach Fort George," Dearborn responded. "The wind is right, and the fog will cover our approach. They will never know what hit them."

From below deck, a newly freed Winfield Scott emerged, clean, healthy, and looking stronger than ever. After a prisoner exchange in Washington, Scott returned to the Niagara Frontier and eventually to Sackets Harbor, where he again joined the war effort aboard the USS Madison.

Dearborn had taken a particular interest in Scott after he had heard of his efforts and bravery at Queenston, his capture, and eventual imprisonment. Dearborn had arranged for Scott to return to Sackett's Harbor and personally serve under him aboard the American fleet.

Scott saluted Chauncey and Dearborn. "All my troops are briefed and ready for action, sir," Scott said.

Scott kept his soldiers, both artillery and infantry, highly disciplined. Regular exercise, daily duties, and regimented sleep would be the cornerstone to their success.

"You are now a Brigadier General, Mr. Scott. Much will be expected of you," Dearborn said. Scott reminded Dearborn of George Washington: ambitious, straightforward, strategic, loyal, and honourable.

"I thank you both for the promotion. Let my first act as a Brigadier General be to request leading the invasion force at Fort George in the morning," Scott asked as Dearborn and Chauncey looked at one another. "My men are well-trained and ready for duty."

"Granted, of course, Brigadier," Dearborn said.

Dearborn knew from the beginning that he had made the correct decision by promoting Scott and bringing him aboard. Not only was he a good soldier, but he was enthusiastic and determined.

"You are an eager young man," Chauncey added.

"Eager to do my duty. It can also be said that I would like to be at the head of an army that can win a siege, with my reinforcements behind me, instead of watching from across the river," Scott said, with a sly, sarcastic tone.

Dearborn turned to Chauncey. "No doubt anger fuelled by the soldiers, or lack thereof, at Queenston last fall."

"Indeed, sir. Though I do not understand why General Van Rensselaer has retired from the frontline," Scott said, knowing exactly why he had not returned.

"It was a voluntary act, I assure you, Scott. Young man, you will see generals come and go throughout your career, not by their choice, but for fear of public outcry. Often, these generals are replaced by erratic, inept officers, who only think of themselves and do not see the big picture of things," Dearborn said, reflecting with military wisdom that gleaned over decades.

"Come Scott, let me show you the map of Fort George and the embankment-landing point," Chauncey said as he led Scott to a map of the Niagara theatre. "You are to advance 300 paces across the beach toward the high bank, then wait for the 1500 infantry under General Boyd. You will guard his flank with the riflemen. Then move in the mentioned three columns to Fort George."

"Understood, sir," Scott said with a surge of adrenaline that came with thinking about his crucial role in establishing the beachhead.

"We will move in towards the Canadian shore with the fog. In the morning, as it clears, our vessels will arc around Fort George and open fire," Chauncey said. "Rest well, eat a big breakfast, and get ready to push the British out of North America."

The soldiers of Fort George were anticipating an attack, but nothing like what was about to come. Governor General Prevost had called General Sheaffe to Kingston to discuss the events and explain the loss at York.

After abandoning York in what many viewed as cowardice, it was clear to leaders at most levels that Sheaffe had outlived his usefulness. Though he had helped rally the troops and forced the Americans off the Heights at Queenston when General Brock had been killed, he was about to be berated for his actions at York.

At York, the British also lost their flagship, the Sir Isaac Brock. Realizing the naval importance of the Great Lakes, Sheaffe understood that if their massive warship fell into American hands, it would likely be the turning point in allowing them to dominate.

As a result, Sheaffe ordered the ship to be set ablaze as they retreated.

The army stationed at Fort George was the only thing left keeping Upper Canada together. After a decade of service there with the 49th, General Sheaffe would not be apart of the army's future actions.

John Norton and John Brant had returned from the Iroquois settlement along the Grand River with 50 warriors. While those 50 were ready and prepared for war, the long, cold winter had reduced the anticipated numbers.

British Brigadier General John Vincent, a tall, refined, stern-looking man, welcomed Norton and Brant. He was a decorated veteran of the 49th regiment, fighting in France, Belgium, the West Indies, and the Caribbean. Vincent was the successor and replacement to Brock and Sheaffe at Fort George and was certainly glad to see his Native allies return. Lieutenant Fitzgibbon and Captain Evans welcomed the Iroquoian friends they had not seen in months.

"Welcome back to Newark, Chief Norton, Chief Brant. It is truly an honour," Vincent said.

"General Vincent, I've just heard the news of York," Norton said as he nodded at FitzGibbon and Evans.

"One-sided, at best," Vincent responded. "Our Lake Ontario flagship has been destroyed."

"Will General Sheaffe be joining our efforts here at Fort George?" Norton asked, thinking of his old friend and ally.

"He was at York during the invasion and has been called to Kingston in a civil capacity," Vincent said, knowing that Sheaffe was being judged for retreating. He also knew there must have been some reasonable grounds for Sheaffe's actions, and so he protected the integrity of his contemporary and colleague.

The men strolled into the officer's mess, where Superintendent of Indian Affairs William Claus sat at the central table. Norton recognized his nemesis immediately. Claus had spread false rumours, looked down upon his people, and cold-heartedly tarnished Norton's reputation in several circumstances.

"Gentlemen, Indians," Claus said in a cantankerous tone.

"Captain Norton, Captain Brant, you remember Mr. Claus," Vincent said. "He has joined us here at Fort George."

Norton and Brant could only nod their heads at Claus. They reviled the man and would have him killed or replaced if it were within their control.

"Mr. Norton, how are your distribution rights going? Are your followers happy with a White man telling them what to do?" Claus asked, raising his eyebrow.

"They are much happier without your frequent visits, war or no war," Norton said disdainfully as he turned to General Vincent and Lt. FitzGibbon. "The enemy forces in the fort opposite are stirring about. We have heard and seen a great bustle of commotion," Norton said.

"It is doubtful they would attack a freshly supplied Fort George with a thousand British regulars here," Claus said.

"Their main body is still at Sackets Harbor; information we acquired from enemy deserters," Brant said, addressing General Vincent.

"Come, let us stroll a while," Vincent said as he grabbed Norton's arm, and they went outside. "The attack is inevitable. If we can meet them here at the beach and stall them, we can perhaps reinforce our batteries and give ourselves a chance of repelling," Vincent strategized. "The enemy is not prepared to delay any further. Despite what Claus thinks and enemy deserters are saying, the Americans will be here soon."

"Understood, General Vincent. We will do our best to prepare," Norton said.

As Norton and Vincent discussed the upcoming conflict, The Coloured Corps, led by Richard Pierpoint, entered the fort. Pierpoint, followed by Jupiter, Vanpatten, Martin, Hector, Bob, and the rest of Butler's rangers, was a determined, battle-hardened group ready for their next engagement.

FitzGibbon went to welcome the newly arrived allies. "Pierpoint, you old dog. Are you still alive?" FitzGibbon joked as they shook hands.

"I am and don't look as old as you do," Pierpoint said jokingly.

"The enemy is stirring, Pierpoint. I hope you boys are ready for a battle," FitzGibbon said.

"We are ready to lay down our lives," Pierpoint stated.

The 30 or so Black soldiers mingled with the rest of the newly arrived militia from around Niagara. Norton and Brant came over to Pierpoint and FitzGibbon.

"We're glad to see you lion-hearted warriors are back for some more action," Norton said to Pierpoint. "You did us Haudenosaunee proud at Queenston."

"We're nothing like you Shawnee and Iroquois fighters," Pierpoint said as he shook Brant and Norton's hands. "You and your rangers will join us at the beach if the attack comes in the morning, which I'm sure it will," Norton said to Pierpoint.

"We'll be glad to join you," Pierpoint said with assurance.

The next morning, Winfield Scott stood at the bow of his boat, leading a force of ten rowboats containing 200 American regulars. Their job was straightforward: establish the beachhead and secure the landing area for the rest of the army.

As the dense fog began to clear off Lake Ontario, the American fleet was revealed to the soldiers at Fort George. Seventeen ships and more than 150 small boats painted a grim picture for the British and their allies. Deserter reports had stated they were at Sackets Harbor but were, in fact, just across the river from Fort George.

General Vincent, Norton and the other leadership had been up since 5:00 am in anticipation of the combat and noticed the armada so close to Newark and Fort George.

"Sackets Harbor, you say?" Vincent said.

"Some enemy reports can be more reliable than others, General," Brant said, raising his eyebrows.

"That's a rather sizable force. I suppose they will open up their cannons any time now," FitzGibbon said.

"I warn you, sir, I have a force of only 50, and seeing this, I fear it will be much reduced in size," Norton said, as he feared for his warriors and their family's safety.

"Norton, Pierpoint, take your men to the beach and meet that force. I will arrange for the Glengarry Newfoundlanders to support you at the ridge," Vincent said. "Give them hell, boys. Take refuge behind the embankment after your first volley. Remember, you must stall them until the regulars arrive from the fort."

Norton and Pierpoint left with their soldiers to meet Winfield Scott's forces on the beach.

Scott's forces rowed hard as he cheered and urged them on. "Today is our day, gentlemen. Nothing will stop us. Row harder, you damned beautiful bastards!" Scott yelled.

As Scott and his forces continued to row, the American ships opened their cannons on Fort George. The dozens of cannons firing caused explosions everywhere in and around Fort George. The British battery also began to fire on the gigantic fleet of ships. Winfield Scott did not flinch and stood proudly aboard his vessel, carrying 20 determined soldiers.

"Remember not to be foolish with your lives. There appears to be little resistance on the beach," Scott said as a cannonball exploded in the water 20 feet from his boat.

"They will retreat at the sight of us!" a soldier yelled.

"We will be met at the beach," Scott said. "Be assured of grapeshot once we land on shore. We will secure the left flank as Boyd's forces push forward. Row hard fellows. We're almost there."

A cannon blast from the USS Madison exploded at the battery in Fort George, sending four British soldiers flying through the air to their deaths. FitzGibbon was able to jump out of the way, avoiding any serious injury. He got to his knees, brushed the debris from his uniform, and began leaving the battery to join the rest of the regulars. He looked down at the mangled men for signs of life but could not find any.

The Grand River warriors, Pierpoint's men, the Glengarry Newfoundlanders, and a handful of militiamen formed up to meet the oncoming Americans. John Decew and Nathan Davis stood nervously among the militia forming on the ridge.

"There's thousands of them," Nathan said.

"I've never seen an armada that big," Decew followed.

"I don't like our chances," Nathan said.

"I think we just need to stall them," Decew added.

"Whatever happens, tell Victoria I love her," Nathan pleaded as he tightened his clothing.

"Victoria knows you love her, just like Catharine loves me. What we need now is an intervention from God," Decew joked.

Aboard the USS Madison, General Dearborn and Commodore Chauncey watched the first wave, led by Scott, approaching the shore.

"He is a very admirable young man, isn't he," Chauncey said, referring to Scott.

"Indeed, Commodore. A born leader," Dearborn said from his wheelchair.

"Has he insisted on retaining the 2nd artillery, even after becoming an Adjacent General?" Chauncey asked.

"He has. He remains committed to those boys. He may be president someday," Dearborn joked.

"Commendable. General, we shall see the stars and stripes flying at Fort George before noon," Chauncey said with a smile.

Norton's forces, Pierpoint's soldiers, a light infantry regiment known as the Newfoundland Glengarries, John Decew, Nathan Davis, Joseph Willcocks, and the rest of the militia approached the beach landing.

"We are here to do our duty, not to seek security. Those who desire only that should remain home. The warrior knows no anxiety about his safety. He only hopes to be truly safe when his body is underground, and his soul is gone above," Norton said to his surrounding warriors.

They all scrambled knee-deep into the water, presented a line and fired a smoky volley of musket balls at the oncoming American boats. Scott stood tall without flinching. The volley hit a handful of American rowers, but they pressed forward through the choppy waves.

After the first shot by the warriors and militias, they all turned to dash up the bank to hide behind the cover of the sandy dune.

"Get moving!" Pierpoint yelled to his scrambling soldiers.

Winfield Scott's boat was the first to land ashore. The American force of 200 soldiers exited the ten boats with muskets and fixed bayonets, ready for engagement. They presented and fired into the clambering soldiers.

John Hall, one of Pierpoint's men, was shot through the leg and was among the first to be captured by the Americans. Smoke drenched the entire beach. Dozens more of Glengarries and militiamen fell. Scott raised his musket, took aim, and fired, hitting John Decew in the shoulder, and dropping him to the sandy ground. Having lost sight of his friend in the retreat up the bank, Nathan yelled, "John!" into the smoky confusion.

Decew lay face-first in the sand as Scott and his forces pressed past him. As the Americans made it to the top of the embankment, Scott was attacked by a green-jacketed Newfoundlander. He thrust his bayonet at Scott, but the tall soldier was able to avoid the offensive. Scott lost his footing as he dodged the bayonet and tumbled backwards down the bank.

Aboard the USS Madison, Dearborn peered through his looking glass to see Scott falling.

"He is lost. He is killed!" Dearborn shouted.

Scott rose to his feet and continued to battle to secure the beach.

"Ah! False alarm!" Dearborn said, laughing. "He just lost his footing."

The remaining Glengarries fell back with Norton and Pierpoint's forces into the ravine. Meanwhile, another dozen American boats landed on the smoke-covered shore, led by General Boyd, another fresh face assigned to avenge the Hull disgrace. Thousands of Americans were now forming up.

Captured troops, including John Hall and John Decew, were tied up and escorted back aboard the American ships among the cannon fire and chaos of the battle.

General Vincent led the British regulars to form up and face the Americans on the plain in the ravine. Hundreds of British regulars approached the gigantic, daunting American force atop the bank. Ten yards apart, a massive volley of bullets whizzed in every direction. There were massive casualties on both sides.

Winfield Scott raised his musket in the air. "Charge!" he screamed at the top of his lungs. The stronger, more significant American force began to obliterate the British regulars, who started to scramble and retreat. General Vincent, sensing defeat, left for Fort George on horseback. He knew they would need to evacuate if they would survive another day.

General Vincent entered Fort George under heavy bombardment. He barged into the officer's mess to find Lieutenant FitzGibbon and Deputy William Claus scrambling to gather intelligence that they did not want to fall into enemy hands. Gun fire and explosions were deafening, as chaos was all around them.

"A third column of Americans has landed upriver. Our beach forces are on the retreat," Vincent said. "Gather what you can and start heading west."

"The militia is pulling back to their homes, General," FitzGibbon said.

"We are overrun," Vincent said to both FitzGibbon and William Claus. "William, I need you to spike the guns and blow up the magazine store. Time to evacuate and meet the retreating on the road to St. David's. We might end up at Burlington Heights before the day is over."

"It will be done, General," Claus said as he ran out the door.

FitzGibbon looked at Vincent. "It is alright, General. We were overmatched. We put up a valiant resistance. We will regroup."

"Thanks, Lieutenant. Let us get moving," Vincent said.

Claus entered the magazine in a panic. The dark storage building was packed with barrels of gunpowder, various weapons, and cannon balls. Claus lit a long fuse leading to a powder keg and rushed toward the exit. He picked up an axe leaning against a nearby wall as he left. He approached the central flagpole at Fort George that flew the Union Jack and began to chop fervently. Startled by the loud voices of the American soldiers coming from across the fort walls, he fearfully left his task. He dropped the axe and ran as fast as possible to escape the fort.

Winfield Scott entered the fort on horseback through the newly opened front gate. Hundreds of soldiers followed behind Scott with fixed bayonets. The first thing Scott did was grab a retreating, red-coated soldier by his collar and pull him toward his face for interrogation.

"Why do you run? Why not fight?" Scott asked the scared soldier.

"The magazine has a fuse on it. Make haste!" the soldier said to Scott.

"Damn." Scott dropped the soldier from his grip and galloped toward the magazine. Scott made it within 20 yards of the magazine when it exploded with a thunderous clap and sent him flying off his horse. He landed awkwardly on his collarbone, breaking it in several places. Scott clutched his shoulder and watched as a cloud of fire torched the sky.

Without hesitation, with his ears ringing and fueled by adrenaline, Scott stumbled back to his feet, looked up, and noticed the Union Jack atop the central flagpole. He thought what a prize it would be to finally bring down the flag that should have been his last October.

He reached the flagpole, picked up the axe Claus had dropped, and took some mighty swings until the pole came crashing down. He plucked the flag off with a huge smile and stuffed it in his jacket.

"Damn you, Scott, and your cursed long legs! That was to be my prize!" an American soldier yelled from afar.

With the adrenaline of battle still surging, Scott once again mounted his horse and rallied his men. "The Brits are on the run. Form up and follow me. Let us finish this now!" he yelled. "Be brave, you glorious patriots!"

The American General Boyd entered the fort and saw Scott forming up his men. He rode over to the rallying men. "Colonel Scott, we are to hold the fort. There shall be no pursuit of the enemy at this time. Order the withdraw."

"I have the enemy in my power. In 60 minutes, I will bag their entire force, General," Scott said, pleading to his superior officer.

"Withdraw is the command," Boyd said to Scott.

"In order of your ranking and superiority; of course, General." Scott cancelled his orders with his men. He rode off with the physical pain starting to set in and palpable frustration on his face.

Nathan Davis slowly made his way to Queenston, winded from the day's fighting. He made his way up the front steps of the Secord's home and banged on the door. Laura opened the door with a shocked look on her face.

"My God, Nathan, what has happened? Is everything alright?" Laura asked.

"Thousands of Americans have landed on the beaches."

"Come inside," Laura said.

"Fort George is overrun," Nathan said.

Laura and Nathan joined Catharine Decew and Victoria in the dining room.

"Nathan!" Victoria jumped up and into his arms.

"Fort George is in American hands. Remaining British forces, the Indians, and the Glengarries march towards Burlington," Nathan said, catching his breath.

"I hope the retreat is swift and timely," James said.

"Where is my husband, Nathan?" Catharine intervened, and everything went silent.

"He was hit, Catharine." Nathan paused. "I saw him lying wounded on the beach. I cannot be sure if he is alive or dead. We were pulling back as he was hit in the shoulder. I could not go back for him. There were hundreds of soldiers landing, and smoke and bullets were everywhere. At best, he is just injured and been taken prisoner. I'm so sorry, Catharine."

Catharine broke down in tears as she slumped in a dining room chair. Laura put her arm around her dear friend and tried to console her as best as possible.

"He is just injured, Catharine. Everything is going to work out," Laura said.

Victoria sat down beside Catharine and, together with Laura, did her best to comfort her friend.

"Their force was in the thousands. The regulars that confronted the enemy were, much to say, ineffective," Nathan said to James. He then turned to Catharine. "You, me, and Victoria should go to your house. Let us avoid any further confrontation with the enemy on this day."

"James and I shall stay here and be as hospitable to the enemy as one can be," Laura said. "I'm going to set the animals free."

"Please be smart. The American forces will be here in moments. Judging by what they did at York, I would hide anything you don't want to get stolen or burned," Nathan said. "FitzGibbon told us they were ruthless; they spared nothing."

"We'll be fine," James said. "We've done our best to prepare."

"John will be okay, Catharine. Have faith in his resilience and his love for you. He will return." Laura was trying her best to soothe Catharine's pain.

"Goodbye, James. Goodbye, Laura. We shall see each other soon," Nathan said.

Victoria, Nathan, and Catharine left through the front door as the sun began to set. Victoria threw her arm around Catharine's shoulders as they walked to the rear of the property.

James and Laura were left standing, looking north toward Fort George, waiting, and watching for the incoming American forces.

Aboard the USS Madison, Scott, Dearborn, and Chauncey observed the American flag waving at Fort George. Injured British, members of the Glengarry Light Infantry, Canadian militia, and Indians lay across the deck of the ship. Among the captured, John Decew and John Hall sat slumped against the ship's side.

John Hall's leg was soaked in blood and wrapped in blood-red bandages. DeCew's right arm was in a sling and covered in blood. Both men appeared to be at death's door.

Scott, Dearborn, and Chauncey strolled the deck, investigating the newly captured prisoners.

"It was an overwhelming victory, General, but somewhat incomplete," Scott said to his superiors.

"Incomplete, General? We have achieved complete victory," Chauncey said as they dodged between the injured prisoners.

"General Boyd had the enemy force within his grasp, and he just let them go," Scott urged.

"You will get your victories, young General," Dearborn said as he lit his pipe. "Boyd did what he was ordered: hold the fort."

"We could have captured the entire Upper Canadian army, sir," Scott said.

"Remember, Winfield, these people are our friends and neighbours. We have broken bread with them, played sport, and shared many stories. We do need to maintain some ration of civility," the wise Dearborn said. "I'm going to prepare for the journey inland to Fort George."

"Your journey will not be met by the enemy, sir. They are amid a hasty retreat," Scott said proudly.

"I'm to guide the fleet to Sackets Harbor," Chauncey told Dearborn.

Dearborn turned to Chauncey. "Well done, Commodore." Dearborn then turned to Scott. "Rest a few hours before you take the prisoners to Albany."

"Yes, sir," Scott said.

The Americans had won the day. Their primary goal, the siege and capture of Fort George, had been accomplished with hardly any casualties. The Americans had launched a surprise amphibious landing, and while it was overwhelmingly successful, Winfield Scott seemed to be the only subdued American. He knew that if they had pursued the enemy and destroyed the entire British army, the Americans would have nothing standing in their way. Instead, the British had retreated and were now regrouping about 30 miles away at Burlington Heights.

As he strode from bow to stern, Winfield Scott looked at all the wounded prisoners along the sea deck and felt a sudden surge of pride.

The captured John Decew and John Hall sat beside each other on the ship's deck. They overheard the entire conversation between Scott, Dearborn, and Chauncey.

"It looks like we're going to Albany," Decew told Hall.

John Hall and a few other Black soldiers knew their future was bleak. They would never see family or friends ever again in Upper Canada. Even if they were able to avoid the gallows or firing squad in Albany, they would, in all likelihood, be sold back into the southern slave market and find themselves on the plantation fields once again.

"We're going to get sold and shipped down to those damned southern fields," Hall said. "I don't think I will make it."

"I'll do what I can to ensure that will not happen, John," Decew said. "For now, we must keep our mouths shut and do as we're told."

"I can't go south, Decew," Hall said as he slumped his head between his knees and began to cry.

"Close your eyes and rest awhile. It is going to be a long ride." John Decew leaned back against the boat, closed his eyes, and slowly drifted off to sleep.

Chapter 12 ~ Occupation

As Fort George fell to the Americans in May 1813, Joseph Willcocks became increasingly disillusioned with British rule, and believed the United States would control the entire North American continent. He, along with about thirty men, marched under a white flag into the American held Fort George and surrendered their service to the American effort.

Willcocks was awarded a Majorship in the American army because of his knowledge of Niagara and its people. Throughout the spring, he was able to grow his force to around 150. Most of them were once Americans who had immigrated to Upper Canada. Ironically, the unit called themselves the Canadian Volunteers.

The United States was now in complete occupation of Fort George and the town of Newark. They had taken over houses, public buildings, and the streets in general. Only the American, blue, and grey-coated soldiers were allowed to walk the streets. If they saw a British soldier or militiaman on the roads, their orders were to arrest them immediately.

Willcocks loved his new American policing position, which allowed him to regulate citizens' movements, make reports, and interrogate prisoners. He took pleasure in taking retribution on Loyalists who supported the King and his tyrannism.

It had been two months since the capture of Newark and Fort George, and things were getting increasingly worse for the citizens of Niagara. Led by their new enemy, Joseph Willcocks, Americans had begun looting and pillaging the homes, burning out-buildings and barns, and treating civilians with indignance and disdain. All the captured British soldiers were imprisoned and sent to Albany or Philadelphia to carry out their sentences and await their fate. Most homes were either empty or left with only women, children, or the elderly. Fear was constant and looming, while resentment and contempt were rising amongst the Upper Canadians.

The citizens of Upper Canada had fallen on difficult times. The economy had halted, trade routes were blocked, fields were left unseeded, and animals were left wild and unattended. Many families migrated west, away from the Niagara frontier, and stayed with family members far removed from the dark cloud of war. As was the case 30 years ago, Niagara was left in ashes.

Though the British remained 30 miles away from Newark and Fort George, they were not idle. They would not be passive victims and did their best to resist American incursions. Night raids, secret missions, and surprise hits were how they were now fighting the war. FitzGibbon and his soldiers were making it arduous for any American who decided to leave the comfort of Fort George and venture off on their own.

General Vincent and his regulars, John Norton and the Iroquois warriors, and Richard Pierpoint and his troops made preparations at Burlington Heights for a possible confrontation in the near future. They spent several weeks digging a fort with earthen walls on the high ground with clear lines of sight for their cannon crews.

Lieutenant FitzGibbon and his men went from Burlington Heights to Queenston, where they would try to capture wandering, careless Americans. FitzGibbon had taken on more of a leadership role since the American occupation and was quickly gaining a reputation for his ruthless military cleverness in the forests of Upper Canada.

This particular night, FitzGibbon was on the lookout for the notorious Captain Cyrenius Chapin, a Buffalo doctor turned raiding marauder. Under the direction of Major Joseph Willcocks, Chapin, at the head of 50 men, was looting every building he could find.

FitzGibbon watched carefully and quietly from the bush at the side of the road to Queenston as two young American soldiers made their way into the local tavern. Only a few people were there, including Decew's wife, Catharine, and Victoria Davis, who had rendezvoused to help the Secords. Catharine turned her head to see the newly arrived American soldiers. She then looked at Victoria and smiled. She rose to her feet and calmly made her way outside.

Catharine knew FitzGibbon was nearby and wanted to warn him of the new American arrivals. She pulled a white handkerchief from her dress and casually waved it about on the cobblestone road.

Through the bushes at the side of the road, FitzGibbon burst onto the road on horseback, wearing the dirty grey uniform of an American soldier. Catharine turned and waved her handkerchief at the mounted FitzGibbon.

"Hello, Lieutenant FitzGibbon. Take flight. You must flee. I've just seen Chapin and about 50 Americans up the road. A couple Americans just entered the tavern, and I'm sure they will not be the last. I must insist that you disappear," Catharine said with urgency.

FitzGibbon dismounted his horse and gave Catharine a big smile. "Thank you for your forewarning and genuine concern," he said.

Inside the tavern, the two American soldiers ordered a beer and sat at a table, seemingly without a care in the world. FitzGibbon ignored Catharine's advice and barged into the tavern with rosy cheeks and a big smile.

"Good evening, everybody!" FitzGibbon shouted to the handful of customers.

He approached the two Americans sitting at a table and extended his hand to greet the unassuming soldiers.

"Colonel FitzGibbon. Good to see the two of you." FitzGibbon shook their hands firmly.

"Private Simpson," the first soldier said.

"Private Miller," the second soldier said. "I cannot say that I recognize you, Colonel. Are you new to the area?"

As FitzGibbon shook Miller's hand, he grabbed Simpson's leaning musket. Miller, noticing this, pulled his pistol from his belt and pointed it at FitzGibbon. FitzGibbon grabbed the barrel of Miller's pistol and pointed it at Private Simpson. Everything happened quickly; Catharine and Victoria looked on, confused by the scene before them.

"Surrender!" FitzGibbon yelled at the Americans.

"No," Private Miller responded adamantly.

"No?!" FitzGibbon questioned, surprised by his response.

FitzGibbon managed to wrestle the pistol free from Miller and threw it across the room. FitzGibbon was a giant man compared to the two young privates. He grabbed them both and wrestled them outside.

FitzGibbon exited the Queenston tavern and pushed the two Americans before him. As he was pushed away, Private Miller was able to pull FitzGibbon's sword from his sheath. Catharine and Victoria came out the door to help FitzGibbon.

After months without her husband, Catharine, full of confidence and anger, kicked the sword from the American's hand. Private Simpson drew his pistol and aimed at FitzGibbon. Victoria saw her opportunity and seized the weapon from Simpson.

FitzGibbon's 240-pound frame pinned the helpless Private Miller to the steps of the tavern while Catharine and Victoria began scuffling with Private Simpson. Victoria dodged an American's wild swing and countered by slapping Private Simpson's face. The enraged soldier turned and faced Victoria with rageful intent.

Catharine quickly picked up the sword from the ground, putting the blade against Private Simpson's neck. "Enough, please!" Catharine shouted, catching her breath.

"Surrender, or I'll kill you both!" FitzGibbon yelled at the frightened soldiers.

"We surrender," Private Miller struggled to say under the weight of FitzGibbon.

FitzGibbon turned to Catharine and Victoria. "Well done," he said.

"You best get moving, Lieutenant," Catharine said. "There will be more soldiers arriving shortly."

"Thank you," FitzGibbon said as he got to his feet. He picked up the pistol and walked the two American soldiers off at gunpoint. "We shall see each other soon. Well done, Mrs. Decew and Mrs. Davis."

FitzGibbon walked the soldiers into the darkness through the thick bush as Catharine brushed the grass and dirt from her dress.

"Well done, Victoria," Catharine said with a smile.

"You saved my life," Victoria said, straightening herself out.

"It was a team effort," Catharine said modestly. "But I am glad I could help."

"I could kiss you," Victoria said. "We should probably leave the area."

"Agreed," Catharine said as the two ladies descended the dark dirt road.

The sun set atop the escarpment. Karighwaycagh and John Norton sat side by side, enjoying the summer air and scenery. Though things seemed perfect when together, war always weighed heavy on Norton's mind. The Americans were encroaching on his community, and he could not help but feel anxiety and anger in the wake of the American spring offensive.

Karighwaycagh was young but wise enough to understand her husband's feelings. "Are we going to be forced from our lands again?" she asked.

"Let us not dwell on moments that may or may not happen. Let us love the moments we are in. You will be safe here, always, I promise," Norton said as he looked her in the eyes.

"I am not afraid. However, I have heard the elders speak of revised provisions. They have been consulting at the fire without much hope. Fear envelopes many villages, Sawatis."

"Though traitors are becoming increasingly prevalent, please understand our Chiefs' decisions to stand beside the King. We will again overtake these lands, our lands. The Americans do not adore these lands as we do. It is a few rich, greedy pocket of Americans who feel the need for war and violence. Let us not forget the thousands of soldiers who will soon be arriving since Napoleon Bonaparte's collapse." Norton rose to his feet.

Karighwaycagh was curious. "Napoleon Bonaparte?" she said, standing up.

"This small French emperor is bullying the entire European continent. He foolishly marched his entire army into Russia, a faraway place, much like this one, with cold, numbing winters and inhospitable frozen wastelands. Napoleon grew too confident and did not prepare for the oncoming, bleak winter," Norton said. "His whole army is either dead, captured or missing, only a few remain."

"Perhaps the Americans will retreat soon," Karighwaycagh said.

"The Canadas and the States will soon be allies again, in great fortune and prospering with one another. Britain has defeated Napoleon's depleted army and will reinforce these new colonies. America is a nation of only eight million souls, but she is not ready to contend with Britain's great navy. Many American leaders know this to be true."

Despite the invasion of the American army, Norton was optimistic about the future of Canada and his people.

"What you are doing is important, Sawatis. You must continue your effort. Without you and your warriors, we may all find ourselves enslaved by the Americans."

"Karighwaycagh, I must leave again tonight, my love."

"I figured so."

"I know you understand the importance of these days, my love. I set forth for the Decew house and am uncertain when I will see you again," Norton said as he embraced his wife.

"Be cautious, use good judgement, and let your heart guide you."

"Walk with pride and spread the news that this war will soon be over," Norton said.

Norton and Karighwaycagh strolled back to the village as the sun tucked behind the hills of the Grand River Valley.

James Secord continued to stay at his home in severe physical distress. His shoulder had healed; however, his torn-up knee prevented him from doing anything. Fortunately, the Americans had allowed Laura to stay and look after Secord, whom they had dismissed with contempt as an insignificant husband.

James and Laura Secord sat on the front step of their rundown home. They were both distraught, as Americans had thoroughly plundered their home again as they sat and watched helplessly. Their house had first been ransacked during the Battle of Queenston Heights. Now it had happened again, except this time, the invaders had killed much of their livestock and stolen the silverware, artwork, candle holders, pots, pans, and precious family heirlooms - even their dinnerware had been pilfered.

Laura began crying as she laid her head on her husband's shoulder.

"We will endure, my love," James said.

"Why does this keep happening? After everything we have built. Our home, destroyed by our neighbours again," Laura said, weeping. "This war is so damned foolish."

"It will be over soon, my love," James said, trying to reassure Laura.

"As soon as it ends, another war will manifest itself," Laura said, shaking her head. "This Niagara frontier does not seem worth the cost or effort of what we have endured."

"We can rebuild. We can grow more crops, raise new animals, and start fresh."

"You can hardly walk. We have five children that need us, James," Laura pleaded. "It will take years to rebuild."

"And we will do it together," James said. "Napoleon Bonaparte is on the run, my dear. British reinforcements will be here soon. Let's go inside now, and we will pick up the pieces together."

Laura stared off and wondered what the coming days and weeks might look like. Usually, she would have the foresight to think about the months and years to come, but the war had hindered her ability to plan beyond a few days.

Laura helped James get to his feet, and together, they made their way back inside the torn-apart home and began cleaning up slowly.

The Decew house, home of John and Catharine, became a secret base of operations for the British and Upper Canadians in the spring and summer of 1813. It was deep in the middle of the Niagara Peninsula and challenging for the Americans to locate. Most American leadership suspected operations were being planned there, but they had more significant concerns, like General Vincent and the British forces at Burlington.

Inside the Decew house, John Norton, John Brant, a handful of Iroquois warriors, Thomas Evans, and a few other British officers were reviewing a map atop a large wooden table.

"I believe the Americans are growing concerned," John Norton said. "Our hit-and-run tactics throw them into chaos and confusion."

"Our raids are keeping them contained. Your warriors are brave, my dear friend," Evans said to Norton and Brant. "If we keep up this warfare on the Americans, they will be forced to abandon Fort George and retreat to American soil."

"I have received word that 200 warriors, led by Dominique Ducharme, are coming from Lower Canada. Our Indian forces will number around 400," Norton said.

"We must not let the Americans feel comfortable," Evans added.

FitzGibbon, still in his dirty grey American uniform, entered the room with a big, confident smile. "Norton, I am glad you and your warriors are still with us. How are you, my good man?" he said as he threw his coat and hat on a nearby chair.

"Well, well, if it isn't old Fitzy," Norton said as he looked FitzGibbon up and down. "The uniform highlights your best qualities."

"Ha! My Green Tigers love the grey, which usually means some sort of carnage is on the horizon."

Everyone shared a laugh as the night was winding down. Catharine entered the room carrying a tray with tea and cookies.

She set it down on the corner of the table and smiled at the surrounding soldiers.

"Hello, Mrs. Decew," Norton said.

"Good evening, gentlemen," she responded.

Catharine had not received any word from her husband over the past few months, and it had taken its toll on the Decew household. Catharine had been rationing food for her family since there was no money or means to buy food. She had help from her in-laws; however, things were not improving. The Secord and Davis families tried their best to make her life more comfortable, but the anxiety and uncertainty surrounding her husband's capture weighed heavily.

"Thank you, Mrs. Decew," Evans said, smelling the pot of tea.

"You're most welcome," Catharine said as she smiled at FitzGibbon.

"Catharine helped me with a few no-good Americans a few nights ago. She kicked the sword from the enemy's hand, picked it up, placed it at his throat and yelled 'surrender'." Catharine could only smile as FitzGibbon told the story to his fellow soldiers.

"You exaggerate," Catharine said as she left to go into the kitchen.

Catharine Decew and her children stayed upstairs while FitzGibbon and his troops occupied the downstairs with operations, tactics, meetings, and strategies. She did not mind losing the space but focused more on her husband's well-being and caring for her eleven children. She knew John had been shot, but was he alive or dead? She could not be sure.

The house, although bustling with soldiers, still seemed empty without the cheer and laughter of her husband. The children missed their father's security and adventurous spirit as the war dragged on. There had been no word since John's capture at the Battle of Fort George. For all she knew, John was killed by a firing squad, died from his injuries, or sat rotting in a prison in Albany or Philadelphia. Although depressed, she knew she had to press on and continue with her onerous responsibilities around the house in such a challenging time.

FitzGibbon sat down at the dining room table with Norton and the other officers, poured a glass of wine, and contemplated the map before him.

"Norton, we must get to Burlington Heights and support General Vincent. They're digging in, building ramparts and earthen works. We need to protect them as best as we can," FitzGibbon said. "Word through the wind is that Americans are planning a march on Burlington."

"I'll gather my forces and depart in the morning," Norton said.

"Godspeed, Captain Norton," FitzGibbon said.

"Thanks, Fitzy. We will see you around," Norton said as he departed out the front door with John Brant and his fellow warriors.

FitzGibbon leaned back in his chair and stared at the ceiling. He knew the fate of Upper Canada would teeter over the next few weeks, and he would need to be at his best.

FitzGibbon missed his friend and ally, Isaac Brock and contemplated what he might do in the coming days. They had fought and bled together on the battlefields of Europe, North America, and the open oceans. He missed their witty banter, especially in such tumultuous times. He promised himself to do right, be courageous, and put his life on the line.

"Alright, let us march to Burlington and repel any American advance," FitzGibbon said. "We depart at first light."

"Aye, Lieutenant," Evans said.

Chapter 13 ~ Ambuscade

The United States began the 1813 spring campaign with more organization and better strategy. Led by Henry 'Granny' Dearborn, the Americans had invaded Upper Canada and were preparing to continue their conquest west and eradicate the British forces at Burlington.

Oliver Hazard Perry had successfully taken control of Lake Erie with the U.S. flotilla, and William Henry Harrison was preparing to retake Fort Detroit and push Tecumseh and his warriors back into the Thames Valley. Having learned from their initial failures and embarrassments in the first months of the war, the Americans were now putting sound strategy into action and looking like a professional army.

John Norton and 200 warriors from the Six Nations joined the British forces at Burlington, along with Nathan Davis and the rest of the local militia. FitzGibbon had also recently arrived with his Green Tigers and was preparing for a potential confrontation with the Americans stationed at Fort George.

The early June night was calm but ominous. As the soldiers began trickling into their tents for the night, a sense of insecurity swept Burlington. Most soldiers knew that any day now, they could be called into action.

Richard Pierpoint, Bob and Hector Armstrong, Roger Jupiter, John Vanpatten, George Martin, and the rest of the Coloured Corps were now part of Butler's Rangers as an integrated unit in the Upper Canadian militia stationed in Burlington. They all sat around a small fire, covered by the newly formed earthen embankments and the surrounding hardwood forest. Although they had been forced to retreat from Fort George, they felt slightly more confident as more warriors and soldiers arrived, joining the main force at Burlington. Despite being outnumbered, the growing confidence made most soldiers believe in their ability to keep the Americans from pressing on into the rest of Upper Canada.

"Why do you suppose the Americans are not making a move on us?" Hector asked his father.

"Well, my best guess is that they are feeling confident and don't have a real reason to come and engage," Bob said to his son.

"I hope Hall is alright, the poor bastard," Vanpatten said as he thought about his captured friend. Vanpatten had stood directly beside John Hall on the beach at Fort George as he was shot scrambling up the beach dune. "It could have been me that got shot and captured."

"Man, I hope he's alive," Jupiter said.

"He's gone, friends," Pierpoint said, shaking his head. "We need to remember his legacy and what he fought for. Let us pray for our brother John Hall."

The men around the fire bowed their heads in prayer. As the men began to pray, a young teenage boy burst through the forest on horseback. Pierpoint and his troops all looked up, grabbed their weapons, rose to their feet, and aimed at the newcomer.

"Americans! At least 3000!" the young boy yelled.

"Calm down, boy!" Pierpoint yelled back. "What have you seen?"

The boy dismounted his horse. "My name is Billy Green, and I've just come from Stoney Creek, east of our position," he said. "Thousands of Americans, with heavy artillery, are camped out and looking to engage at first light."

"God damn!" Bob said as he looked at Pierpoint.

"3000?" Hector said.

"They're everywhere, disorganized and overly confident," Billy said. "I observed their positions and can lead you to them."

"Come with me, Billy. I need you to share this news with the General," Pierpoint said.

Pierpoint led Billy Green to General Vincent and the rest of the officers, where they quickly decided not to delay engagement. They would strike at the unsuspecting Americans in the middle of the night. All 1500 soldiers would march in absolute silence, remove their flints from their muskets, destroy the unsuspecting sentries, and capture the American artillery before they could mobilize or even realize what was happening.

"Billy Green, you've done a great service today," General Vincent said to the young man. "Can you lead our column to the American positions?"

"Of course, General," Billy said confidently.

Word spread through the ranks of the 49th and 8th regiments. The entire Upper Canadian force gathered their belongings, ate a hurried, hearty meal of oatmeal and walnuts and began the 10-mile hike from Burlington to Stoney Creek at around 11:30pm under cover of darkness.

Billy Green led the army to the American force's location in total stealth. They trekked past rivers and streams, climbed hillsides, and travelled across the rocky, forested terrain. Upon their arrival, they found the American forces sound asleep, except for a few sentries and cooks preparing food for the next day. Only the crackle of a couple dying fires could be heard as the soldiers moved into position.

FitzGibbon and a few of his soldiers crept behind an unsuspecting sentry post and waited for the perfect opportunity. The American soldier leaned his musket against a tree to adjust his belt; FitzGibbon saw his chance. He slowly emerged from the dense bush, grabbed the sentry, covered his mouth and slit his throat. To ensure the body was concealed, he then dragged it back into the forest.

John Norton carefully maneuvered into position and prepared to take down another American sentry. He plunged his sharp hatchet into the back of the unknowing American's skull, and he dropped instantly.

The sentries were dispatched one by one as the British army moved in. With fixed bayonets, muskets began to sound, breaking the eerie silence as the nighttime ambush began.

The weary, confused Americans emerged from their tents, buttoning their pants, and putting on their jackets. Their lack of organization allowed the British to swarm among them, unleashing their bloody surprise attack.

The redcoats devastated the camp; chaos reigned everywhere. Americans struggled to load their muskets as Iroquois forces whooped and hollered in their attacks. They used war clubs, gun stocks, knives, daggers, swords, and bayoneted muskets in their frenzied close-quarter attack.

Pierpoint, Bob Armstrong, Jupiter, and Vanpatten managed to capture one of the American cannons and began to defend it. Beginning their brave defence, George Martin and Hector Armstrong captured an American general who seemed more confused than distraught. When an American soldier sprang from the dark woods and plunged his dagger into Vanpatten's shoulder, Jupiter sprang into action and tackled the soldier to the ground. They struggled with clenched jaws before Jupiter eventually plunged his knife into the chest of the American.

Vanpatten lay on the ground writhing in pain. Jupiter approached his friend. "Hold still!" Jupiter said as he grabbed the dagger and pulled it from his friend's shoulder.

"You alright?" Pierpoint screamed as he fired a musket shot.

"I'll survive," Vanpatten said, clutching his bleeding shoulder.

The Americans had no idea what was happening, let alone the number of soldiers surrounding them. There were one on one fights between soldiers—struggles, fist fighting, and bayonet skirmishes throughout the wooded area. Before long, the ranks on both sides began to form up and exchange musket volleys in firing lines. Smoke filled the forest floor, creating an even more chaotic, blinding environment.

Amid the bloody battle, the Americans sounded the retreat and began heading back down the road toward Fort George. They were now even more disorganized, given that two of their generals had been captured—one by Hector Armstrong and George Martin, the other by FitzGibbon and a few Glengarry Newfoundlanders.

It was a brazen raid by the British and Indians. Dead soldiers lay everywhere, hundreds wounded. While the British regulars withdrew, John Norton assembled his warriors and began following the retreating Americans. Facing Norton's warriors back to Fort George was demoralizing. Additionally, most soldiers had run out of ammunition and were severely dehydrated. They were running for their lives as they sought refuge in the fort walls.

The British had captured hundreds of soldiers and had landed a significant blow to the American effort. Pierpoint, Bob, and the rest of the soldiers returned to Burlington Heights with the prisoners just before daybreak.

Fueled by rage and adrenaline over the long march back, Bob and Hector arrived at their tent, threw down their muskets, took off their boots, and lay down utterly exhausted and parched after the all-night affair.

"You did really well tonight, son," Bob said as he lay down thinking of his dear Fannie.

"Thanks, Dad," Hector said with a smile.

"No matter what you hear or think, what you do here matters. Do you understand me? Do not second-guess yourself or your actions, son."

"I understand, Father," Hector said.

"I know you are too young to see such horrible violence, but you are fighting for an honourable cause, Hector. You are a bloody saint, and everyone for a thousand years will thank you for your courage and your sacrifice," Bob said.

"Thanks again, Dad," Hector said, smiling.

"You're one of a kind, kid." Bob laid his head down and shut his eyes.

"Hey, Dad, do you think Mom is alright?" Hector asked.

Bob thought of Fan, her toughness and resourcefulness. "She is doing just fine, Hector. Do not go worrying about Mom. She's tougher than most of these Americans."

Hector smiled at the thought. He eventually got comfortable and closed his eyes. As the sun rose on Lake Ontario, he and his father slowly drifted to sleep.

Chapter 14 - Espionage

Although occupied by Americans, Fort George lay in a disorganized state. Norton, Brant, FitzGibbon, and their troops harassed the soldiers coming to and from the fort for weeks. They had adopted guerilla tactics, including wearing green to blend in with the natural environment. They wore disguises, set traps, created decoys, and made life a nightmare for any American wandering outside the fort walls.

Inside the officers' mess at the occupied Fort George, Captain Wool, General Winfield Scott, General Boyd, General Dearborn, and the newly arrived General George McClure, Lieutenant Colonel Charles Boerster, and Captain Cyrenius Chapin sat around the same table where Brock and Sheaffe once had tactical discussions.

Chapin, the expert marauder, appeared intoxicated as he plopped down in a chair with a thud. Everyone turned and looked at the commotion as Chapin smiled back at everyone. Cyrenius

Chapin was a Buffalo doctor, a drunk who swore abundantly, an expert plunderer, and second in command to Lieutenant Colonel Boerster.

General Boyd turned his gaze away from Chapin toward General Dearborn. "The constant raiding has placed a great fright in the camp, sir. Nobody wants to leave the fort walls."

"They're cowards, sir," Chapin blurted.

"What Dr. Chapin means is that they are hiding and disguising themselves quite well, sir," Boerster said.

"They have become quite the burden outside these walls," Dearborn responded. "Our defeat at Stoney Creek has us in a bind."

"The raids are coming from, and being planned at Beaverdams, sir. Lieutenant FitzGibbon stations his Green Tigers there. They are a nuisance and need to be eliminated," Winfield Scott said as he slammed his fist on the table.

"I know the Decew family owns a two-storey stone house there. That's where FitzGibbon is when he's out of action," Captain Wool added.

"Those Green Tigers are why we still sit here at Fort George. Instead, we should be trying again to eliminate the forces at Burlington," Scott said, looking at Dearborn.

"We shall strike FitzGibbon and his 'Bloody Boys' with a force of 500," Dearborn said as he lit his pipe. "If we take the Decew House, we will be in a position to drive the British right out of Burlington and Upper Canada and into Québec. Our western forces are in the Thames Valley and ready to join us."

General Boyd interjected, "John Decew was one of the prisoners taken at the battle for Fort George."

"Where is John Decew now?" asked Dearborn.

"I believe he is in Philadelphia with the rest of the prisoners taken that day, sir," Boyd replied.

"So, I suppose his wife remains there with their children. We shall plan to take the house and the forces there on June 23rd, three days from now." Dearborn said as he spun towards Boerster and Chapin. "Colonel Boerster, you will lead this force under cover of darkness. Stealth will be your ally, as we do not want to alarm any scouts or spies in the area."

"Understood, General. Upper Canada will be ours in less than a week," the confident Boerster said.

"I am looking forward to burning their precious little house down," Chapin said with a smile as everyone turned to look at him. "What? It sounds like fun."

John Decew had been in prison in Philadelphia since May. The wound in his shoulder had almost fully healed since having the musket ball removed while he was aboard the prisoner ship.

Upon arrival in Philadelphia, John Decew and John Hall were separated. Hall continued south aboard another ship, whereas Decew was shuttled to the prison within the city of Philadelphia. Decew had promised to do everything in his power to find Hall and bring him back to Canada but knew it would almost be impossible.

John Decew was smart and meticulously catalogued everything he saw or interacted with in his day-to-day routine at the maximum-security prison. He noticed guard changes, mealtimes, other prisoners, mannerisms, weather, and everything else that might play a role in his escape.

Once his shoulder healed, Decew was assigned stone sawing duties. He welcomed the hard labour over the stitching or laundry duties. The manual labour helped him rehabilitate his shoulder and gain strength and stamina as he prepared for a potential escape back to Niagara.

He missed his eleven children dearly: their inquisitive nature, different types of humour, and creativity. Working during the day usually kept his mind from dwelling on thoughts of his family and whether he would see them again.

Nighttime was the worst part of most days. It was solitary, cold, damp, and claustrophobic. Each floor of the building had only one fireplace, and the inmates were constantly battling sickness. The prison was not a welcoming place. It was overcrowded with the mentally ill, serious, and petty criminals, and soldiers captured during the war. Sleeping was difficult, as those who had mental illnesses often caused some commotion during the night.

The sun began to rise on the Pennsylvania prison as the prisoners gathered in the walled courtyard to receive their five ounces of cold portage and black coffee. John Decew brought his prison-issued spoon and dish and ate the bland food as he reflected on his next steps. He remained highly motivated to escape Philadelphia and make his way home.

The prison grounds were in downtown Philadelphia, bustling with pedestrians and thoroughfare. First, he understood that he would need to escape at night under cover of darkness.

Decew had only trusted a handful of prisoners, one of whom was Albert Bishop, a young man who had lost his arm at the Battle of Sackets Harbor a few days after the Battle of Fort George. Bishop had served under Governor General George Prevost, who led the battle to the American naval dockyards on Lake Ontario. Bishop helped by drawing maps of Philadelphia in the dirt – he outlined the streets and surrounding area with detail. He knew navigating at night would be tricky, and having a proper sense of direction would be crucial for escaping.

Once over the wall, he would head north toward Montréal, where he might find a route back to Upper Canada. Travelling through New York State would be too risky, especially with all the activity surrounding Albany, Sackets Harbor, and Fort Niagara. Decew would head through Massachusetts, New Hampshire, and Vermont, eventually crossing the St. Lawrence River into Montréal. The Appalachian Mountains would provide the perfect path into Lower Canada.

The coffee was cold, and the portage lacked flavour, but a smile came over his face as he reminisced about his home and the milling operation in Niagara. He thought of the smell of the freshly cut timber, his children swimming in the nearby creek, and his beautiful wife on the beaches of Lake Erie in the summertime.

The next problem Decew would have to solve is safely escaping to the roof and scaling the 40-foot walls without being detected. Being caught trying to escape would almost certainly mean facing a firing squad or a rope at the end of a gallows.

Inside the Secord home, Colonel Boerster, Captain Chapin, and a few other American officers made themselves at home and spoke freely of military plans. They demanded food, drink, and hospitality while discussing the importance of securing Beaverdams and flushing out FitzGibbon at the Decew house. They dined on Laura and James' food, showing little gratitude and respect for the frontier woman who waited on them hand and foot. Laura did not protest, though. She would do anything to appease the Americans and provide anything they demanded, as her ailing husband and five children were upstairs.

"We need only to concentrate our forces on that damned FitzGibbon, capture the Irish fool, and advance on Burlington Heights," the drunk Chapin said.

"Once captured, that position will mean Upper Canada is all but ours," said Colonel Boerster.

"The Decew house needs to be burned," Chapin said, smiling.

Laura stood near the doorway, out of sight of the American officers but close enough to hear their conversation. She kneaded bread to disguise her presence so close to the dining room. She was quiet, kneading slowly and deliberately. She could not help but overhear their desire to burn Catharine and John's house down.

"The 23rd, we shall move under the cloak of darkness," Boerster said, gulping wine.

Laura considered the urgency of the situation as her heart rate increased. She needed to consult her husband about what to do next. Sweat dripped from her brow as she kneaded the bread with more urgency and haste.

"Mrs. Secord!" Boerster yelled from the dining room.

Laura froze as she put her hand on her chest. Had they seen her trying to overhear their conversation? She tried to steady herself and catch her breath. She thought about running out the back door but quickly realized the foolishness of the act and decided against it.

"Mrs. Secord, come in here for a minute!" Boerster yelled again.

Laura was not sure what to do. Still frozen, she gripped the counter with all her might and thought about grabbing a knife and slipping it under her apron, but she realized it would be incriminating if found. Eventually, she crept into the dining room, where the Americans all sat looking at her sternly in the dimly lit room.

"Ah! You are there," Boerster said.

"Hello, gentlemen," Laura said, looking down to avoid eye contact.

"Don't be frightened, Mrs. Secord," Boerster said. "We don't mean any harm."

"Thank you, sir," Laura said, trembling. "Is there something else I could do for you?" The tension was mounting as Laura still did not know what they wanted.

"We appreciate your hospitality, and I am terribly sorry for the recent looting of your home and property. As gentlemen, we would never have allowed such action to happen to a dignified, beautiful woman," Boerster said as Chapin sat smiling.

A few days earlier, Captain Cyrenius Chapin and a handful of his men had raided several homes throughout Queenston, including the Secords, without Boerster knowing or receiving his superior's consent.

"Thank you, sir," Laura said.

There was a long, distinct, motionless pause.

"Have you heard anything spoken here tonight?" Boerster asked.

Laura shook her head.

"Ha!" Chapin laughed in disbelief.

"I have not heard a single thing. I have been busy in the kitchen, making fresh biscuits for guests such as yourselves." Laura's heart was beating a mile a minute, and she hoped the Americans believed her portrayal of oblivious innocence.

"Just because you're baking doesn't mean you can't use your inquisitive little ears," Chapin said.

"Through the years, I have come to ignore conversations about war, as they only bring about feelings of frustration and melancholy," Laura said as she cleared her throat. "I can assure you; I haven't heard a thing."

Boerster and Chapin looked at each other and then at the seemingly poor woman who didn't have the stomach or inclination for war.

"You see, gentlemen, she didn't hear a word of it," Boerster said laughingly to his fellow officers. "A simple, oblivious frontier woman, cooking biscuits, and ignoring men's conversations about war."

The Americans laughed as Laura nodded in affirmation. A part of her was relieved, but they were still in her house, and she was still uneasy.

"Can I get you gentlemen a spot of tea or something else this evening?" Laura asked cordially.

"I do not think so, Mrs. Secord. You have been a terrific host here in Queenston. I appreciate your hospitality." Boerster rose to his feet. "I hope to see you again, Mrs. Secord. We depart for Fort George." Boerster, Chapin, and the other officers made their way to the front door.

Laura watched to ensure she was out of impending danger. The soldiers all left, but just as Boerster was about to exit, he spun around on the heel of his boot, taking a few slow, deliberate steps toward the frightened Laura. She swallowed hard and trembled at the thought of what might follow.

"Are you quite certain you have not heard what was communicated here tonight?" Boerster asked, a mere foot away from her face.

"Not a word, Colonel," Laura said, shaking her head. "I assure you; I have not heard a single thing."

Boerster paused and stared at Laura with a furrowed brow as if he was closely analyzing her face for signs of dishonesty or malice.

"Excellent. Adieu, Mrs. Secord. I wish you and your family the best."

Boerster made his way out the front door, and Laura shut it behind him, collapsing against it. She threw her hands over her face and began to cry, struggling to catch her breath, as she was overcome with emotions. Never before had she felt such overwhelming anxiety or been so close to such a dangerous encounter.

"Honey!" James yelled from the top of the stairs.

Laura could not respond.

James hobbled down the stairs, cane in hand. "Laura! What's wrong?" As he reached the bottom of the stairs, he noticed his wife crying as he leaned against the front door. "What happened? Is everything alright? Tell me, what is going on?" James stood above her and leaned down, using his cane for support. "Have they hurt you?"

Laura suddenly rose to her feet in a panic. She took her bonnet off the coat rack and tied it swiftly.

"Talk to me," James persisted.

She then brushed past James into the kitchen, wrapped a loaf of bread in a cloth, and put it in a satchel that she slung around her neck.

"Laura, what is all this fuss? Slow down." James was confused as he observed Laura's rare anxiety. "Talk to me, dammit!" James yelled, losing his patience.

His sharp words helped to snap her out of it. "I've heard word of an impending attack at John and Catharine Decew's house," Laura said. "They are going to burn it down. Catharine and her children are there."

"FitzGibbon's headquarters. Of course. When is this attack supposed to happen?" James asked.

"On the morrow. I just heard those obnoxious soldiers talking about it," Laura said.

James grabbed her by the shoulders and looked her in the eye. "Laura, please slow down and look at me. Is the information credible?"

"Enough to warrant alarm." Laura broke from his grip and went upstairs to grab another dress that would better suit her journey.

James sat on the parlour couch and waited for Laura to come down the stairs.

"Slow down, my love. Come here," James said. "Are you sure you've overheard an impending invasion at the Decew house?"

A nervous but more focused Laura made her way to James on the couch. "Yes," she said.

"We have come to a place that I am not prepared for. Please sit." James thought about delivering the message himself but knew he would never make it, nor would anyone else in the area.

Laura sat down beside her husband. "Nor am I quite prepared, James, but I believe I have a solid plan."

"It looks as though you're planning a venture to deliver FitzGibbon this message yourself?"

"I believe I have no choice, James. You are certainly in no condition. I am a simple frontier housewife; even if confronted, I won't be suspected of anything treacherous," Laura said.

"Certainly not, but I'm sure someone else will be willing to make the trip besides yourself."

"All able-bodied men are either at Burlington or John Decew's house. I believe I am the most fitting person for the job," Laura said, looking at her husband with determination and sincerity.

James thought for a moment. "Make your way to St. David's, then Shipman's Corners thereafter. It will add a few miles to the journey, but young William Merritt is there. Perhaps from there, he can find you a relay messenger. If you are stopped, tell them you are going to visit your sick brother-in-law in St. David's."

Laura was finally coming to grips with the fact that she was about to embark on a dangerous journey with multiple threats. Wolves, cougars, enemies, injury, and dehydration posed real dangers she might have to confront. "I'm scared, James."

"Stick to the paths and be wary of your footings; no one is around if you break an ankle or twist a knee. If you feel panic setting in, sit down." James gave his wife a big smile. "You are a fearless woman, my love. I know your strength will guide you. Remember to pace yourself in the heat. The sun beats hard on these mornings. Take plentiful water breaks and take extra good care of your feet."

Laura gave James a forced, half-hearted smile and hugged and kissed him. "And what of you?" she asked.

"The children and I can manage; don't worry about us. Save the lives of FitzGibbon and his soldiers." James struggled to the dining room, opened the cabinet door, removed a sheathed dagger, and brought it to Laura. "Keep this with you in the event you run into trouble. Keep it hidden from any American you see."

Laura felt a sense of duty calling to her. The morning was a few hours away, and she thought it best to leave the village without anyone seeing her. If an American sentinel were to inquire about her destination, she would tell them of her dangerously ill brother Charles and hopefully pass without suspicion or incident.

James hugged and kissed Laura one last time and watched her exit through the front door into the darkness of night.

Chapter 15 – Duty

It was still pitch black outside but humid and stifling in the midsummer heat. Laura walked gently through the small town of Queenston without a single soul in sight. Fireflies dotted the forest floor, and only the sound of the odd cricket disrupted the stillness. She stepped lightly in the night's still silence, knowing she would need to escape the town without being noticed to avoid immediate danger.

She turned west, around the last home on the block, toward St. David's and eventually Beaverdams and the Decew house to warn FitzGibbon. In the distance, Laura could make out two dark figures straight in front of her, but she did not hesitate at the sight. She kept moving forward, taking a deep breath, knowing this moment might come.

"Hello there!" the dark figure yelled.

"Hello," Laura responded.

"What brings you out at this time of night?"

Laura recognized the two dark figures as American sentries that regularly patrolled Queenston. "Hello, gentlemen. I am just trying to beat the morning heat. I am going to visit my sick brother Charles in St. David's. His health is fast deteriorating, and he needs constant attention. He has been coughing up blood, vomiting, diarrhea. It is rather grim…"

"Okay, okay, Mrs. Secord. Fine, fine. We understand. Have a safe journey." The two Americans continued past Laura without a hint of suspicion.

"Thank you, gentlemen. God bless you," Laura said, smiling.

Relieved, she continued her journey, knowing this was just the beginning. Aware of the daunting 20 miles separating her from the Decew house, she remembered the importance of pacing herself. However, adrenaline was surging through her body.

Before long, the sun began to rise, and light appeared through the canopy of leaves above her. The temperature rose quickly, and she felt her face flush red. It took about two hours to reach the nearby town of St. David's. There, she made it to her brother Charles' house and could rest for a few minutes. She drank some water quickly and urged them that she must press on.

Laura's sister-in-law, Hannah, insisted her daughter Elizabeth accompany her for a stretch of her journey. While Laura made it to St. David's, she needed another explanation for her solo venture if she was stopped at Shipman's Corners. Hannah and Elizabeth had family there, so it could be used as an excuse if they were stopped en route.

Laura remembered to stay off the main road into Shipman's Corners. Instead, she and her niece, Elizabeth, took to the ravines and forests, which made the journey much longer and more treacherous. Each step meant avoiding ferns, saplings, fallen trees, stumps, and rocks.

Laura and the young Elizabeth pressed on along the ridge overlooking the Black Swamp, something they needed to avoid. Diverging into the swamp would cost them precious time or, potentially, even their lives. The sun beat down on Laura and Elizabeth as they stopped at 10-Mile Creek for a water break. Laura rubbed her feet and then shared some bread with her niece under the shade of an old oak tree.

Laura observed Elizabeth's developing blisters. "You're going to have to wrap those up."

"They hurt, Auntie," Elizabeth said.

"Only a few more miles to your uncle's house. Then you can rest and wrap those wounds."

Laura and Elizabeth pressed on under the hot sun until they reached Shipman's Corners and Elizabeth's uncle's house. Laura was exhausted, with feet hurting as much as Elizabeth's, but she knew she had to keep going. Having been up for almost 36 hours, she was beginning to feel somewhat delirious as the result of dehydration combined with exhaustion. After a bite to eat, some water, and a short rest, Laura felt her second wind prop her up and she sensed the motivation to finish the last leg of the journey.

Laura was fine with Elizabeth leaving to return to St. David's. Despite being young, delicate, and developing painful blisters on her feet, Elizabeth showed incredible bravery by accompanying her. Laura had children and understood how they would only slow her down at this stage. Not using time to share information with Elizabeth's family, she said her goodbyes and continued on her journey, determined to reach FitzGibbon.

The next and most challenging stretch of the journey took Laura into the 12-Mile Creek ravine, which meandered its way through the dense forest. She knew she would need to cross the wide river at some point, but she had to determine the best spot. The bridge had been washed out a few years earlier, and finding an alternate way to cross it could prove treacherous.

After a few more gruelling miles along the bank of the raging river, she found a tree that had fallen across to the other side, and she knew this was her opportunity. Laura struggled on the log; it was slippery with algae and moisture, and the bark was completely saturated. She got on her hands and knees and shimmied herself across. It was time-consuming, dirty, and exhausting, but she knew this was likely the only way across. After many hours into her journey, fatigue was now settling in. Her feet hurt, her back was aching, and she was filthy, sweaty, and dehydrated.

Once across the treacherous log bridge, she paused and took a needed drink from the river's edge as the sun set on the forested escarpment before her.

James and his children sat at the dining room table in the bare Secord house. They ate a rudimentary meal of beef from the Grand River and potatoes from their backyard that Mary and Charlotte had recently dug up. The invading army had helped themselves to everything throughout the house except for the vegetables in the small garden at the back of the house. Throughout the invasion, Laura had been forced to cook for any soldiers who found themselves in her home. This often-meant food for the Secords was in short supply.

James was silent and tense at the dinner table and seemingly vacant with his children as he knew Laura would be exhausted at this stage. If she had managed to escape the immediate dangers, she would be hungry, dehydrated, and vulnerable in the final steps up the escarpment. With every bite he took, he fought back the tears.

"When's mommy coming home?" little Charles asked.

"Not until tomorrow, Charles," James responded.

"Why didn't she say goodbye?" the little Harriot asked.

"She needed to leave early, to miss the hot midday sun." James was trying his best to hide the gravity of the situation.

Mary, James and Laura's oldest daughter, did her best to steer the interrogation away from her father. "Sometimes Mother goes away, and sometimes Father goes away too. They run a business; you know."

"Thanks, Mary," James said. "Enjoy your dinner, children. We have a big day tomorrow."

James could not help but think of the worst. Laura could have collapsed, drowned, been attacked, or even captured. He wouldn't know of anything until the next day.

There was a loud knock at the front door, which made all of the children jump. James grimaced as he got up with his cane, reached the front door, and cautiously opened it. It was Hannah, James' sister-in-law.

"Hi, James," Hannah said.

"Hannah, this is a surprise," James said.

"Laura made it to Shipman's Corners. From there, she was alone as she made her way to Twelve-mile Creek. Elizabeth told me she was in good spirits and more than willing to continue on her way."

James stumbled forward out the front door. Hannah took him by the shoulder, and they sat down on the step.

"Everything is going to be alright, James," Hannah said.

"Was she tired? Did she seem sick?" James asked.

"She is strong, James. She only needed to cross 12-Mile Creek and make it up the escarpment."

"I hope she can navigate at night." James slumped on the front step, clearly shaken but somewhat relieved.

"She is strong, James," Hannah said.

Though his house was in shambles, his body was failing him, his business was gone, and his wife was in the most treacherous stretch of danger, James managed to compose himself and stay relatively optimistic.

"Thanks for coming by the house," James said. "It means a lot."

"No problem, James," Hannah said. "She's going to be alright."

Laura was exhausted; her feet throbbed with sores and blisters, her vision blurred, and her throat was parched dry. She was about to encounter the most challenging, steepest part of the journey.

The escarpment was about a half-mile long, incredibly steep, rocky, and thickly forested with hardwoods and softwoods. Laura would need to take her time, find her proper footings, and carefully calculate each step.

A few minutes into the climb, her left leg buckled, and she fell face-first into the ground. Frustrated, she took a deep breath and got back on her feet. She brushed the debris from the front of her dress and pressed on up the escarpment. She would need to be more careful, as her legs had built up lactic acid and were starting to cease.

Laura was anxious as she could barely make out where she was going. Darkness had set in, and only the moon and stars illuminated her way. The wilderness was quiet; she snapped twigs and displaced leaves on the ground with each step. Step by step, Laura grew more delirious. Eventually, she reached the summit of the escarpment and found herself crossing one of Decew's overgrown wheat fields.

Once through the field, in the distance, she noticed a small flickering light amongst the trees. Relief set in, as she did not care who it might be, whether Indian, American, or English. As she got closer, she noticed a couple of fires and realized it was a group of camped-out Indians.

A few warriors noticed the strange figure and started to whoop and holler at Laura's presence. At this point, Laura was too exhausted to be frightened. Her legs were weak, and she was dehydrated, but her determination to do her duty fueled her.

"Woman!" a young Caughnawaga warrior yelled.

"I am Laura. I need to speak with FitzGibbon." Laura could hardly speak. "Lieutenant FitzGibbon."

The young warriors did not understand her and asked her to follow them. As they guided them onto the encampment, Laura felt relief that they were not overly hostile.

"Sawatis!" the warrior yelled.

John Norton came out of his tent and stretched as the early morning sun began to reveal itself. "Good morning," he said. "This is rather peculiar."

"John Norton!" Laura yelled excitedly.

"Mrs. Secord, what on earth are you doing here?" Norton asked. "How did you get here?"

"I have an urgent message for FitzGibbon, and the men stationed here. They are in immediate danger," Laura said.

"Are you able to keep moving?" Norton asked.

"Yes," Laura responded.

"Follow us. It is only one mile to the Decew house," Norton said.

John Norton and a few young warriors guided Laura along the narrow path to the Decew house. As they entered, a young British lieutenant noticed Mrs. Secord's state and immediately offered her some water.

"You must be exhausted. Sit down. Relax," the young officer said.

"I have come from Queenston. I have been walking for over 24 hours with an urgent message for Lieutenant FitzGibbon," Laura said, taking a drink of water.

As she sipped the glass of water, FitzGibbon came into the dining room, buttoning up his jacket. "Mrs. Secord. My, my, what brings you out here this early?"

"There is a plot to destroy you and your army. I have overheard them planning to send heavy cannons and 500-plus soldiers to overrun the Beaverdams and the Decew house."

"When is this plan supposed to happen?" FitzGibbon asked.

"The 23rd; on the morrow," Laura responded. "I've come with great haste from Queenston."

FitzGibbon looked around with concern at Norton and the other officers present. "How did you overhear this information, Mrs. Secord?"

"Colonel Boerster and another officer, Captain Chapin, were divulging the plan at my God-damned dinner table," Laura said, leaning back in her chair. "Mr. Secord, my injured husband, could not carry the message, so I decided to take on the duty. I left Queenston about 28 hours ago."

"My God, you must be exhausted. Lt. Jarvis, take Mrs. Secord to Mrs. Turney's house so she can rest awhile," FitzGibbon said.

"Yes, sir," Jarvis responded.

"Mrs. Secord, you have gone beyond the call of duty. Your courage and determination will not go unnoticed. Now, gentlemen, we need to plan how to surprise our oncoming enemy," FitzGibbon said. "Thank you for your sacrifice," FitzGibbon said to Laura with a smile.

Norton looked at FitzGibbon. "Looks like there is work to be done."

Laura, guided by Lt. Jarvis, arrived at Mrs. Turney's small home with great relief. She had been awake for almost 48 hours; her feet were swollen, she was delirious, and her vision was blurred by exhaustion. She was happy that her message might save the lives of hundreds of soldiers and protect her friend's house and livelihood.

Mrs. Turney came to the front door and welcomed Laura inside. An old widow with a spare room, she would welcome anyone needing a bed and a warm meal.

"Come deary, you look like you could use a nap," Mrs. Turney said.

Laura smiled and nodded at the understatement. "Thank you kindly. It has been a terribly long couple of days."

"I have many soldiers come through here. Often, they're looking for a comfortable bed and a warm meal. Lay down. I'll bring some hot soup and bread when you wake up. Sleep as long as you need."

Laura sat on the single bed. "Thanks again, Mrs. Turney." Laura removed her shoes and felt immediate relief. She untied her bonnet, put it on the nightstand, lay down and fell asleep almost immediately.

Chapter 16 – Beaverdams

To disguise the number of troops leaving for Beaverdams, 500 Americans left Fort George before daybreak. Lieutenant Colonel Charles Boerster planned to march his 500 men undetected to the Decew house; the artillery would take the main road, and the other detachments would take other unsuspecting routes to help disguise their numbers. Upon engaging with FitzGibbon, they would join forces and destroy the British contingency.

Inside the officer's mess at Fort George, Winfield Scott and Henry Dearborn watched Boerster and Chapin lead their men out of the fort onto the road to Beaverdams.

"Why have you not assigned this Beaverdams mission to me, sir?" Winfield Scott asked Dearborn.

"There are great things beyond these forts of wilderness, my young friend; this is not a mission for you to undertake," Dearborn replied.

"This is a country of burgeoning power…"

Dearborn interrupted Scott. "...Before you continue, this mission is going to see casualties. There is truly no officer who knows these lands intimately, certainly not yourself. There are hostiles all about the outskirts of these walls, not a place for a man of your rising rank and national pride. Also, winter is approaching faster than our supplies are advancing. So, as you can see, there are many variables, Mr. Scott."

"I fear the commands from Washington will be to settle in for the winter. They may even call us back to the east bank of the Niagara," Scott said.

"Please accept these orders, General Scott; it is for your own good," Dearborn said.

"Of course, General Dearborn. Perhaps it is just my frustration that is coming through right now. I am troubled by our army's faults so far in this war. At Queenston, I was not reinforced and was eventually captured. At the Battle of Fort George, we could have done so much more in our efforts had I been supported."

"Boyd's judgement to not advance on the British was vacillating and imbecile beyond all command; however, his orders were to hold the fort. Van Rensselaer's strategy and lack of enthusiasm and support were unwarranted and outright shameful. There will be better outcomes in your future, Winfield. Trust me, your story has yet to be written." Dearborn treated Winfield like a son and was doing his best to mould and condition him to be a tolerant, wise leader.

"Now we are forced to wait on these tactical hit and run missions that will be far from successful." Winfield was clearly frustrated with the languorous performance of his country's army.

"Of course, I understand you are not happy with the orders, but this course of action is for the best," Dearborn said.

"It is not my unhappiness, but rather, I loathe the truth that all of this could have been completely circumvented," Scott said.

Dearborn smiled. "This war will be over soon. We will go back to being neighbours with the people of Upper and Lower Canada. We will start trading with the Indians again. It won't be long, Winfield, before we must discover a new enemy to engage."

Winfield paused and reflected on his impulsiveness and ambition. He hoped that one day he might be as wise as General Dearborn.

"Come, Winfield, let's smoke for a while." Dearborn took his pipe from his jacket pocket. "Take pleasure in the little things, Winfield."

Scott looked at Dearborn in his wheelchair and smiled at the sensible old man smoking his pipe; the once brave soldier who had helped create the country.

Norton and FitzGibbon help devise the plan to ambush Boerster and the American army near Beaverdams. Dominique Ducharme had arrived from Lower Canada with 200 warriors ready and willing to engage the enemy together.

William Kerr, Dominique Ducharme, John Norton and John Brant were to lead the Native forces. They would form small groups along the road to Beaverdams and communicate by a series of assigned messengers. They would scout the oncoming American forces and relay their message to the other parties until they were ready and willing to engage.

It was a hot, stifling, and foggy morning as the Indigenous forces moved out and took up their positions in the bush alongside the road.

A few hours into the morning, a Haudenosaunee warrior spotted Boerster's incoming forces. He slipped back into the bush, stealthily moved to Norton, Ducharme, and Brant's main body, and relayed the message of the incoming enemy.

"Comrades and brothers — be men. Remember the fame of ancient warriors, whose breasts were never daunted by odds of number. You have run from your encampments to this place to meet the enemy. We again have found what we came for," Norton said to his men.

The three Indigenous leaders prepared their warriors. Norton moved along the rear of his fellow allies and patted each man on the shoulder without saying a word. This subtle gesture emboldened each man and told a thousand words.

Boerster and Chapin, both on horseback, led the force of 500 men, a dozen cavalry, and four heavy cannons being pulled at the rear of the column. The soldiers were weary, dehydrated, and needing rest after 10 miles of marching in the humid summer heat.

Norton held his arm up to signal the attack. He held his arm high, waiting for Boerster to lead his forces in between the waiting ambush.

Norton saw Boerster and Chapin trot by, and he yelled: "Now!" as he dropped his arm, signaling the ambush.

A massive volley of musket fire erupted, shattering the silence of the hot morning. Dozens of confused Americans fell upon the first deadly volley. Boerster, in a panic, rode his horse towards the rear of his forces. He planned to organize the artillery to push back the enemy. Before he could get there, his horse was shot, and he was thrown to the ground.

Most of the Natives remained in the bush, firing shot after shot, while the Americans did their best to organize themselves into firing lines. Though the American force was much larger in number, they were almost ineffective against the well-covered warriors in the dense beechwoods.

After falling from his horse, Boerster managed to get to his feet and reach the rear of the column, where Captain Chapin cowered behind the artillery cover.

"Get to your feet, Captain Chapin!" Boerster yelled. "Get your troops in this battle. Aim the artillery into their forces at once!"

The heat was intense as the Indians kept up their unrelenting fire from the bush. Once the American artillery began, it was nearly ineffectual.

Boerster tried to move his forces but kept confronting the invisible enemy from every direction. The whoops and hollers from the forest haunted the exhausted Boerster and the rest of the unnerved Americans.

Word had reached FitzGibbon, who had arrived on the battlefield with about 50 British regulars. He surveyed the situation and was confident in its outcome. The Indians were pushing Boerster back, and the American cannons were useless in the dense bush. Fierce battling continued for hours as the firing lines broke up and the fight became more irregular.

A few warriors and dozens of Americans continued to fall as Boerster tried his best to rally his troops. Boerster took a bullet through his shoulder and fell to his knee but quickly rose to his feet and continued to fight. He bravely led his forces into a nearby hollow to avoid a potential massacre. On the move down the embankment, Boerster was shot again through the leg. He collapsed to the ground in agony while two soldiers dragged and laid him in the back of a nearby pull cart.

"Where is Captain Chapin?" Boerster yelled in agony.

FitzGibbon had arrived with 50 regulars and saw his opportunity. The Indians pressed forward while the Irish Lieutenant called his troops forward. He attached a white cloth to the end of a musket and waved it at the enemy. The firing eventually stopped as FitzGibbon approached where Boerster lay.

"Your men are surrounded, General!" FitzGibbon yelled. "We demand your surrender!"

"To hell with you!" Boerster yelled back.

"Hundreds of regulars are minutes away, and we have thousands of Indians here! We can not guarantee you or your army's safety. Let us avoid a slaughter here today!"

"Damn you to hell!" Boerster responded.

"Please, General, these Indians are much injured and thirsty for blood," FitzGibbon said, using his old friend Brock's tactic.

Boerster had the same fear that many Americans shared; like General Hull at Detroit, he needed to make a quick decision. "Alright, dammit, we surrender!" he yelled, seeing no other option.

"That was a smart, admirable decision, General," FitzGibbon said. "Your soldiers will thank you later."

The Americans threw down their arms and put their hands in the air. It had been an overwhelming victory. About 400 Americans surrendered, while about 100 lay dead on the forest floor. FitzGibbon and the Indian allies confiscated a massive bounty of guns, powder, and two cannons that would help the future effort.

A part of FitzGibbon was relieved, as the Americans still outnumbered the British and Indian forces. Without his persistence and the threat of the Indians, the Americans surely would have overrun FitzGibbon and his forces.

Norton smiled at John Brant and Dominique Ducharme as their ambush had worked flawlessly. He thought of the brave Laura

Secord and her 20-mile journey to warn the Canadian forces. He would surely need to thank her in the coming weeks.

Chapter 17 – Withdraw

Laura Secord had returned home and not shown an ounce of pride or triumph in her duty. She felt loyalty and commitment in helping to save the lives of friends, family, and neighbours. Her legs and feet were sore the following day, but she felt fine otherwise. Laura had slept soundly at Mrs. Turney's house and had returned home on horseback with William Hamilton Merritt from nearby Shipman's Corners.

James was relieved and jubilant upon Laura's return. He had spent nearly 40, sleepless hours with a frantic sense of uncertainty, as he did not know Laura's whereabouts or well-being. He would have been completely lost in her absence. She was his life, a modest and discreet woman, and James was incredibly proud that she could make the trip to Decew's.

Once again, James and Laura sat on their front porch and enjoyed the breezy summer evening while the children played in the front yard.

"Did you run into any problems out there?" James asked.

"Just the sentry at the edge of town," Laura said. "My heart was racing like a hummingbird's wings. There was also the crossing at 12-Mile Creek. I had to squirm along a slick log like a caterpillar. It felt like it took hours to cross."

"I cannot believe you made it. It was the worst two days of my life," James said. "I was thinking about the Black Swamp, the wild animals, the treacherous terrain…"

"I should have been afraid of the Indians approaching me in the middle of the night, in case they thought I was the enemy, but I was so tired, I seriously could not have cared less. My legs were giving out, and I was just happy to see somebody."

"Who were the Indians? Did you recognize them?"

"I think they were mostly Cayuga. None of them could understand English until I mentioned John Norton, and they started yelling, 'Sawatis, Sawatis.' They brought me to Norton, who, in turn, brought me to FitzGibbon. It was quite the adventure."

"I would say. You have done well, Mrs. Secord," James said with a smile.

Laura smiled at her husband's kind words. "I hope this helps to end this terrible war. I do not think I can take much more."

General Dearborn sat at a desk at Fort George, smoking his pipe and drinking a bottle of wine. He tapped a letter on the desk while looking at the ceiling.

Winfield Scott came into the office. "You called, sir?" he said, noticing Dearborn's carefree, drunken demeanour.

"Do you know what this is?" Dearborn asked. "The accumulation of failures has led me to be recalled to American soil, to New York. Above all else, on an administrative command! Can you believe it?"

"General Dearborn, they were well-thought-out plans, just executed by incapable soldiers," Winfield said. "How could the enemy possibly know about Boerster's forces? Hundreds of Indians could not have just stumbled upon them. Something is rotten."

"True, true. Maybe a traitor in our midst. Or that damned Willcocks or one of his men is playing both sides." Dearborn said.

"There are spies everywhere, General Dearborn. It is best you escape these unstable conditions while you can. Our command and leadership cannot do anything without reproach."

"You are so right, Winfield. I am quite fortunate to leave this frontier and return to my wife; she misses me dearly," Dearborn said as he finished his glass of wine.

"May I see the letter, sir?" Winfield asked.

"Sure, General," Dearborn said as he handed him the letter. Winfield read from the letter:

...climax of continual mismanagement and misfortune... unfortunate and unaccountable events that continue. The nation calls for your immediate removal and the recall of all American soldiers to U.S. soil.

"The nation calls for my immediate removal. Ha!" Dearborn laughed as he poured and slurped some more red wine.

"A better climate might fare you well, General. All of us want you to return safely home anyway. The nation will always desire to point its collective finger at somebody; in that way, it does misleadingly feel a false sense of closure. We all know of your great qualities, General. That is what matters."

Dearborn smiled at Winfield. "Thank you, Winfield. I will cherish your words. Part of me now thinks I should have allocated you to the Beaverdams mission."

"It is in the past now, General. Let us put this behind us and look forward to better days," Scott said.

"Cheers," Dearborn said as he raised his glass.

Victoria Davis had been staying at her aunt's house in Shipman's Corners. She was safe from Americans in the home. However, she had not seen or heard from her husband, Nathan, in weeks. The last news she had heard was the retreat from Fort George to Burlington. She still managed to spend time with the Secord children; however, travelling to Queenston was fraught with danger.

Nathan Davis was now riding with William Hamilton Merritt, the young Captain with the British Dragoons. Merritt, though young, was a great leader, a superb horse rider, and mature beyond his years. Nathan and Merritt had been great friends since the outset of the war and were now delivering messages for the British army and relaying vital information where needed.

The two young men travelled to Shipman's Corners to check on the citizens and deliver various messages to them, including the house where Victoria was staying. Nathan had been looking forward to this moment, as he missed his wife and was desperate to let her know about his well-being.

"We need to stop at my father's house," Merritt said, galloping along a narrow dirt path. "I have a message for him, and he will have food and fresh water."

"My wife is staying just down the street. I would love to see her and let her know I am doing well," Nathan said.

"It should not be a problem," Merritt said, snapping the reins.

The two young men arrived under darkness to deliver messages of progress, well-being, espionage, and military movements to various families in the area, including Merritt's father, Thomas.

Merritt and Nathan tied their horses in the forest just outside the little town and proceeded on foot. As they made their way to the edge of the woods, they heard the peculiar rumble of dozens of horses on the ground.

"Do you feel that?" Merritt asked.

"I do," Nathan said.

"Take cover."

The two young men hid behind a fallen maple tree as they watched Joseph Willcocks ride into town, leading 25 mounted soldiers. Willcocks was now at the head of a unit called the Canadian Volunteers. The defectors now fought for the United States regulating the ongoings of Niagara citizens and reporting enemy movement in the area.

Now a Major, Willcocks had become disillusioned with the British and joined the side he believed would win the war. Many of his parliamentary and newspaper supporters had become his officers, and he had about 125 recruits from throughout Upper Canada. American leadership valued his love for liberty and hatred for the King. Leadership in Washington also valued his local knowledge and his uncanny zest for capturing, arresting, and punishing his former neighbours.

Merritt and Davis watched as the column of Willcocks' soldiers stopped in front of his father's house. Irate, Merritt could do nothing as Nathan put his arm in front of him.

"What the hell does he think he's doing?" Merritt cried.

"It's that damned traitor Willcocks," Nathan said.

"It looks like he's an officer now." Merritt was scathing through his teeth. "What the hell is he doing at my father's house?"

Willcocks dismounted his horse and removed his leather gloves as he ordered four men into the house. Willcocks waited patiently on the front porch. After a few minutes, the soldiers emerged from the house with Merritt's 60-year-old father in pajamas.

"What the hell does he want with my father?" Merritt was livid.

"Due to your support of the British Crown and your Loyalist leanings, you are under arrest, Thomas Merritt," Willcocks stated. "Now, where is your Dragoon son, William Hamilton?"

"I have no idea where he is," Thomas Merritt said. "He hasn't been here in a year."

"Don't play me the fool, Mr. Merritt," Willcocks said. "Take him away. Perhaps prison will refresh his memory."

Merritt wanted nothing more than to jump out and confront the treacherous scum and put a bullet in his head. This was too personal for Merritt. Throughout his scouting of the Niagara area, he had heard reports of Willcocks finding and arresting Loyalists, but this experience had sent him into a fiery rage. Merritt's father was an older man and was not a part of the war effort.

"Where is your son, William Hamilton Merritt?" Willcocks asked again.

"I have no idea," Thomas said.

"Bind his hands!" Willcocks ordered.

Nathan held his enraged friend back.

"Take him to Fort George!" Willcocks barked.

Two soldiers marched Thomas Merritt down the road to Fort George, where he would be sent to prison in Albany or Philadelphia. Willcocks mounted his horse with a big smile on his face.

"These damn volunteer traitors. I would slit every one of their throats," Nathan said to Merritt.

As Nathan and Merritt could only watch, Willcocks and his Canadian Volunteers rode off towards Fort George.

"I am going to make it my personal mission to capture that coward and make a goddamn example of him," Merritt said.

William Hamilton Merritt and Nathan Davis arrived at Burlington to deliver the troops' movements over the past few days. General Vincent, FitzGibbon, and the rest of the Canadian leadership had just received word of a great victory at Crysler's Farm in Québec. They also discovered that the great Shawnee leader Tecumseh had tragically been killed at the Battle of Thames. Oliver Hazard Perry's fleet now controlled Lake Erie, and William Henry Harrison pushed the war into Canada, across from Detroit. Tecumseh and his forces had fallen into a swamp without the British regulars and were severely beaten.

The death of Tecumseh left many of his supporters in a state of disillusionment. Those tribes dreaming of a united Indian nation were now left in disbelief and uncertainty about their future.

"I think it is time we sent soldiers to the edges of Fort George," General Vincent said.

"They don't venture too far from the walls," FitzGibbon said. "When they do, it is only for moments."

"The only one scouting the area is that traitor Joseph Willcocks and his damned Canadian Volunteers," Merritt said. "He has a group of about a hundred men, and they're burning every Loyalist house and barn they set their eyes on."

"It won't take much to send them packing," FitzGibbon added. "They've been on a gradual retreat for days."

"Alright, FitzGibbon, take 400 men and establish a line of defence at 40-Mile Creek. If we feel it prudent, we will move to 20-Mile Creek thereafter," General Vincent said. "We need to protect the citizens from these arrests and these barbaric raids."

Merritt was glad they were finally going on the offensive. The Americans were wounded, and he would be happy to swing the finishing blow.

A few weeks after the British moved troops back into Niagara to protect the citizens from Willcocks and his Canadian Volunteers, the Americans began preparations to fully evacuate Fort George and move their army back across to American soil at Fort Niagara. Supplies were running low, food was scarce, and winter had set in.

On a cold, snowy December morning, Captain William Hamilton Merritt led a group of mounted troops, including Nathan

Davis, searching for Willcocks along the Niagara River. It was early morning, snow fell and drifted two to three feet in some areas. There had been little troop movement from Fort George. However, John Norton and his warriors had spotted an American unit on its way to Queenston just before dawn.

Norton stood above the transcendent Niagara Falls, admiring the peacefulness that surrounded the thunderous and raging waters. He was waiting for Merritt and his Dragoons to arrive so he could pass word of any troop movements or enemy sightings.

It had been a month since Norton had been home, and today, he was incredibly homesick. The temperature had plummeted below zero, and he daydreamed about home and the warmth of his bed on the Grand River with his loving wife and baby boy.

Norton saw Merritt and his Dragoons approaching on the road along the Niagara River connecting Fort Erie and Fort George. The road was muddy, and half-frozen as snow fell on the picturesque landscape.

"Captain Merritt!" Norton yelled.

"Captain Norton!" Merritt yelled back.

Merritt pulled on the reins and dismounted his horse. "How goes it, Norton?" Merritt asked.

"All is well, young man. We spotted a couple hundred infantry moving north towards Queenston just before dusk. Their numbers were too great to engage," Norton said.

"I'll try and scatter their forces," Merritt responded, looking north towards Queenston.

"Merritt, it looks like they are on the full retreat across to Fort Niagara; they're protecting their rear," Norton said. "Be careful with your lives."

"We will," Merritt said as he mounted his horse.

"Oh, and Merritt," Norton said, grabbing the reins of Merritt's horse, "Willcocks was with them, and he and his troops had torches in hand."

Merritt's eyes went deep red as he thought of Willcocks and his unforgiving treachery. Nathan Davis looked at Merritt, who was swelling with anger, and felt for his friend.

"Merritt, let's go find this son of a bitch," Nathan said to his friend.

Merritt and Nathan mounted their horses and galloped off towards Queenston while Norton and his few warriors followed on foot through the snowy mess.

Willcocks ordered two soldier teams to go door to door in Newark to evacuate the homes. There were few men in the homes around Niagara; the majority were women, children, and the elderly.

A young girl named Amelia Ryerse looked through her bedroom window at the hundreds of Americans, led by Willcocks, marching ominously over the ridge with torches in hand.

"Mom!" Amelia yelled down the hall. "Soldiers are coming!"

Amelia's mother ran out the front door, followed by Amelia, into the frigid cold.

"Please, sir," Amelia's mother pleaded with Willcocks.

Willcocks grabbed her by the shoulders. "You need to evacuate your home," he said.

"I am a widow with children. Our home is all we have," she said.

"I civilly and respectfully regret that I have my orders," Willcocks said.

Willcocks lit the curtains inside the front door and the window frames on the front porch. He then walked to the bottom of the main stairs and lit the railings and dining room table on fire. Willcocks walked out the front door, down the steps and past the crying Amelia and her mother as the house fire became a raging inferno.

William Hamilton Merritt, Nathan Davis, and the other mounted Dragoons made their way into Queenston to find dozens of homes on fire and streets engulfed in black smoke.

Nathan froze and looked west toward the Secord's house; afraid the worst may have happened to his friends and their home. He broke away, riding as fast as possible to check on Laura, James, and the children. It was only a couple of blocks away, and upon arriving, he was relieved to find the house unmolested by Willcocks and his marauders. The windows were still boarded up, and he assumed everything was okay. He pivoted his horse and rode back to join Merritt and the rest of the Dragoons.

Merritt nodded at Nathan as he returned. "Everything alright?" Merritt asked.

"Yeah, just checking up on some friends," Nathan answered.

Merritt and Nathan were both disgusted by these heinous acts by treacherous, opportunistic men. The thought of Willcocks and his traitors taking pleasure in punishing his former neighbours for whatever real or imaginary slight disgusted Nathan and Merritt.

"This is goddamn deplorable," the young Merritt said as he spotted the end of the American column.

"There's only a few houses they haven't torched," Nathan said.

"Goddamn animals." Merritt was fuming.

Merritt led the Dragoons after the Americans and engaged them with musket fire and charging into their ranks. Nathan fired a shot into the back of one of Willcocks's men, who was carrying a torch. He dropped instantly, and his torch extinguished and sizzled in the drifting snow.

Merritt unsheathed his sword, plunged it into the back of an unsuspecting Canadian Volunteer, and sliced the chest of another soldier. Merritt was taking vengeance on these former Canadians, and the marauders could sense his and the Dragoons' rage.

Several Canadian Volunteers began scattering into the woods, and others surrendered as they were no match for the mounted soldiers.

The young Captain Merritt looked further north and noticed a large black plum of smoke coming from Newark.

"Lieutenant Davis, Dragoons, with me!" Merritt yelled as he pointed his sword and charged toward Newark with his troops.

In Newark, Willcocks climbed the stairs of the Dickson home with a torch in hand. He ordered two soldiers into the home, and moments later, they brought out a single bed with an old, ill-stricken lady covered in a quilt. As Willcocks ignited the house, the two soldiers placed the bed without care on a nearby snowbank.

Months earlier, Willcocks had arrested Mr. Dickson and knew the house was empty, except for the old lady. As he walked past Mrs. Dickson, she completely ignored Willcocks and looked on at her burning home in disbelief. Willcocks took a little pleasure in vengeance against his neighbour and smiled at the thought.

After the Canadian Volunteers caused maximum damage in Newark, Willcocks returned to Fort George, along with his 100 or so troops. All of Newark was on fire. Black smoke filled the sky above. Hundreds of women and children stood watching, helpless and in disbelief, as their houses burned to ashes. Snow deepened, temperatures dropped, and the winds began to pick up as more and more people were left outside in the elements. The vulnerable citizens stood in nightgowns and pajamas as exposure would soon set in on the helpless Newark and Queenston victims.

Captain Merritt charged the retreating Americans on the outskirts of Fort George. The main body of the scattering Americans were Willcocks' Canadian Volunteers. Merritt grinned as he charged and stabbed a soldier through the back. Nathan Davis followed close behind, firing his freshly loaded musket. Merritt's Dragoons routed the retreating enemy, taking several prisoners and leaving several dead volunteers.

Merritt only regretted that he could not find Willcocks in the mayhem. Merritt and Nathan looked west to see every building in Newark smouldering in black smoke. The glowing embers were a stark reminder of the hundreds of townspeople left in the cold. Merritt knew they would need shelter immediately if they were to survive.

"Butler's Barracks!" Nathan yelled to Merritt.

"What about it?" Merritt yelled back.

"The townspeople, they are going to need shelter quickly. That may be the only building still standing," Nathan said.

"Do your best to round them up, Mr. Davis. I am going to continue the pursuit," Merritt said.

Nathan galloped toward the streets of Newark and helped guide the citizens toward the shelter and safety of the barracks near Fort George. Nathan could not believe his eyes as the roads were littered with furniture and desperate people looking for warmth. Some people walked towards the farmlands for sanctuary; others frantically built makeshift shelters against their still-standing fireplaces. There were already several elderly frozen to death on the streets as he beckoned to the people who were able to follow him.

In the gradual retreat, the Americans burnt every building they could in Newark. As they had done at the Battle of York, the American army burned the library, stores, homes, barns, and any outlying structure they could get to. Fort George was in relatively good condition, but the unsuspecting town was burnt to the ground.

It was a tactic devastating to the local population and would remain firmly lodged in the minds of the British, Natives and Upper Canadians as they tried to pick up the pieces of their shattered lives. Once again, Niagara lay in ashes.

Laura had to watch her friends, kindred, and the labours of 30 years swept away by the barbarity of warfare. The Secords, along with hundreds of other families, would need to start the process of rebuilding. Given the neighbouring carnage, Laura and James were grateful their house was in relatively good condition and their children were safe.

Nathan, Victoria Davis, and Catharine Decew arrived that winter evening to help Newark citizens and spend some time with

Laura and James. Catharine's husband was still in the Philadelphia prison. However, she had received a letter notifying her that he was still alive but would be serving a lengthy sentence until a prisoner exchange could be arranged.

The Secord children were sound asleep and warm in their beds as Nathan, Victoria, Catharine, James, and Laura sat at the dining room table after a long day.

"I'm glad you're doing alright," James said to Nathan.

"The poor people of Newark. They did not deserve this. It is that damn Joseph Willcocks. He and his volunteers were ordered to burn everything," Nathan said. "I rode here from the main road to check on you and your house, and it was one of the only homes not in flames."

"Thank you for checking on us," James said.

James, Laura, Nathan, Victoria, and Catharine all felt a sense of relief as the American force was no longer on Canadian soil, and the fires had all gone out.

"You've received a letter from John?" Laura asked Catharine.

"I have. He has written that he is serving a lengthy sentence, meaning it could be years before he is released." Catharine paused as everyone looked on, clearly being sensitive to Catharine. "I wonder what the conditions are like in Philadelphia," the upset Catharine said.

"I am certain it is not the cleanest place, but I am sure he is getting hot meals," James said.

"The memory of you and the children is keeping him alive, Catharine," Laura said. "He would be lost without you."

"I dread the thought of him being in pain," Catharine said.

Victoria squeezed Nathan's hand under the table.

"He's going to be alright," Victoria said.

"He's the toughest man I know," Nathan added.

Chapter 18 - Escape

John Decew sat in his lonely prison cell with a copy of the Washington newspaper, The National Intelligencer, an influential and widespread publication in the United States. Governor General George Prevost had written a long letter to the citizens of Canada and the United States following the aftermath of the burning of Newark.

It became a matter of imperious duty to retaliate against America for the miseries that the unfortunate inhabitants of Newark had been made to suffer from the evacuation of Fort George. Accordingly, the villages of Lewiston, Black Rock, and Buffalo have been burned...

...It will hardly be credited by those who shall hereafter read it in the page of history that in the enlightened era of the nineteenth century, and the inclemency of a Canadian winter, the troops of a nation calling itself civilized and Christian, had wantonly, and without the shadow of a pretext, forced 400 helpless women and children to quit their dwellings and to be the mournful spectators of the conflagration and destruction of all that belonged to them.

Decew could not help but think of all his friends and family in Newark and Queenston who would be exposed to the frigid elements. He worried about the Secords, Nathan and Victoria, but especially his wife and their children.

The burning of Newark infuriated Decew, as this type of warfare had not been used since the Middle Ages. Decew threw the newspaper on his bed and thought about the urgency of his situation.

Decew had assessed the Philadelphia prison for almost a year. The daytime was too risky to escape; guards were too plentiful, and the streets were full of pedestrians. He gathered information from inmates about guard schedules, routines, and behaviours. He had done the math, and it was, barring any setbacks, going to take about three weeks to get to Montréal. From there, he would take a ship home to Newark, hoping to catch a ride aboard a proper vessel. During those weeks, he would need to forage for food, build shelters, and survive unforgiving conditions and challenging circumstances. He would rely heavily on his mental fortitude and focus, as he navigated his way back to Catharine and the children.

The chimney at the end of the hall, nearest to the street, was large enough to fit a man through. Decew and his fellow prisoners had spent the past four months carving out the mortar surrounding the iron gate atop the chimney that was preventing escape. Every night, they would disguise the bars with charred black paper to convince the guards they had not been tampered with. After hundreds of hours of intensive labour, Decew and the rest of the inmates had successfully removed the iron bars and prepared an escape route.

Tonight was the opportunity. He and eleven others would wait until around 10pm, when only two guards were patrolling, to begin the dangerous journey. If they failed, it would mean extended prison time, hard labour, or even death.

As the evening settled in, a dozen prisoners quietly escaped their cells and climbed up and out of the chimney. They made their way across the roof's edge and descended the 40-foot makeshift rope made of tied bed sheets. Decew was the last prisoner to climb down and found himself at the end of the rope the previous man had just broken. Decew looked down, unable to make out how far he was from the ground in the darkness.

"Let go!" a prisoner whispered to Decew.

"How far down is it?" Decew asked.

"Not too far," the fellow escapee said. "Just let go."

Decew let go of the rope about 20 feet from the ground. He dropped and landed on his feet, but his ankle buckled, and he fell and smashed his face on the brick wall of the prison. Blood ran from his mouth and nose as two fellow prisoners picked him up on their shoulders.

Decew was concussed and lightheaded as his vision blurred, and there was ringing in his ears. The prisoners helped Decew move along into a nearby wooded thicket.

"Leave me, make your own escape," Decew said.

"Nonsense," the prisoner helping Decew said.

His fellow inmates ignored his plea and carried him off toward the outskirts of Philadelphia in the darkness of night.

At the beginning of 1814, John Norton was getting over a terrible sickness. The last few years had been rough. He and his people had been dislodged, and they were fearful, hungry, and uncertain of their future. The United States had come close to the Grand River settlement a few months earlier, and the Iroquois were now in a desperate fight to start 1814 in a positive way.

Norton had received a personal letter from Sir George Prevost recalling him to Québec for consultation regarding the role of Native support. He and his wife Karighwaycagh made the long, cold journey to Lower Canada and were warmly welcomed. Hundreds of people lined the Capital city streets and applauded his efforts throughout the past two years. Until this point, Norton had not been aware of the public support. He was not accustomed to such praise, though he did welcome the positivity after two years of bloody war.

Norton and his wife were given private accommodations in Québec and were delighted with the hospitality and view from their room. Norton left his wife to wander the city and explore the different shops in the area while he travelled to see Governor Prevost.

Norton walked into Prevost's office with little expectation of what was to come. The office was modest and highly organized. Bookshelves and maps lined the walls as Prevost sat writing a letter.

"Governor Prevost, what a grand welcome," Norton said.

"You deserved every moment, Captain Norton," Prevost complimented, as he stood and shook Norton's hand. "So glad you have made the wintery journey. How is your wife? Are you comfortable in your accommodations?"

"We both have just overcome an unpleasant sickness, and we are grateful it is over," Norton said. "I must say, Governor, my wife and I were pleasantly surprised to see so many people lining the streets to welcome us," Norton said. "I honestly did not expect this type of support for our efforts."

"Well, you are a celebrity now," Prevost said as he picked up a couple of letters from his desk and read: "His services are the most efficient of any in that Department, and he is the only one who personally leads Indians into action." Prevost shuffled to the next letter. "...Prioritizing and zeal for public service were constantly in evidence."

"Quite flattering words, Governor," Norton said with modesty.

"You have created quite the reputation, John Norton. Whomever I speak with, they sing your praises and your diplomatic ability." Prevost grabbed another letter from his desk. "I was just finishing up a letter to Superintendent William Claus."

"Between ourselves, I must say that the man is vile and knows nothing of the Indian," Norton said.

"That is precisely why I've called you here to Québec. He has interfered with you and your affairs for too long," Prevost said.

"That is an understatement," Norton replied. "No offence, Governor."

"General Sheaffe and the late General Brock were absolutely correct in trusting you. You have shown, time and time again, throughout this war, that you were able to bring warriors to the battlefield and engage the enemy without reserve. That is why I am giving you three-eighths of the Indian budget in Upper Canada to distribute as you see fit."

"Without the input from William Claus or the department?" Norton asked.

"Absolutely not. That man has shown that he is incapable of maintaining relations with the Indians," Prevost replied. "He is forbidden to interfere with your dealings along the Grand."

"This is terrific news, Governor. The Grand River people are in desperate need of supplies. This past year has been taxing on their families, and it is hard for them to trust anyone outside their immediate circle." Norton envisioned all the different seeds, farm equipment, weapons, tools, and materials the Grand River people needed immediately. "We will need to focus on proper harvesting and planting this spring, as we have been unable to maintain anything substantial or reliable these past years."

"Napoleon Bonaparte has capitulated to Britain and her allies. As we speak, one hundred warships sail toward the eastern seaboard of North America. The Americans will attempt another desperate invasion on the Niagara Frontier to control the area before British reinforcements arrive."

"They may try to occupy Fort Erie instead of Fort George this time around," Norton suggested.

"Your instincts are probably correct," Prevost said. "I understand if your Grand River warriors are not as enthusiastic or willing to leave their homes this spring."

"I will try my absolute best. They have suffered, Governor, but I think I could still recruit a few dozen. It is for the best that I return to the head of the lake as soon as possible in order to establish those relations and organize a troop willing enough to engage the Americans once more," Norton said.

"Spring is almost upon us, Captain Norton. I wish you the best in 1814," Prevost said.

"Thank you, Governor. I will forever be grateful for all you have done for the Haudenosaunee," Norton said as he shook Prevost's hand.

"Travel well, John Norton."

After a short recovery in the cover of the bush on the outskirts of Philadelphia, John Decew continued his journey alone. After a few hours of walking slowly and silently with a nagging broken ankle, he came to a farmhouse with a light on at the edge of town. Decew knocked on the door and spoke with the owner about sleeping the night. The owner agreed he could sleep in the barn loft, to which Decew happily agreed.

Decew was relieved to get off his broken foot and lay in the soft hay. He thought about the next day and which direction he would need to take. It wasn't long before he was sound asleep.

The following day, before the sun was up, Decew awoke with the homeowner waving a leaflet in his face.

"There is a $100 reward for the capture of each escaped prisoner. Anyone harbouring or assisting their escape would be tried for high treason and have their property confiscated," the old man said with a frown. "Why didn't you tell me you were a convict?"

"Best I be on my way," Decew said.

"Hold it!" the homeowner said.

Decew rose to his feet, still feeling tremendous pain in his foot and bruised face. "Yes, sir," he said.

"The way I figure, you are not going to make it ten miles with that bum foot of yours," the old man said. "So, I have decided to let you go."

"Please don't tell anyone you saw me," Decew said as he rose.

"I'll be sure I don't," he said, returning to his house.

The broken bone in his foot was still incredibly painful and necessitated long rests. Miles and miles, he continued on his way North towards Québec. The Niagara frontier was geographically closer, but he knew crossing the Niagara River would almost be impossible.

After weeks of travelling on foot, sleeping under makeshift shelters, and eating nuts and berries, Decew found refuge in a swamp where he concealed himself for a few days. He placed his swollen, inflamed foot into the cool, black mud, and it immediately soothed the pain. At the end of each day, he would try the same therapeutic poultice. The next morning, after each treatment, he found walking much more manageable.

Weeks later, Decew finally made his way into Montréal where he engaged with a general who was surprised and proud of Decew's endurance and perseverance. After the general heard the entire story, he gave Decew $20 and a free pass to Newark aboard a merchant vessel. It would only be a few more days until he saw Catharine and his family again. The hardest part was over. Decew, through sheer will, had made it this far; only a few more days and his journey would be complete.

Once again, Reverend George stood before his congregation with serious intention. Richard Pierpoint, Bob and

Fan Armstrong, their son Hector, Roger Jupiter, and John Vanpatten were all in attendance.

The ongoing conflict had taken its toll on the community. Several people were missing, so the mass was much thinner than before the war. John Hall, amongst others, were captured at Fort George and sent to various plantation fields in the southern United States. Several families moved west or north to avoid the continuing bloody conflict and the threat of re-enslavement. Others suffered from food shortages and poverty, people lost their jobs, and citizens lost their homes.

Reverend George saw the trauma and worry in their eyes and wanted to tread carefully and wisely as he attempted to guide his flock with God's wise words.

"Ladies and gentlemen, my dear brothers and sisters, this summer's day, we gather in the house of the Lord to ask our dearest God to bring an end to the War of 1812. Though these times have been incredibly unyielding and stone-hearted, we must give time for reflection, gratitude, remembrance of the countless blessings bestowed upon us, and the peace in our future. This War of 1812 is a great struggle and we have sacrificed much for our new nation. This war is testing our resolve and challenging our unity, but through it all, we remain steadfast in our faith and trust in the Almighty. We pray for strength, courage, and a swift resolution to the conflict engulfing our young Canada."

Bob squeezed Fan's hand a little tighter. After all they had endured together, their love for one another was a pillar of strength that had risen above all the blood, misery, and tragedy. Bob looked at Fan and smiled at the thought of them strolling the beaches again, raising grandchildren, and watching the everlasting sunsets together.

Reverend George continued: "One day, when this is all over, we will look back at these challenging days with gratitude in our hearts. We will remember the brave men and women, including John Hall, who fought for our freedom and preserving our way of life. We honour those who made the ultimate sacrifice and extend our thankfulness and sincerest gratitude to their families for their unwavering support and love."

A few mass members began to cry as they remembered John Hall and the other captured men at Fort George. The thought of them being taken to the plantation fields in chains was emotional and made worse because there was nothing that anyone could directly do. They could not pursue them nor reason with any of the politicians. This particular trauma was something everyone would have to cope with as life continued to move forward.

"Remember that our ancestors clung to their faith. They sought solace in the house of God, just as we do on this hot summer's day. They lifted their voices in prayer, asking the Lord to grant them deliverance from the trials of war. They prayed for peace and the safety of their loved ones, and by God's grace, our ancestors' prayers were answered. The wars came to an end." Rev. George smiled at the mass. "I know if we continue to pray, this bloody War of 1812 will end, and peace will establish itself. Our nation and our people emerged from these conflicts stronger and more united. We learned the value of peace and the importance of coming together as one people."

The whole mass shouted: "Amen!"

As the mass continued, they sang hymns, prayed in silence, and rose to give thanks to God. They felt better as each minute passed.

"Let us not forget the lessons this war has taught us. Remember that we can overcome even the most formidable challenges through faith, prayer, and unity. Our ancestors' faith sustained them during their darkest hours, and that same faith continues to guide us today."

"Amen!" the mass shouted again.

"In closing, let us offer our gratitude and servitude to the Almighty for His divine intervention in bringing peace to our land. Let us pray for His guidance and protection as we progress as a united and blessed nation. May we always remember the lessons of our history and remain steadfast in our faith. Amen, and thank you, Lord."

"Amen!" the mass shouted, as they all rose to their feet.

After the two-day trip on the merchant boat, the bearded John Decew finally limped towards his homestead near Beaverdams with a cane in hand. The grass was overgrown, the mills were not running, but things smelled sweeter than ever. It felt as though he had not been there in over a decade. Decew thought about what words he might say to Catharine. He knocked loudly on the door and patiently waited for his wife to answer.

Catharine opened the door and immediately jumped into her husband's arms. They kissed several times, and both cried tears of joy. It seemed their separation had strengthened their unity even more. John spun his wife in a circle as they laughed and kissed a few more times.

"It's nice to be home," John said.

"It's nice to have you home," Catharine said, crying and laughing simultaneously.

"Oh Lord, do I have a story for you."

"Why the cane?" Catharine asked.

The Decew children came running downstairs and tackled their grizzled father in the doorway. Decew looked at his wife, grabbed her around the waist, pulled her close to his body, and kissed her as tears began to roll down his face.

Chapter 19 - Last Foray

Napoleon had just been exiled to Elba, off the coast of Tuscany, and Europe was in relative peace. British warships began a blockade of all American imports and exports. They sent 100 ships of war along with thousands of fresh, veteran troops from Wellington's army to reinforce the North American colonies.

President James Madison had just promoted the young, ambitious Winfield Scott from Colonel to the station of Brigadier General. He quickly ascended the military ranks within two years of war. He had been captured at the Battle of Queenston Heights, imprisoned in Québec, paroled back to Washington, and led a significant victory at the Battle of Fort George. Now, Scott was in a position of responsibility where he would develop strategies and policies, supervise, and oversee major military components.

Henry 'Granny' Dearborn played a significant role in Scott's quick ascension up the military ranks, as he greatly believed in his potential as a future leader in the United States.

Dearborn had pressed other generals and many people in Washington to have Winfield Scott promoted to such a high ranking in such a short period.

In the spring of 1814, 3500 Americans had marched into Upper Canada, led by Scott and newly arrived General Jacob Brown, and decisively captured Fort Erie at the south end of the Niagara River. Winfield Scott, a few days after capturing Fort Erie, had led two brigades and won a decisive victory at Chippewa Creek, pushing the British all the way back to Fort George.

On the 25th of July, the Americans and the British were about to clash at Lundy's Lane in Niagara Falls. British Lieutenant Governor of Upper Canada, Lieutenant General Gordon Drummond, had just arrived at Fort George to take personal command of the Niagara Peninsula. John Norton, at the head of over 200 warriors, Captain Merritt, Nathan Davis and the Dragoons, and John Decew had returned to action in support of pushing the American army back across the river.

Drummond's troops and 2000 regulars and militia controlled the cannons on the high ground of Lundy's Lane. In the late afternoon, the American 1st Brigade of Regulars under Winfield Scott and a major artillery company emerged from a forest into an open field. The British artillery and the Indian forces under Norton badly mauled them.

Massive waves of American regulars surged the British positions but did not give way to the blue coats. Volley after volley, wave after wave, the battle continued into the early evening.

Now a Brigadier General, Scott sent the 25th U.S. Infantry to outflank Drummond's artillery forces atop the hill. Scott discovered a small path leading to a landing stage on the river and used it to pass around the British flank. In their manoeuvre, they surprised the British cannons and killed hundreds of artillery men and infantry.

The hours of bloody combat continued until the day turned into night. By 10pm, both sides were utterly spent. Hundreds were dead; hundreds more lay wounded. Blood ran the hills red, and, in the darkness, water was difficult to transport along the line, and finding injured soldiers was almost impossible.

In the final American push, Winfield Scott charged the last artillery position with 50 soldiers. Leading the way, he was among the first to be shot. He took a musket ball through the thigh, which made him stumble, then a second shot through his abdomen. Two of his soldiers eventually found the severely injured General in the darkness and stretchered him off the battlefield. With supplies and water running short, General Jacob Brown and the Americans ordered a retreat back to Fort Erie.

In the final minutes of the battle, as the Americans withdrew, William Hamilton Merritt had carelessly charged into their retreat and was shot through the leg. He fell to the ground and was eventually captured and dragged off the battlefield by the Americans. Like all prisoners, he would, in all probability, be sent to Albany or Philadelphia and await sentence or prisoner exchange.

The battlefield was the most deadly and ferocious engagement of the war, and after all the bloodshed, it was a stalemate. The nearly six-hour battle had been a hard-fought deadlock, with nobody gaining significant ground.

William Hamilton Merritt and the rest of the captives from Lundy's Lane were kept out all night near the battlefield, as there were no tents or nearby buildings. The next day, they were shipped and marched to Buffalo, where they could finally lay their heads down and have a decent meal.

Merritt couldn't help but be angry and frustrated along the journey to Albany. He would not get the opportunity to find and kill Joseph Willcocks, the traitor, treasonous villain, and ruthless arsonist who had burned his hometown.

A few days after the bloody Battle of Lundy's Lane, General Drummond began the siege of Fort Erie to remove the Americans from Upper Canada again. The Americans had made significant modifications since occupation: they extended walls, built embankments, and added gunner positions. Though the British lost several men at Lundy's Lane, fresh troops arrived weekly to continue the effort on the Niagara frontier.

Drummond and his 3000-strong opened their guns on the fort. Day after day, the walls held up against the British cannons. Days turned into weeks; before long, a month had passed in the attempted siege.

The British and the Natives camped night after night along the north shore of Lake Erie and were growing tired and impatient with the lack of progress. American General Jacob Brown felt just as impatient as he knew his supplies would not last forever.

John Decew and Nathan Davis helped guard one of the British artillery guns outside the fort. Davis peered through his telescope, looking for potential weaknesses and gaps in the fort's defence. Nathan had made a promise to himself and to William Hamilton Merritt to find and kill Joseph Willcocks after the burning of Newark. He owed it to every woman, child, and elderly person in the area to find the heinous villain and put a bullet through his head.

Joseph Willcocks was the most hated man in the British Empire. Nathan knew Willcocks was inside Fort Erie because he saw his loyal followers inside and around the fort. Nathan was constantly on the lookout and doggedly determined to find Willcocks and kill him.

"I know he's in there," Nathan said to Decew. "He just has to show his face, just once."

"This standoff is on the brink of disaster. The cold is coming, and neither we, nor the Americans have the food or supplies to last the winter," Decew said.

"Who is going to pull out first?" Nathan questioned.

Just before sunrise, as Nathan kept a close eye on the fort walls, he saw a group of about 50 American soldiers exiting. Nathan ran towards the battery, awakening everyone along the way. Decew followed close behind.

The American sortie erupted in musket shots as they tried to take out the British cannons. Sunbeams came through the clouds along the horizon and pierced the smoky haze of the artillery position.

Nathan and Decew both joined the battery defence. They took aim, fired, and ducked down to reload. Nathan took out his telescope again, looked at the attacking soldiers, and noticed Joseph Willcocks leading the American division.

Willcocks looked at his fighting soldiers and recognized they had not surprised the enemy and were taking heavy casualties. "Retreat to the fort!" Willcocks yelled.

Seeing the American retreat, Nathan Davis stood up and looked for the retreating Willcocks. He spotted him from a distance, raised his freshly loaded musket, carefully aimed, drew a deep breath, exhaled slowly, and pulled the trigger. Through the puff of smoke at the end of his musket, the red-hot ball of lead flew through the air and went straight through the throat of Willcocks and splattered blood on the grass in front of him. He immediately fell face-first into the ground as Nathan ducked behind the battery embankment.

Nathan looked at Decew. "I got him. I think I nailed him."

"Willcocks?"

"Right through the neck," Nathan said, smiling. "I killed him, John."

The two friends shared a laugh behind the sandy embankment, and the last Americans retreated inside the fort.

A few days later, following a month-long siege, with winter around the corner, the Americans, once again, retreated across the river. This time, the British would pursue with 4,500 men and march straight to the capital of Washington and burn every public building on the way.

President James Madison, members of his government, and all of the military personnel evacuated the city of Washington after a victory at Bladensburg, just outside of the capital city. They had caught wind of a massive British contingency moving toward them, intent on taking revenge for the burning of York and Newark.

The British burned only the public buildings and no personal property, unlike the horrors at York and Newark. After setting fire to the Capitol building, the British regulars moved up Pennsylvania Avenue and lit the Whitehouse on fire. The British finally displayed their full power, and President Madison lost his appetite for war.

Luckily, as the White House burned, a hurricane stormed up the East Coast and put out all the surrounding fires. A few hours into the storm, the British marched back to Upper Canada. The hurricane rains put out all the fires in Washington and cast a massive, destructive tornado up Constitution Avenue.

Both the British and the Americans had grown war-weary and tired of conflict, so peace negotiations finally began at Ghent in Belgium around Christmas 1814.

Chapter 20 ~ Burying the Hatchet

Ghent, Belgium, was chosen to begin peace talks because of its neutral state. Britain and America each sent delegations of five diplomats to resolve and come to agreeable terms.

The American delegates decided not to present President Madison's terms, which suggested handing Upper and Lower Canada to the Americans. So, they let Britain begin with their propositions.

The most critical proposal was Tecumseh, Norton, and Brant's dream of an Indian nation. The British delegates proposed the creation of an Indian barrier state in the southwest territory, the area of Ohio, Indiana and Wisconsin. They made it clear that they would sponsor the Indian State until they had a stabilized form of government.

The next day, the Americans refused to consider the proposal of a buffer state, nor would they include or consider the Indians in the creation of the treaty whatsoever.

Henry Goulburn, one of the British negotiators who took part in the treaty negotiations, wrote in his journal:

Until I came here, I had no idea of the fixed determination which prevails in the breast of every American to eradicate the Indians and appropriate their territory.

The British were persistent in their fight for the tribes of North America. They wanted everything restored to the way it was, to 'all possessions, rights and privileges which they may have enjoyed, or been entitled to in 1811'. However, the British delegates could only influence the Americans so far.

On Christmas Eve, 1814, terms were eventually reached, with productive discussions and pledges on both sides to end the slave trade. News of the treaty spread slowly, and word of peace did not reach the American and British armies for some time.

There were two bloody months of unnecessary fighting throughout America, including a prominent American victory in New Orleans, led by Andrew Jackson, and the engagement of the USS Constitution and the HMS Cyane and the Levant.

Though the two countries lay in ashes, much like the aftermath in Europe, the people were glad it was over. It was now time to pick up the pieces and rebuild.

The warring tribes had come to bury the hatchet. It was the only true tradition arising from the bloodshed, pain, and trauma of the war. The Grand River chiefs invited the Seneca and people of Buffalo Creek to carry on with the ancient traditions and ceremonies of healing and rekindling the mutual friendship established before the war.

The Grand River was bustling with activity, and many weapons were about to be passed back to their allies and buried beneath a 500-year-old oak tree they called the 'Tree of Peace.'

Red Jacket and Little Billy led hundreds of their followers along the north shore of Lake Erie to the Grand River settlement, where they would express their condolences to their friends and allies. They offered to wipe the tears of their families and friends and were ritually cleansed to ease the hatred and mourning they felt.

John Norton and his wife shared in the celebration, and both were glad they could settle down, raise crops and livestock, and watch their son grow in peace.

Norton joined Chief John Brant near the Tree of Peace.

"Your father would be proud," Norton said to Brant.

"I hope he has travelled well," Brant said, smiling.

"He sees you and what you have accomplished here. We are on the right path, John Brant," Norton said.

Brant suddenly got up the nerve to address the entire pow-wow: "We, the several Nations residing at the Grand River, salute you from the other side. We are the same people with you; we are relations of the same colour, notwithstanding having been opposed to each other in the field during the late contest between our Father, the King of England and the Americans. The Niagara River, which separates us, is open so we may have a free passage at all times. The roads are cleared of all briars and rubbish so we can renew that friendly intercourse between us. I now speak to you on behalf of the Indians residing on the Grand River, and I desire to assure you that all ill will is removed from their hearts towards you."

All the people cheered at Brant's words, and the Great Peace was again restored.

"We must stand by these words, young Chief Brant. Let us keep our hearts and minds clean. We must sustain and prolong our grandfather's heritage and fight any encroachment or evil that will retake our glory or tradition," John Norton said, shaking hands with Brant.

The citizens of Queenston and Newark had begun the slow process of rebuilding their lives. The local mills were working around the clock to provide people with lumber to start rebuilding their homes, though many families were left impoverished and unable to afford the reconstruction.

James and Laura Secord were picking up the postwar pieces in the spring of 1815. Laura had planted a massive spring garden crop filled with squash, corn, beans, carrots, potatoes, and any other seeds she could get her hands on. James was in ongoing agony and was still having trouble getting around but was nonetheless in better spirits than the previous couple of years. He had slowly replaced the house's smashed windows and purchased a few new animals for the farm.

Though they were feeling the financial burden of losing everything they owned and feeling the postwar woes, the Secords hosted a modest Sunday afternoon party with friends to celebrate the war's end and spring's arrival. Everyone made the trip to Queenston, including John and Catharine Decew, their children, Nathan and Victoria Davis, Bob, Fan, Hector, and other friends from the Queenston and Newark community.

The children played in the yard, and the adults talked and laughed for what seemed to be the first time in three years. They ate assorted fruits, nuts, cheeses, cured meats, freshly baked bread, and biscuits.

"So glad you returned to us," James said to Decew.

Decew would never take his life for granted again. Prison in Philadelphia gave him a new perspective. He promised to cherish the little things he had taken for granted: hot meals, warm blankets, friends, children, and, most importantly, his wife Catharine. Decew looked at his wife, holding their three-year-old, and gave her a subtle wink.

"It was a long walk," Decew said to James.

"Philadelphia to Montréal?" Nathan asked.

"Without the Quakers, I never would have made it. When I jumped from the prison wall, I broke my ankle, and a local doctor set the bone and put it in a splint."

"How far was the drop?" Nathan asked.

"It must have been 20 feet. It was pitch black as I fell, and I smacked my face on the prison wall; it nearly knocked me on conscious," Decew answered.

"Sounds painful," James added.

"Honestly, the first couple of hours, nothing really hurt. Adrenaline was coursing through my body. It wasn't until the morning that I realized I broke a bone and gave myself a black eye," Decew described. "How's your knee, James?" he asked.

"It will never be the same. Unfortunately, I will likely be using a cane for the rest of my life," James said.

"We're all here for you, James," Nathan said.

"Thanks, Nathan," James responded.

Victoria came from inside the house and approached James, Decew, and Nathan. "I wonder if I might steal Nathan for a few minutes."

"Of course, madam," Decew said. "No need to return him," he said, laughing.

Nathan and Victoria went inside and stepped into the kitchen.

"Would you help me with a cheese tray?" Victoria asked, smiling at her husband.

"Is that what this is about?" Nathan asked coyly.

Victoria grabbed Nathan by the shirt with two hands and pulled him in close. They kissed passionately as the peacetime and spring air had taken hold of the new couple.

Outside, Richard Pierpoint, Roger Jupiter, and John Vanpatten arrived at the Secord house and were welcomed by James, Laura, Bob, and Fan. Bob immediately shook Pierpoint's hand.

"Great to see you, old man," Bob said to Pierpoint.

"You too, old-timer," Pierpoint responded.

Pierpoint, against all odds, had survived yet another tumultuous time in his life: Muslim enslavement in West Africa, the transatlantic voyage, working on the plantation fields, the Revolutionary War, and now, the War of 1812. He had fought hard and spent the past few months at home in Grantham planting a new apple orchard. He also began looking at prospects in the York area.

Bob and Fan's son, Hector, had noticed Pierpoint and the others' arrival and came rushing over to greet them. "Hello, Mr. Pierpoint," he said.

"There's the young Hector," Pierpoint said. "How are you, young man? You have done terrifically these past couple of years. You truly have become a man."

"Thank you, Mr. Pierpoint," Hector said.

"I'm pretty proud of the young man," Bob said. "Richard, you remember my wife, Fannie."

Pierpoint kissed the back of Fan's hand and smiled.

"So, you made it without having a heart attack, eh, Mr. Pierpoint?" Fan joked.

"Doing just fine, Mrs. Armstrong," Pierpoint said, laughing.

"Mr. Pierpoint, thank you for keeping my silly husband alive," Fan said.

"He kept us alive, Mrs. Armstrong," Pierpoint said. "We are so proud of all his hard work and diligence. We are all free, thanks to acts of valour by your husband and son. I hope this is the last time that North Americans will fight amongst each other."

James limped over with his limp and shook Jupiter, Vanpatten, and Pierpoint's hands. "Mr. Pierpoint, it's great to have you here."

"Thanks for the cordial invitation, Mr. and Mrs. Secord," Pierpoint said as he shook James and Laura's hands.

"Bob and Hector have told me a lot about you fellows," Laura said to Vanpatten, Jupiter, and Pierpoint.

"I trust it's all good," Pierpoint said, laughing.

Lt. FitzGibbon arrived with his new wife and was happy to see familiar faces after the unstable wartime. The conflict had taken its toll on FitzGibbon. He lost many friends and fellow soldiers throughout the war, including his longtime companion, Isaac Brock. FitzGibbon joined the 49th Regiment of Foot in 1799 and came under the command and instruction of Brock in North America. Brock had always encouraged and tutored FitzGibbon, knowing he was an intelligent, capable soldier. In 1809, Brock made him a lieutenant and believed in his abilities despite being rough around the edges. FitzGibbon cried the day they buried Brock at Fort George, as they had accomplished so much together. Now, he would carry on with the 49th alone. FitzGibbon noticed John and Catharine Decew and walked over immediately. "It is wonderful to see you both," he said. "Without your home, I don't know if we could have held on."

"I am glad it could be put to good use. It is truly lovely to see you again," Catharine said. "You look much better dressed in red than in grey."

"Ha! Those grey uniforms did come in handy," FitzGibbon said. "Mr. Decew, how are you, sir?" he said, shaking his hand.

"Quite well, Lieutenant, quite well," Decew responded.

"Has your wife told you the story of when she held a sword to the throat of an American?" FitzGibbon asked Decew.

"No, she has not, but I am certainly interested to hear the tale," Decew said as he turned to look at his wife.

FitzGibbon raised his fist to tell the tale. "I dragged a couple of no-good Americans into the street, and in the struggle, they dropped their sword. Catharine picked it up, placed it at his throat and said: 'Enough, please!' as we regathered ourselves and brush the twigs from our coats."

"Incredible! Why didn't you tell me this story?" Decew asked Catharine.

"They exaggerate," Catharine said.

FitzGibbon saw Laura out of the corner of his eye and grinned. "Now, there is another lady I would like to thank," he said, pointing at Laura.

"Lieutenant!" Laura yelled across the yard as she walked over to meet the newcomers.

"It is terrific to see you, Mrs. Secord. You look well," FitzGibbon said. "This is my wife, Eleanor."

Laura and Eleanor shook hands. "Thanks, Lieutenant. Pleasure to meet you, Eleanor," Laura said.

"It's actually Captain now," FitzGibbon said with a smile.

James came walking over. "Captain FitzGibbon, that's got a nice ring to it."

"James, how are you?" FitzGibbon said, shaking James' hand. "You ought to be quite proud of your wife. We managed to scare and capture over 500 Americans into submission, no thanks to Laura's intelligence."

"She is quite remarkable," James said, putting his arm around Laura's shoulder.

"Things might have ended up differently had she not taken that long walk," FitzGibbon added.

"I'm glad I asked Miss Ingersoll to be my wife," James said, kissing Laura on the cheek.

"James, there is something I need to tell you," Laura whispered to James.

"What is it, darling?" James responded.

"Can I tell you inside?"

"Can it not wait? We have guests, you know," James said, sipping his drink.

"It will only take a minute," Laura said, grabbing him by the hand.

Laura and James excused themselves and entered the house to find Nathan and Victoria in a heated embrace. They quickly broke their affections and flushed red at the surprise.

"You two having fun?" James joked.

"Quite sorry, Mr. Secord. We are just so happy that the war is over, and we can spend more time together," Victoria said.

"I'll say," Laura added.

Nathan and Victoria embarrassingly walked back to the party as Laura led James to the parlour sofa and sat him down.

"Those two are so endearing," James said.

"James, my dearest, my love," Laura said as she looked James directly in the eye, "I am with child."

"You are! Are you sure?" James stood and grimaced at the pain in his knee.

"One hundred percent!" Laura exclaimed as she rubbed her belly.

James couldn't contain himself. He took his cane, quickly limped out the front door, and yelled, "Laura's going to have a baby!"

Everyone turned to the Secords, yelled, and clapped with excitement as James and Laura shared a rare public kiss in front of their friends and family.

A year later, John Norton, his wife and small boy were summoned to London, England, to be rewarded for his efforts in the war and for building relationships between the Indigenous tribes and the Crown. They had sailed across the Atlantic Ocean, the journey taking about a month, and the family had intended to spend a good amount of time in Britain. It was pleasant for Karighwaycagh, who had never sailed before, and it was even more astonishing and overwhelming for their little boy, whom they planned on schooling in Britain while overseas.

When the family arrived in London, their ship was welcomed by a large crowd who applauded them as they set foot on the royal dock. Norton had felt confused by such alien people giving him so much gratitude and acclamation.

Norton and his family were guided to Buckingham Palace by one of the King's carriages and instructed on the specifics of bowing and being introduced to royalty. King George III was determined unable to perform the King's duties, as he had rheumatism, was nearly blind, and developing dementia. George IV was named regent and arranged to meet with John Norton. After being gifted a lavish set of pistols and a ceremonial sword, Norton and his family were invited to the Royal ballroom in central London to celebrate his efforts throughout his time in North America.

At the reception, after Norton was given his gifts, he found himself surrounded by an elite, dignified group who applauded him as he entered the grand ballroom. Norton and Karighwaycagh were completely unsuspecting and welcomed the warm reception.

Norton and his wife sat at the head table at the front of the room, along with old friends Sir Roger Sheaffe and Sir George Prevost. Sheaffe and Prevost waved and smiled at Norton as he sat down while the crowd continued to applaud his efforts throughout the war. Though he knew his endeavours were important, he never understood how much they were appreciated throughout Britain.

"Welcome, Captain Norton," Prevost said.

"How are you, you old dog?" Sheaffe asked above the noise of the applause.

Norton could only smile at such admiration from the crowd.

"It is my pleasure to share the story of John Norton, who has been summoned here to London and bestowed with a most remarkable gift from the King. This man's tale is a testament to the enduring spirit of courage and the deep bond between a nation and its people." As the master of ceremonies spoke, Norton's face flushed red.

"Years ago, at the outset of the War of 1812, a period of great conflict and uncertainty, Captain John Norton, a valiant hero, was called to action. He fought many gallant battles at Queenston, Fort George, Stoney Creek, and several other engagements during the War of 1812. The King learned of his unwavering loyalty and fearless acts of valour in defence of the realm and his country and thus called him here to England. Norton, Chief of the Six Nations, renowned for his unyielding commitment to his Mohawk and Iroquois people, is hereby recognized by the British kingdom as a symbol of honour and duty."

The crowd applauded Norton once again, and he smiled and blushed at the overwhelming response. Though he had been a leader and orator throughout his life, he had never learned how to accept praise or gratitude. It was a completely foreign concept, and he felt undeserving of such flattery.

"Upon his arrival in the grand city of London, Norton was greeted with a warm and joyous reception. Crowds of people gathered to welcome him; their cheers echoed through the streets as he made his way to the royal palace. His presence, demeanour, loyalty, and honour were a beacon of hope during the troubled times of 1812. At the palace, Norton was received by the Regent King, who recognized his extraordinary service and commitment to the crown and its people. This pair of exquisite pistols and a sword of unparalleled craftsmanship are not just any weapons; they are symbols of the King's trust, gratitude, and recognition of Norton's valour."

The crowd applauded the symbolic gift of gratitude and Karighwaycagh looked at him and smiled. She reached for his hand under the table and grasped it tight. Norton looked back at his wife and smiled.

"The King's gift is an acknowledgment of Norton's dedication and the sacrifices he had made to protect the kingdom and the people of the Grand River nation." The master of ceremonies indicated that Norton should stand.

Norton slowly rose to his feet. "The King's gesture deeply moves me, and I humbly accept these gifts with humility and honour. I also pledge to protect the people of Upper Canada and promise to spread the word of God throughout the Kingdom. This esteemed position, though unexpected, has reassured me that my steadfast morals and strong values have a purpose in this land."

Everyone in the room rose and raised their glasses to Norton. "Hear, hear!" they shouted.

The master of ceremonies once again spoke to the crowd: "This story of John Norton serves as a reminder of the profound spirit of bravery and dedication to family that can inspire an entire nation. It is a tale of honour, loyalty, and the powerful symbol of a gift given from the heart of a king. Hear, hear, John Norton. We salute you!"

Everyone in the room raised and drank from their cups to recognize John Norton and his sacrifice.

Epilogue

In the wake of the War of 1812, a profound transformation swept across the nations involved. The cannons fell silent, and the smoke of battle gradually dissipated, leaving behind a new chapter in the histories of the United States, Britain, France, and the Indigenous peoples who were deeply affected by the conflict.

The war symbolized a moment of national identity and resilience for the United States. It played a critical role in the young nation forging a distinct sense of unity and purpose. The Star-Spangled Banner, penned by Francis Scott Key amid the bombardment of Fort McHenry, would become the national anthem, forever linking the struggles and triumphs of those days to the American spirit.

Across the Atlantic, the war became a footnote in the broader tapestry of British imperial history. The British Empire, facing challenges on multiple fronts, sought resolution and negotiation rather than the subjugation of its former colonies. The

Treaty of Ghent in 1814 ended the hostilities, and the borders largely reverted to their pre-war lines. British North America, now Canada, was profoundly affected by the conflict. It solidified a distinct Canadian identity, and the war is remembered as a struggle for survival against American forces.

For the Indigenous peoples, who often found themselves caught between the great powers, the war brought both hope and disillusionment. Tecumseh's death disbanded any hope of a grand, united Indigenous nation. Even the hopes of safeguarding their lands and autonomy were often dashed as the post-war treaties and encroachments continued to displace Indigenous communities, paving the way for westward expansion in the United States.

At the Treaty of Ghent, British diplomats stated their case first, demanding the creation of an Indian barrier state in the American Northwest Territory (the area from Ohio to Wisconsin). It was understood the British would sponsor this state. For decades, the British strategy had been to create a buffer state to block American expansion. Britain also demanded naval control of the Great Lakes and access to the Mississippi River. On the American side, the American diplomats sent to Europe were instructed to try and convince the British to cede the Canadas, or at least Upper Canada, to the U.S. At a later stage, the Americans also demanded damages for the burning of Washington and for the seizure of ships before the war began. Money exchanges and settlements were agreed upon, and on Christmas Eve, 1814, The Treaty of Ghent was signed by the diplomats and arrived in North America soon after.

All prisoners were released, including William Hamilton Merritt, who was eventually released from Albany after three months of captivity. On returning to Canada, he stopped in Mayville, New York and found his future father-in-law. Shortly thereafter, he married his American wife and began a family together. In 1818, John Decew and William H. Merritt set out to survey and plot a route for the first Welland Canal that would open in 1829.

As we look back upon the War of 1812, we are reminded that history is a complex tapestry of human endeavours, where the actions and decisions of individuals and nations ripple through time. It reminds us of the sacrifices made and the lessons learned in the crucible of conflict. The war left an indelible mark on the collective memory of the nations involved, shaping their futures and offering enduring tales of courage, resilience, and unity.

The War of 1812 may have ended, but its legacy lives on. It is a testament to the human spirit's capacity to endure and adapt in the face of adversity. It serves as a powerful reminder that, even in the darkest hours of history, there is a light that guides us forward and an unwavering resolve to build a better future together.

Bibliography

Alderman, Clifford Lindsey. *Joseph Brant: Chief of the Six Nations*. Julian Messner, Inc. New York, 1958.

Allen, Robert S. "The British Indian Department and the Frontier in North America, 1755-1830," *Canadian Historic Sites: Occasional Papers in Archeology and History*, no. 14 (1975).

Babcock, James L. (ed.). "The Campaign of 1814 on the Niagara Frontier," *Niagara Frontier*, vol. 10 (1963).

Beirne, Francis F. *The War of 1812*. New York: Dutton, 1949.

Benn, Carl (ed.). *A Mohawk Memoir from the War of 1812*. University of Toronto Press, 2019.

Bidwell, Barnabas. *Statistical Account of Upper Canada* Volume 2. Simpkin & Marshall, 1822.

Biggar, E.B. "The Battle of Stoney Creek," *Canadian Magazine*, vol. I (1893).

Bonney, Catharina V.R. *A Legacy of Historical Gleanings*. 2nd edition, volume I. Albany, New York, 1875.

Borneman, Walter R. *1812: The War that Forged A Nation*. Harper Collins Publishers 2004.

Boylen, J.C. (ed.) "Strategy of Brock Saved Upper Canada: Candid Comments of a U.S. Officer Who Crossed at Queenston," *Ontario History*, volume 58 (1966).

Brown, Roger Hamilton. *The Republic in Peril: 1812*. New York: Columbia University Press, 1964.

Berton, Pierre. *The Invasion of Canada 1812-1813*. Anchor Canada 2001.

Berton, Pierre. *Flames Across the Border 1813-1814*. Anchor Canada 2001.

Callcott, Margaret L. (ed.) *Mistress of Riversdale: The Plantation Letters of Rosalie Stier Calvert, 1795-1821*. Baltimore: John Hopkins University Press, 1991.

Carnochan, Janet. "Sir Isaac Brock," *Niagara Historical Society Publications*, no. 15 (1907).

Chapin, Cyrenius. *Chapin's Review of Armstrong's Notices of the War of 1812*. Black Rock, N.Y.: D.P. Adams, 1836.

Claus, William. "Diary," *Michigan Pioneer and Historical Collections*, volume 23, 1895.

Coffin, William F. *1812: The War, and Its Moral: A Canadian Chronicle*. Montreal: J. Lovell, 1864.

Coles, Harry L. *The War of 1812*. Chicago: University of Chicago Press, 1965.

272

Colquhoun, A.H.U. "The Career of Joeseph Willcocks," *Canadian Historical Review*, vol. 7 (1926).

Crooks, James. "Recollections of the War of 1812," *Women's Canadian Historical Society of Toronto*, Transaction no. 13 (1913/14).

Cruikshank, E.A. (ed.). "Campaigns of 1812-1814: Contemporary Narratives," *Niagara Historical Society Publications*, no. 9 (1902).

Cruikshank, E.A. (ed.). *The Documentary History of the Campaign upon the Niagara Frontier 1812-1814*. 9 volumes. Welland: Lundy's Lane Historical Society, 1902-1908.

Cruikshank, E.A. *The Battle of Queenston Heights*, 3rd ed. Rev. Welland: Tribune, 1904.

Currie, J.G. "The Battle of Queenston Heights," *Niagara Historical Society Publications*, no. 4 (1898).

Dictionary of American Biography, 22 vols. New York: Charles Scribner's Sons, 1928-58.

Dictionary of Canadian Biography, vol. 9: 1861-70. Toronto: University of Toronto Press, 1976.

Dictionary of National Biography, 22 vols. Oxford: Oxford University Press, 1885-1900.

Douglass, David Bates. "An Original Narrative of the Niagara Campaign of 1814," edited by John T. Horton, *Niagara Frontier*, vol. II (1964).

Edgar, Matilda. *General Brock*. Toronto: Morang, 1904.

Edgar, Matilda. *Ten Years of Upper Canada in Peace and War, 1805-1815; Being the Ridout Letters*. Toronto: W. Briggs, 1890.

Eisenhower, John S.D. *Agent of Destiny: The Life and Times of General Winfield Scott*. New York: Free Press, 1997.

Gleig, G.R. *The Campaigns of the British Army at Washington and New Orleans*. Totowa, N.J.: Rowman and Littlefield, 1972.

Goodman, Warren H. "The Origins of the War of 1812: A Survey of Changing Interpretations," *Mississippi Valley Historical Review*, vol. 28 (1941).

Graves, Donald E. *Where Right and Glory Lead! The Battle of Lundy's Lane, 1814*. Toronto: Robin Brass Studio, 1997.

Hanks, Jarvis. "A Drummer Boy in the War of 1812: The Memoir of Jarvis Frary Hanks," edited by Lester Smith, *Niagara Frontier*, vol. 7 (1960).

Hatzenbuehler, Ronald L. "The War-hawks and the Question of Congressional Leadership in 1812," *Pacific Historical Review*, vol. 45 (1976).

Heidler, Jeanne T., and David S. Heidler (eds.). *Encyclopedia of the War of 1812*. Santa Barbara, California: ABC-Clio, 1997.

Hull, William. *Memoirs of the Campaign of the North Western Army of the United States, A.D. 1812*. Boston: True and Greene, 1824.

Irving, L. Homfray. *Officers of the British Forces in Canada during the War of 1812-15*. Welland: Tribune Print. For Canadian Military Institute, 1908.

Jacobs, James R. *The Beginning of the U.S. Army, 1783-1812*. Princeton: Princeton University Press, 1947.

Johnston, C.M. "William Claus and John Norton: A Struggle for Power in Old Ontario," *Ontario History*, vol. 57 (1965).

Jones, Elwood H. (1983). "Willcocks, Joseph". In Halpenny, Francess G (ed.). *Dictionary of Canadian Biography*. Vol. V (1801–1820) (online ed.). University of Toronto Press. Retrieved December 15, 2011.

Ketchum, William. *An Authentic and Comprehensive History of Buffalo*, vol. II. Buffalo: Rockwell, Baker and Hill, 1864-65.

Kirby William. *Annals of Niagara*. Welland: Lundy's Lane Historical Society Publications, 1896.

Lajeunesse, Ernest J. (ed.) *The Windsor Border Region*. Toronto: University of Toronto Press, 1960.

Lavender, David. *The Fist in the Wilderness*. Garden City, N.Y.: Doubleday, 1964.

Le Couteur, John. "List of Losses Claimed on Houses Burned in Niagara Dec. 13th, 1813," *Niagara Historical Society Publications*, no. 27 (n.d.)

Lossing, Benson J. *The Pictorial Field-Book of the War of 1812*. Glensdale, New York, Benchmark Pub. Corp., 1970.

Lower Arthur R.M. *Canadians in the Making: A Social History of Canada*. Toronto: Longmans, Green, 1958.

Lucas, Sir Charles P. *The Canadian War of 1812*. Oxford: Clarendon Press, 1906.

MacDonald, Cheryl. *Laura Secord: The Heroic Adventures of a Canadian Legend*. Altitude Publishing Canada Ltd. 2003.

Mahon, John K. *The War of 1812*. Gainesville: University of Florida Press, 1972.

Malcomson, Robert. *Burying General Brock: A History of Brock's Monuments*. Niagara-on-the-Lake, The Friends of Fort George, 1996.

McKenzie, Ruth. *Laura Secord: The Lady and the Legend*. Toronto: McClelland and Stewart Ltd., 1971.

McKenzie, Ruth. *James FitzGibbon, Defender of Upper Canada*. Toronto Dundurn Press, 1983.

Moir, John S. "An Early Record of Laura Secord's Walk". *Ontario History* Vol. LI (1959) No. 2, 105-108.

Murray, John M. "John Norton," *Ontario Historical Society Papers and Records*, vol. 37 (1945).

Norton, John. *The Journal of Major John Norton*, edited by Carl Klinck and James J. Talman. Toronto: Champlain Society, 1970.

Pike, Zebulon. *The Journals of Zebulon Montgomery Pike*, edited by Donald Jackson. Norman, Okla.: University of Oklahoma Press, 1966.

Prevost, George. *"To the inhabitants of his Majesty's provinces in North America: A Proclamation"*. Published 1814.

Randall, E.O. "Tecumseh the Shawnee Chief," *Ohio Archeological and Historical Society Publications*, vol. 15 (1906).

Redway, Jacques W. "General Van Rensselaer and the Niagara Frontier," *New York State Historical Association Proceedings*, vol. 8 (1909).

Roach, Isaac. "Journal of Major Isaac Roach, 1812-1824," *Pennsylvania Magazine of History and Biography*, volume 17 (1893).

Ryerson, Adolphus Egerton. *The Loyalists of America and Their Times, from 1620 to 1816*, 2 vols., 2nd ed. Toronto: W. Briggs, 1880.

Scott, Winfield. *Memoirs of Lieut.-General Scott*, Written by Himself, 2 vols., New York: Sheldon, 1864.

Shankman, Andrew. *The World of the Revolutionary American Republic: Land, Labor, and the Conflict for a Continent*. Routledge. 16 April 2014.

Sheaffe, Roger Hale. "Documents Relating to the War of 1812: the Letterbook of Gen. Sir Roger Hale Sheaffe," *Buffalo Historical Society Publications*, volume 17 (1913).

Stagg, J.C.A. "James Madison and the Malcontents: The Political Origins of the War of 1812," *William and Mary Quarterly*, 3rd ser., vol. 33 (1976).

Stanley, George F.G. "The Indians in the War of 1812," *Canadian Historical Review*, vol. 31 (1950).

Stanley, George F.G. "The Significance of the Six Nations Participation in the War of 1812," *Ontario History*, vol. 55 (1963).

Tupper, Ferdinand Brock. *The Life and Correspondence of Major General Sir Isaac Brock*, K.B., 2nd edition, London: Simpkin Marshall, 1847.

Turner, Wesley B. "The Career of Isaac Brock in Canada." Ph.D. dissertation, University of Toronto, 1961.

Van Rensselaer, Solomon. *A Narrative of the Affair of Queenston, in the War of 1812*. New York: Leavitt, Lord, 1836.

Willcocks, Joseph. *Upper Canada Guardian; or, Freeman's Journal*. Newark, 1812.

Williams, Jack. *Merritt: A Canadian Before His Time*. St. Catharines: Stonehouse Publications 1985.

Zaslow, Morris and Turner, Wesley B. (eds.). *The Defended Border: Upper Canada and the War of 1812*. Toronto: Macmillan, 1964.

Endnotes

Page/Author (source)

27 – Norton, John
34-35 – Willcocks, Joseph
48 – Alderman, Clifford Lindsey
49-53 – Norton, John
59-60 – Willcocks, Joseph
85-88 – Norton, John
93 – Hull, William
96 – Van Rensselaer, Solomon
120 – Scott, Winfield
128 – Macdonald, Cheryl
212 – Norton, John
219 – Scott, Winfield
233-234 – Prevost, George
254 – Shankman, Andrew